MW01170479

When Secrets and Stars Align

Emma Humfleet

PRAISE FOR HEART IN YOUR HANDS

"After reading so many books that were nothing but spicy bits every two minutes this book was such a breath of fresh air with an actual story!"

"I am hooked. I absolutely loved, loved, loved this book. I can't wait for the author's next book to be released."

This is a work of fiction. Names, characters, places, and incidents either are the product of the author's imagination or are used fictitiously. Any resemblance to actual persons, living or dead, events, or locales is entirely coincidental.

Copyright © 2024 by Emma Humfleet

All rights reserved. No part of this book may be reproduced or used in any manner without written permission of the copyright owner except for the use of quotations in a book review.

Author's Note

This book contains profanity, graphic violence, strong sexual language, and content that some readers may find disturbing including mentions of child sexual (not depicted) and physical abuse. This book is intended for readers eighteen years and older.

Table of Contents

Chapter 1...1

Chapter 2...15

Chapter 3...28

Chapter 4...47

Chapter 5...58

Chapter 6...67

Chapter 7...88

Chapter 8...103

Chapter 9...109

Chapter 10...130

Chapter 11...134

Chapter 12...145

Chapter 13...150

Chapter 14...165

Chapter 15...171

Chapter 16...176

Chapter 17...185

Chapter 18...205

Chapter 19...207

Chapter 20...217

Chapter 21...228

Chapter 22...230

Epilogue...240

WHEN SECRETS AND STARS ALIGN

Two souls don't find each other by accident.

-Jorge Luis Borges

Chapter 1
Lawrence

———— * ★ * ————

I run my hands down my face, digging the heels of my palms into my eyes hard enough to see stars as I try to will away the urge to fall asleep, as if I'd be able to get much anyway. I've been doing my due diligence watching this family for nearly two weeks, and every day it's the same mundane boring-ass routine.

My undesirable job is to learn their schedule, making it easier for me to clean up my mess when I make my move. Usually, the people I'm sent to watch give me something, some semblance of entertainment. Sometimes they're cheating on their spouse and sneaking off to meet their secret lover while their husband or wife sleeps peacefully in their bed at home. Other times I get to watch them rip their lives apart without any help from me because all they know how to do is make self-destructive decisions.

Regardless of what it is, I'm usually rewarded with some form of interest from my stakeouts before the real "fun" begins. The Reed family though is about as boring as boring gets. You've got a husband who goes to work, comes home, and sits on his ass in front of the TV ingesting the junk beer–which I'm almost certain takes away from his wife and daughter's grocery budget–he keeps handy until his wife gets home. His wife trudges in the house looking like the day has kicked her ass and slaves in the kitchen making dinner while her useless husband does nothing to help, only getting up to take piss breaks, and her pre-teen daughter stays locked away in her room.

Benjamin Reed looks like your traditional blue-collar family man. The fact that I haven't busted him doing something illegal, divorce-worthy, or even mildly interesting, is boring as much as it is surprising, and irritating considering he's a target in the first place. It makes me think he knows he's on our shit list. He's keeping his nose abnormally clean, and I don't just mean free of chalky white powder. The joke is on him if he thinks walking the straight and narrow is going to pay off his debt. My boss, Biggy, is not a kind man, and he keeps track of every penny owed to him. Five hundred or fifty thousand dollars, he will not let a single cent fall through the cracks.

I reach across the middle console and pull out a bag of chips from my stash, opening it and shoving a few of the salty crisps in my mouth, cursing under my breath when stray crumbs fall on the seat at my crotch. Nothing pisses me off like a dirty truck; I know, ironic considering what I use it for. I swipe the crumbs to the floorboard taking a mental note to sweep them out later before chugging the rest of the stale energy drink that was in the cup holder. I'm thankful today is the last day of watching these people because I'd probably off myself if I had to watch another day of this mundane crap life the Reed family lives.

I suppose there's nothing wrong with living a typical boring life, but for my interest, it would be nice if they didn't have such a mundane routine they stuck to every day.

I check the time on the dash: 11:15 pm on the dot. Little does he know he's working the graveyard shift tonight, and tomorrow he'll be rotting in one.

Right on cue, Reed exits the front door before climbing into his shit box of a car and backing out of the driveway of his two-bedroom suburban box. Maybe if the idiot stopped blowing all of his money on gambling and drugs, he could afford to drive his car without the fear that the floorboard would fall out on him while he's driving.

I wait until he's down the road a ways before turning on my headlights and turning over the engine to follow him on his twenty-minute commute to work, just as I have for the past thirteen days.

I've been meticulous about watching all three of them so I know exactly how to execute my plan and cause the least amount of havoc. Whenever one of my assignments has a spouse or kids, it complicates things. Especially considering I don't like to bring their families into the mix. Luckily, Reed's schedule is the complete opposite as his wife's so it makes things easier for me being able to watch all of them. Typically the wife doesn't have any involvement in these affairs, but I can never be certain, which is why I have to do my due diligence, making sure she isn't playing a role in the situation that I wasn't aware of. From what I can tell, she hardly has any involvement with her husband at all–by his choice from what I can tell–let alone any knowledge about what her husband does behind her back.

She appears to be the only one that gives a shit about keeping their family afloat even if it means sacrificing her happiness. Sure, her husband goes to work each day, but it's not like he's doing it out of the kindness of his heart. They wouldn't be struggling as much if the deadbeat would stop wasting their money.

Pulling into the factory parking lot, I watch as he climbs out of his car and carries his tired frame into work. It irks me beyond measure that his shift starts at 11:30, and he makes it his mission to show up at 11:35 every day, especially considering he has such a strict routine with everything else. It shouldn't surprise me that the guy isn't reliable. The people I'm sent after usually aren't, but I suppose my pep talk tomorrow could include something about his lack of punctuality as well.

I wait twenty minutes, filling my mouth with more sodium-packed junk before making the call that Reed wasn't just putting on a show for my benefit. I put a tracker on his car, so I'll know if he does leave. I'm confident he has no idea I've been watching them for the past two weeks, but I still have to cover all my bases. Anticipation grows in the pit of my stomach as I throw my truck in gear and head home to prepare.

––––––––––

I shove a few more essentials in my duffel bag before zipping it closed and hauling it out to my truck. My cell phone rings, and I groan as I pull it out of my pocket because I know who it's going to be before I even look. Not that I wasn't expecting it, but it doesn't make it any more enjoyable. I accept the call, prepared to answer his typical questions that he always asks before I finish a job, eager to already end this conversation.

I position the cell between my ear and shoulder as I slam the truck bed closed and make my way back to my room.

"Yeah."

"Talk to me," Biggy says. I can tell he's got a cigarette in his mouth as I hear him exhale smoke clouds on the other end. I will never understand the pleasure people get from swallowing foul-tasting smoke into their lungs.

I pop the tab on another energy drink, taking a swig before replying. I don't know how my heart hasn't stopped yet from my caffeine consumption, though some days I wish it would.

"I'm moving in on him tonight. Just send Ricky over here so we can run over the plan." I place him on speaker as I rummage through my dresser, pulling out my favorite hoodie and dark jeans.

"I'm not sending Ricky. I need him elsewhere so I'm sending Terry to help you."

I grit my teeth and resist the urge to scream at him through the phone.

Terry is the dumbest motherfucker I have ever met, and frankly, I'm not sure how he hasn't gotten himself killed with all the dumb shit he says and does. He once took 20 minutes trying to install a silencer before someone had to tell him he was holding it backwards. It's unfortunate he hasn't pulled the trigger while accidentally pointing the gun at himself. He can't do a single thing without screwing something up. The few times I have had the displeasure of working with him upon Biggy's request–no, demand–I've barely been able to keep from murdering him myself. Unfortunately for me, Terry is Biggy's best friend? Brother? Fuck if I know. They look nothing alike, but I don't try to immerse myself in his personal life enough to find out. But I do know he refers to Terry as his brother so ending the numbskull's life would be ending mine even though half the time Biggy acts like he wants to kill the guy, too. I guess being blood would make a difference in keeping Terry's worthless ass around.

Terry is like dogshit on the bottom of your shoe. No matter how many times you wipe it in the grass or spray it with the hose, it never leaves. I could spray Terry with the hose until his skin falls off and the bastard would still come running back because his pathetic existence relies on it. This life fuels him because it's the only place he is accepted. I slip the hoodie on over my head and relish in the comfort it brings. I always wear the same one when I start a job and I've grown a disturbing attachment to the garment. Thankfully it's black fabric and hides stains well, but I've gone through more jugs of vinegar getting blood out of it than I can count.

"Fine," I say through clenched teeth. Luckily, this is going to be an easy task, so I don't foresee it being too much of an issue keeping Terry in line knowing there's zero point in complaining about his choice because he doesn't care about what I want, even if it means doing it all on my own while Terry stands on the sidelines picking his nose.

"You scout everything out? You know what you're doing?"

Leaning forward I plant my elbows on my knees, running my free hand through my hair. I huff, "Yes, Bigg-Boss."

His name isn't Biggy, but I have no idea what his actual name is. Besides, I like not using his real name. It feels too professional and helps me stay disconnected. That's why I like referring to the people Biggy sends me after with their last names or nicknames. It feels weird being on a first name basis with people I'm about to torture and kill so I try to avoid it.

I started calling him Biggy because he's anything but and I found it funny. The dude probably weighs 160 after downing a meatball sub and a couple beers, and is barely five foot seven. Small or not, I have to admit he's an intimidating guy even given his older age. He knows how to kick you where it counts. Not to mention he's got so many sheep in his clutches because of his ability to get anyone "arrested" or killed on the spot.

He has several connections, and I'm not stupid. He's got so many dirty cops in his back pocket that getting me taken in would result in something much worse than just some nasty mush being served to me on a plate in a concrete cell. There would be no fair trial, no privileges, no commissary, no sticking to myself without unwanted attention. I'd be getting the shit beat out of me on a daily basis and some of the torture I've inflicted on my targets would feel like heaven compared to the assault I'd endure from his bitches on the inside. I'm one of those pathetic sheep just waiting for the day I'm led to the slaughter or Biggy decides to set me loose. Though I'm fully aware that day will never come.

Biggy gained his title after he took over for his father several years ago. His family has always been in the drug trade, and though Biggy put up no fight against the topic, from what I've gathered, it was always expected that he would take over the empire when his father no longer could.

His gravelly voice cuts through my phone speaker again, and my head instantly starts pounding.

"Walk me through it."

I suppress my annoyance before spelling it all out: "They're boring. They live a typical low-middle-class life. Reed gets up every night at 11 and leaves the house at 11:15 on the dot every time. He takes the same back road route to the factory."

It's been anything but interesting for me to watch it for the past two weeks but somehow relaying it all to Biggy feels even more dull.

"His wife and daughter are always asleep when he leaves. She leaves the house and takes the girl to school every morning. Reed gets five dollars worth of gas every morning before coming home."

"He runs on five dollars of gas every day? That's only like 2 gallons," he says.

"Apparently he has something against a full tank." Maybe he's hoping his car will break down and give him an excuse out of his pathetic repetitive routine.

"His daughter gets off the bus between 3:10 and 3:20, Reed eagerly waiting for her at the front door." He waits for her with a smile on his face while she seems less than thrilled to see him. But I don't know jack about kids, so who am I to judge? Maybe all pre-teens are like that. I know I was, but I also had anything but a normal childhood. She just seems so much happier around her mom, but her dad doesn't seem like much of a winner. Also not my business how she gets along with her parents.

"His wife gets home around 5 every night before cooking dinner. They eat, and Reed goes back to bed before he has to get up for work. She puts the girl down for bed before going to bed herself at 10. They seem to really like routine."

"And you're sure neither of them are up to something?"

I fight the need to audibly groan my annoyance with the conversation and throw myself back against the couch, resting my head on the cushion, and stare up at the ceiling.

"Yes. I've watched both of their workspaces and even watched the school the girl goes to. I placed a tracker on his car so I could make sure he wasn't leaving work when I wasn't there to watch. I haven't seen him snort a line, pop a pill, or even drop his cigarette butt on the ground. Either he got his shit together and cleaned up his act or he's hoping you'll forget if he keeps on the straight and narrow long enough." The poor bastard is stupid if it's the latter because Biggy doesn't forget anything. Greedy greedy man.

"He couldn't walk on a tightrope of dental floss to get me to forget he owes me twelve grand," he complains.

Biggy gave Reed a loyalty test of sorts, and he failed big time. It's a rarity for Biggy to even offer second chances, so the fact that Reed was stupid enough to risk it speaks volumes about how smart he is. Taking Biggy's money and running away with it as if there aren't little worker bees watching his every move was a mistake he's going to regret soon enough.

Twelve grand seems like chump change to some in the drug world, especially the one Biggy is in. While we aren't the biggest fish in the sea in Portland, we're big enough that most aren't dumb enough to try and screw with us; and we hold our own well enough that other crews keep to their own territory and we keep to ours. It's when people can't stay in their own territory that we have problems. We run the South and East sides, The Snipers keep up North, and Lloyd with his crew has their own thing on the West. As long as everyone stays where they are, we don't have problems. Of course we have the little guys scattered throughout who think they're tough, dealing dime bags and stolen pills, but they're so minuscule we rarely do anything about them.

"So what's your plan?" he asks. I rub my eyes with my thumb and finger trying to grind the headache out from behind them.

"What it always is. I'm going to take care of it." I really don't feel like going through the whole thing with him when I know I'm going to have to explain it to Terry at least six times. I hear Biggy huff on the other end of the phone before erupting into a coughing fit presumably from choking on the toxic fumes he enjoys inhaling.

"Don't get short with me, boy. I don't have the patience for your shit." His condescending term for me has me rolling my eyes. I'm 25, not 12. Not that it matters because no matter how much I prove myself to him trying to dig myself out of the hole I dug that got me into this mess, he never treats me like anything more than an indentured servant which is all I'll ever be.

"I'm not giving you shit. I have yet to fail you one time." Unlike Terry. "Trust that I will get it done."

He grunts, and I hear faint voices on the other end of the line. "You better or it's your ass on the line," he says before the line goes dead.

It's always me on the line. I lie down on the couch, propping my feet up on the arm and grumbling when my legs dangle off the end. I'm too tall for this piece of crap. I close my eyes and will my body to allow some sleep before Terry gets here. My mind won't stop reeling as I lay there staring at the ceiling instead of contemplating how I jacked up my life enough to be in my position.

Thirty minutes later nitwit Terry is pounding on my door like he's got a rabid dog nipping at his heels. I groan as I force myself off the couch and throw open the front door.

"Will you shut up, for crying out loud?" I whine.

Terry shoves his way in, bumping my shoulder in the process, and I almost gag from the smell that emanates from his gangly form. He smells like a skunk crawled up his ass and died. I've always assumed from his lack of upkeep with his appearance that his hygiene was slacking, but to smell like that when you have a working shower is asinine.

"Ever heard of ringing the doorbell?" I ask as I gesture to the button just outside the door.

"I have, I just don't care."

I close the door and turn to see him plopped on my couch. First thing tomorrow I'm burning it. Bugs be gone.

"Ahh yes. Please come in and make yourself comfortable as if this is your house."

He sneers at me with his rat teeth as he kicks his dirty shoes up on my coffee table. Great, now I have to burn that, too. I'm about to toss Terry in the fire with it.

"So what's the plan?" he asks as he sighs and relaxes back into the cushions. I open my mouth to answer but he doesn't give me a chance.

"Breaking in and holding him at gunpoint? Is the wife hot? I call dibs if she is," he squeezes himself through his pants, and I'm about to hold him at gunpoint. The man has zero morals and doesn't care about making a mess because he knows I'll inevitably be the one who has to clean up after him.

"First off, get your nasty feet off my table and stop grabbing yourself." I kick his foot off the table and watch his face as his shoe thuds against the floor, dirt falling off with it. He goes to lift his foot again but I raise my eyebrow in challenge.

"I will kick your ass if you put that boot on my table again."

The moron knows I could beat him senseless without a doubt. I've got 70 pounds on his scrawny ass. He's slim with little muscle, and I'm confident he's never worked out in his life. But of course, he doesn't have to because he relies on anyone else to do the heavy lifting. Like I said, he offers no value, but heaven forbid he be kicked out of the inner circle.

"Secondly, no we're not breaking in. I know they don't have anything worth any value in their house."

"And you know this how?"

I'm convinced this man doesn't think before he speaks.

"Because I've been in the house, you halfwit. I've been watching them for two weeks. You don't think I'd scope the house out to make sure the money wasn't in there? I had to make sure they weren't hiding shit I didn't know about. Unlike you, I cover all my bases."

That was a real challenge too because of their schedules. I had a very short window between his wife leaving in the morning and him returning from work to snoop around. Especially since Biggy wouldn't let me install a single fucking camera. Cheapskate. He just kept saying I needed to do it "the old fashioned way" because it saves him money. It took far more convincing than it should have just to get him to let me put the tracker on Reed's car.

"Plus, they live in a neighborhood. Do you really think I'm going to risk having the neighbors calling the cops? Not to mention he's got a kid. I'm not dragging her into all this mess. It's not her fault that her father is a moron." I relate to the last part a little too well.

He scoffs like he thinks we need to make this as complicated for ourselves, or me, as possible.

"He drives the same route to work every night. I'm going to cut a slit in his gas line ensuring he only gets a few miles down the road before he breaks down. He has a weird habit of only getting a couple of gallons of gas everyday so it won't take much. When he pulls over, we're going to stop and offer him help. I'm going to grab him, and you're going to get the car towed to the lot where you're going to wait until I call you. Got it?"

I know he doesn't, but I ask anyway. Before the words leave his mouth, I know he's going to ask something stupid: "Why do we gotta mess with his car at all instead of busting down the joint?"

Called it.

I lean against the kitchen door frame and imagine my life behind bars. Maybe I would be better off rotting in a concrete cell in an orange jumpsuit than dealing with this moron.

"Because, Terry, I'm not trying to make this a big mess that I'll have to inevitably clean up. I expect this to be an easy job."

He huffs as he sinks deeper into the couch, drenching the cushions with his smell.

"What am I supposed to do once I get the car to the lot?"

"You wait until I call you and tell you what to do."

He gets up, crossing the room before pushing his grimy finger into my chest. He's a good six inches shorter than me, and I can't help but chuckle at his confidence.

"I don't take orders from you and I say we do it my way," he sneers, exposing his crooked and rotting yellow teeth. Biggy isn't a bad-looking guy and is strict on his appearance, always dressing to the nines, so how he could share the same blood with this nasty man–if you can even call him that–I will never understand.

I push off the doorframe and into his shit-stained finger, putting myself at my full height towering over his pathetic frame. Still, he doesn't back down, though I can see the flash of intimidation in his eyes.

"Fine. When we end up with three dead bodies instead of one, preferably zero, I'm not helping you clean it up. You can call Boss and tell him you decided to clean house. See how he takes it. We both know you're on thin ice right now."

I'm not lying. He is on thin ice with Biggy because of an incident last month with one of the jobs he "helped" with, but I also know that no matter how many times Terry pisses him off, he'd never actually follow through with any threats on him. But Terry doesn't know that, so I use it to my advantage. Biggy doesn't appreciate unnecessary messes, so it would no doubt piss him off and earn Terry a tongue-lashing. I can tell he's grinding his teeth resisting the urge to argue with me. He backs off, throwing himself back on the couch.

"You're such a wuss, Lawrence."

Right.

"What, are we in third grade? I've been watching them for two weeks. I know their routine, not you. Now get your crap and let's go."

He shoves past me as he gets up to grab his bag from the car, and I hear him mumble under his breath, "Asshole."

"At least I don't smell like a rotting one!" I yell over my shoulder as he walks to his car.

Chapter 2
Lawrence

———————— * ★ * ————————

There's not a huge window of time for me to cut the gas line between when Reed's wife goes to bed and he gets up for work, so I have to work quickly to also avoid any neighbors noticing me. It's a pretty run-down neighborhood, so people don't really pay attention to what goes on, but still. I was lucky that so many people park on the street in their neighborhood, so it was easier for me to watch from the truck without raising suspicion.

The drive to the Reed house is silent apart from the wind rushing through my window. The instant I got in a closed vehicle with Terry, I wanted to drive with my head out the window like a dog. I'll take the smell over listening to him talk, and somehow, he's managed to stay silent the entire time.

I park down the street from their house, my nerves kicking in when I see the driveway. His wife's van is there, but his car isn't. The routine has been the exact same every single day, both cars in the driveway; the day I make my move cannot be the day he switches things up.

"Where's his car?" Terry asks.

I know if I screw this up, Terry will jump at the chance to try and bury me with Biggy.

"He just parked in the garage today. He does that sometimes," I say, hoping the words are true because otherwise I'm royally screwed. He hasn't once parked in the garage since I've been watching them. I'm not even sure how he would with how much junk is packed in there. It's 10:38

so I've got to get this done if I stand a chance of being back in the truck before Reed wakes up.

"Just stay here, and I'm going to go snip the line."

I open the door expecting a comment from Terry, but he stays quiet as he gestures for me to go. It's at this moment I'm glad I staked out the interior of the house, so I know they don't have any cameras or alarms. Not that it's a surprise given the state of the house, but appearances aren't always accurate.

I make my way down the street staying in the shadows as I get to the side door of the garage. I pick the lock, swing the door open, and release a deep breath when I see Reed's car sitting in the wreck that is their garage. It looks like he shifted what he had to in order to make the car fit and give himself just enough room to open his car door.

I don't know why he didn't park in the driveway like he usually does, but my balls are thanking their lucky stars that it's here because Biggy would have me by them if I screwed this up. I slip the knife from my jeans and grunt as I shimmy myself under the car to cut a neat slice in the line so no gas pours out until there's pressure in the line.

I ease out from under the car and glance around the garage, looking for any indication that something is off but notice nothing. Convenience strikes when I notice a gas can propped next to a rusty push mower by the side door. I pour some of the gas out, letting a small puddle collect. I doubt Reed will notice the smell anyway, but if he does, this works out well in my favor. I make my way back to the truck cursing under my breath when I see it idling with the headlights on. I rip open the driver's door.

"What do you think you're doing? Are you forgetting that the goal is to stay inconspicuous?" I hiss. He looks at me like I'm stupid while chewing on a Twizzler. He's probably too stupid to know what inconspicuous means.

The black truck and black tinted windows make it easy to blend into the shadows, but the idiot is painting us bright blue with the headlights on parked on the street at 11 pm.

"Nobody is out anyway. Nobody cares," he says as he shoves another bite of Twizzler in his mouth. I'm almost certain I'm going to witness him lose one of his rotted teeth from biting the candy.

"This is why I wanted Ricky," I grumble as I climb into the driver's seat and kill both the lights and engine.

"Ricky's nothing special," he says as he opens a bag of chips and shoves a handful in his mouth.

"You're right. Between the two of you, you're definitely the special one."

The meathead smiles, his mouth still full of junk food. Idiot thought it was a compliment.

"Thanks, man," he says as he playfully punches my shoulder. "I know we could be friends if you pulled that stick out of your ass."

I grunt in reply not caring to correct him. There's no way he and I could ever be friends. I lean back in the seat focusing my gaze on the Reed house, hoping Terry takes that as his cue to shut up, but he doesn't.

"How long do we have to wait on this guy? I gotta pee." The sound of his voice has me questioning why I value my life at all and haven't just let Biggy kill me off so I don't have to deal with this. I don't bother looking in his direction as I reply.

"Do you have the bladder of a hamster or something? You peed before we left." I'm sure he missed and got it all over the seat, too.

"Yeah well, I gotta go again. I don't control when nature calls, man."

"Well, hold it."

"Screw that. I'm not holding it." He's reaching for the handle, opening his door before I'm stretching over the console and pulling it shut.

"What are you doing?" I ask.

"Uh, getting out to piss. There're trees right over there." He points to a group of trees by a house caddy corner to the Reed's.

"In someone's yard!" I whisper yell. "If you screw this up by pissing in someone's trees because you have the bladder of a toddler, you won't have to worry about Boss because I'll kill you myself." I turn back to my window ignoring the mumbling under his breath.

I see the bathroom light in the house flip on. Checking the time on the dash, it's right on cue so it's safe to assume it's Reed getting up for work. The blinds in the bathroom and the daughter's room are the only two rooms with curtains that offer actual privacy, so I can't say for certain, but I'm confident it's him.

I start running through the plan in my head, my brain repeating it over and over. A trickling sound pulls me out of my thoughts and snaps my head in Terry's direction.

"Are you serious?"

"What? You told me I couldn't piss in the trees, so this is me not peeing in the trees," he says as he finishes relieving himself into the bottle before screwing the cap back on and dropping it on the floorboard of my truck.

"Terry, I swear, you get that bottle off my floorboard or so help me I will chop off that tiny green bean you call a dick."

Reluctantly he reaches down and grabs the bottle, placing it in the cupholder between us. That's not any better, but at least I don't have to worry about it spilling on the floor.

I watch the clock with impatience as it hits 11:15, and there's no indication of Reed leaving. Having Terry in the car is making me antsy, and I don't like it. I should have done the job myself.

"Isn't he supposed to have left by now?" Terry asks, my eyes still trained on the house. I glance at the clock, my nerves kicking in when I see it's 11:30. I've been staring out the window for more than fifteen minutes. Shit. He never leaves this late, and that in combination with him parking in the garage has me on edge that something is off.

As I start playing out possible scenarios in my head, the garage door opens and his tail lights illuminate the driveway as he backs out, waiting for the garage door to close completely before pulling off. Game time.

I wait for him to pass my truck and get to the end of the street before turning over the engine to follow him, keeping the headlights off.

"I still think breaking in would have been a lot more fun," Terry whines beside me. "For me anyway," he adds as he nudges me with his bony elbow.

I know he's referring to the wife, and the thought makes my stomach churn. I've tortured and killed my fair share of people for Biggy. People who ripped him off, stole from him or wronged him in some form, so I've grown mostly immune to the lifestyle. Assaulting innocent women is where I draw the line. I don't tend to enjoy inflicting pain on those I torture. It's by far not my dream profession, but I try to not let it bother me like it used to. It actually made me sick. But after years of being forced to do it, I learned to make the most of it. I could do so much more with my life, but until I play my cards right, it's a trap I'm stuck in.

"I like it when they fight back."

I nearly break my neck as I snap my head in his direction. Considering his appearance, I'm not surprised the only way he can get a woman is unwillingly, but it makes me want to drag him on the asphalt behind my truck. Perverts like him are wasted space.

"Will you please shut up about that and tell me the plan?"

"It's your plan; why do I need to tell you?"

"So I know you paid attention and know what to do," I bark.

"And here I thought you were starting to thaw."

Yeah right. I will never thaw with him, or anyone for that matter. I'll stay a freezer-burnt cube of ice.

I've been keeping track of the miles in my head to remember how far we've driven. We're three miles from the house, so Benny Boy should be sputtering to a stop pretty soon. I'm keeping my distance as he slows at a stop sign. My chest hurts as he turns left. What the hell? He never goes that way. Right is a straight shot to the factory. Turning left means we only have two miles before the street lamps in town start illuminating everything, and the nightlife becomes an issue.

"Uh, is there a reason you aren't moving?" Terry asks.

I realize I haven't moved as I see Reed's tail lights starting to fade down the road. I'm thankful that Terry doesn't know Reed's route to work and doesn't realize my entire plan may have just gone down the drain. This man is really trying to give me a mess tonight. Turning on the headlights, I step on the gas, turning left. As I get closer, I see his car is stopped on the side of the road. The car finally ran out of gas, his hazard lights illuminating the empty road.

"You know what to do," I say as I nod to Terry.

"Yeah, and if he doesn't want our help?" he asks.

"We don't give him a choice."

Pulling up beside Reed's car, I idle, waiting for him to notice. His head is resting on the steering wheel. A quick honk of my horn has him nearly jumping out of his seat. Even from my side of the truck and the minimal lighting, I can see his eyes bugging out of his head and the panic on his face. My gut churns. Something is off. Terry motions for him to roll down his window so we can talk to him.

"You okay? Need any help?"

"Oh. Uh no. Just ran out of gas. I'm good," Reed says, his eyes shifty.

"Doesn't seem like it. You sure you're okay?" I ask as I lean over the console, suppressing a gag at my proximity to Terry's filth.

"Yup, all good. You can go on." He motions at the road in front of him.

Don't make this difficult, buddy.

"There's a station up the road a bit. We don't mind taking you up there to fill up a can," I reason.

"No, that's okay, really."

Don't do this, Reed.

His eyes are darting around the car, his gaze bouncing between us and his surroundings. He notices our intent to help and persists.

"You know, it's probably actually just something under the hood. I've been having issues with the hunk of junk. I'll get it taken care of, no worries."

I throw the truck in park, exiting the vehicle before rounding the hood and rolling up the sleeves of my black hoodie.

"I'm pretty good with cars. Why don't you pop the hood and I'll take a look?" I am good with cars, but I'm not helping buddy ol' pal here with his car troubles. He *is* the trouble.

He's still white-knuckling the steering wheel, and I suppose for a second, it's possible that he knows I've been tailing him, but I've gotten the feeling that he's too dumb to look for signs like that.

"No really, it's okay. You can go."

I'm not going anywhere, he is, and he's starting to realize it if his demeanor is any indication.

Walking to his driver's door I grip the frame so he can't roll up the window. Not that it would matter, but I'm not going to get his hopes up.

"Get out of the car, Benny Boy," I demand quietly but sternly. His eyes go wide at the realization that I know who he is, and he tries without success to turn over the engine. Desperate moron.

"Either you get out of the car willingly, or I drag you out. You choose."

I can see him weighing the options of whether he should put up a fight or not. While I have no doubt I can beat him unconscious one-handed, he's a hefty guy probably weighing close to 300 pounds. I'd rather he cooperate so I don't have to wrangle his fat ass out of the car, but I will.

Just as I think he's made the right choice as he unbuckles his seatbelt, he's scrambling, reaching into his center console, dropping a gun on the floorboard as I reach through the window and bust his face into the steering wheel.

He lets out a high-pitched wail that resembles a twelve-year-old prepubescent boy, and my lips pull at the corners when I see the blood streaming from his nose.

"I can get the money, I swear," he blubbers as blood steadily streams into his mouth, coating his teeth. So, I was right, he knew it was coming.

"Too late for that, buddy," I say as I reach in, unlocking the door and hauling him out onto the pavement before landing another blow to his face, enjoying the crunch of the bone beneath my knuckles.

"Help me get him in the truck, Terry," I hiss as I drag the behemoth to the back of the truck, his groans getting louder as his body drags across the road beneath him. I'm trying not to have to knock him out because then he'll just be total deadweight and I risk him waking up on the drive to the warehouse.

"Terry!" I yell as I deliver a punch to Reed's nose, giving him the message to stop squirming. He must note the look in my eyes that tells him I'll kill him right here if he doesn't stop resisting because he gives up, blubbering like a baby. I feel in his pants and jacket pockets before finding his phone and tucking it in my back pocket.

Opening the bed of the truck, I haul him up and shove him under the covered bed. There's nothing in the back that he can use as a weapon, but I grab some rope and tie his arms and legs anyway.

"Have fun on the ride, roly-poly," I snort as I slam the truck bed shut, Reed's whines becoming much quieter. "Thanks for the help jackass," I sneer at Terry as I bend at the waist, heaving in air. Reed's a heavy dude, and I clearly need to start lifting more.

"Oh, so now Mister 'I can do it by myself' wants my help," he scoffs from the front seat. Asshole.

"Whatever, just tell me you called the tow guy. We have to get out of here." We've been lucky that nobody has driven past us yet. Luckily, it's an odd time, and there's not much out here that has people coming from town.

"Yeah, yeah, he'll be here. Don't get your underwear tied in a knot."

"It's panties in a twist," I mumble. I don't know why I trusted Terry to call the tow truck in the first place. But if I'm going to be forced to deal with him then he's going to pull some sort of weight.

I look down the road in both directions cursing when I don't see any headlights. The guy we use gets paid good money to be at our beck and call no matter the time of day, and most importantly not to ask any questions.

Suddenly I remember the gun that Reed dropped in the car. That pisses me off because there weren't any weapons registered in his or his wife's name, and I hadn't seen the gun in the house. That's not typical for your average blue-collar gambler. I guess maybe he did expect Biggy to come after him. Turning my attention back to Reed's car, I climb into the driver's seat looking for the gun. It's too dark to see where it landed, so I reach my hand down to the floorboard feeling for it with my fingertips. My fingers brush metal, and I grip the gun in my hand before shoving it into the back waistband of my jeans.

Since the dude had a gun I didn't know about, I need to check for any other surprises he might have hidden. I click on the overhead light and open the glove compartment, and find nothing but his expired registration and the car manual. I move onto the center console where he was hiding the gun, again disappointed when I find nothing of interest besides a gold pocket watch with an engraving inside that reads, *For my daddy. I love you- Starlette* that I shove in my back pocket. I don't know why I want it, but I do, and he won't miss it, so I take it without thinking twice. It's when I reach to turn off the light that something catches my attention in the back of the car. It takes me a second to realize what I'm looking at before my brain catches up. What the hell?

Lying unconscious in the back seat is his twelve-year-old daughter, Starlette. Her hair is messily draped over her face, only some of her pale skin visible between the dark black strands. She's lying on her side, her arm dangling over the seat and a blanket covering most of her body. It's then that I panic, my heart nearly falling out of my ass not knowing if she's just knocked out or if she's dead. I quickly climb out of the driver's seat and fling open the back door, bending down to check for a pulse. I breathe in a sigh of relief when I feel a steady heartbeat under my fingers.

"FYI there's headlights coming," Terry booms from the truck. I close the car door gently, making sure her head isn't close enough to get hit.

The headlights get closer and I'm ready to lose my shit when I realize it isn't the tow.

"Everything alright?" a middle-aged man asks as he slows to a stop next to the truck.

"Yeah, man. Everything's good. Just broke down but my buddy here is gonna give me a ride," I explain, gesturing to Terry hoping it's enough to keep the guy from getting out and offering help even though Terry is in the passenger seat.

For his sake, I hope he's smart enough to avoid helping two random strangers in the middle of the night. I'm not one to kill innocent people, but Terry on the other hand doesn't care who gets hurt if he gets enjoyment from it. By the smirk on Terry's face, I can tell he's silently begging for the guy to get out. I have enough to deal with as is, I don't need more. I watch as the guy's eyes travel from me to Terry who's looking like a psychopath with a huge grin on his face, to Reed's car, back to me before deciding.

"Alright, man," he says before pulling off, a look of uncertainty lacing his features as he looks back at Terry before driving away.

"Could've had a two-for-one special," Terry says. I'm too busy trying to figure out what to do about the unconscious girl in the back seat to reply.

I pull open the back door of my truck and assess the situation because there's no way I'm putting that little girl in the bed of my truck with her father. Luckily, she's dainty and there's enough room on the floorboard to fit her. My blood is boiling as I wonder why she's in the car to begin with. I have an idea of why, if her being unconscious is any indication, but I tamp down the thought before I can think too much about it because I may end up stabbing her father right here before I even get the chance to question him about it.

This answers the question about why he had parked in the garage, but now the question is why his daughter is unconscious, and I'm going to find out even if I have to rip him apart.

I remove the blanket from her and arrange it on the floorboard of my truck, taking off my hoodie to provide a pillow of sorts for her head.

"What are you doing?" Terry asks as he twists himself to look at me between the two seats.

"Shut up and keep watching the road," I say, not in the mood to deal with him. Thankfully he twists back in his seat mumbling something about me being an asshole under his breath before grabbing a bag of chips from the floor and shoving a handful in his mouth. I'm convinced the only thing he brought with him in his bag is junk food.

"Incoming," he says through a mouthful of food. Quickly I grab Starlette from the car and gently place her on the blanket in my truck, making sure her head is cushioned by my sweatshirt and wrap the blanket around her so she's hidden if Terry looks in the back of the truck. He's too focused on shoving food in his face to notice what is happening behind him, and I'm thankful for it. Seconds later the tow truck pulls up, positioning his truck in front of Reed's car before climbing out and silently waiting for an order.

"Take it to Lyonel. I'll be in touch," I say as I slam a wad of cash into his open palm. All I get is a grunt in response before he shoves the money in the pocket of his stained jeans and goes to work hooking up the car.

I climb into the truck, my heart and mind racing. I stare at Terry waiting for him to get out and go with the tow.

"I'm not going. You don't get to have all the fun to yourself. If you don't like it, then you can call Shotty and see what he has to say about it," he sneers, baring his nasty teeth. I've never understood where his nickname for Biggy came from, but I've never cared enough to ask.

"Fine," I say through gritted teeth. So much for not having a massive mess to clean up.

Chapter 3
Lawrence

———— • ★ • ————

The warehouse is forty minutes out, and every minute I'm in this truck with Terry feels like I'm waiting for a bomb to explode and rip all the limbs from my body. This is not how the plan was supposed to go. Shit like this doesn't happen to me. I watch them; I know their routine as well as I know the feeling of my dick in my hand. Other than small hiccups, I've never had a plan go to shit like this one is.

Terry is munching on more junk food, and every bite he chews is amplified in my head like nails on a chalkboard, making me resist the urge to reach across the car and rip his throat out so he can never eat again.

"Will you stop shoving shit in your mouth? It's a wonder your stomach hasn't ruptured yet," I snap at him. His eyes turn to me as he shoves half a chocolate bar down his throat.

"You know, I'm gettin' real tired of your bitching," he starts, bits of spit and chocolate flying out between his teeth. "All you do is gripe and complain about the things I do, but you don't let me do a single thing I wanna do. You order me around like a dog, but I ain't no bitch, Lawrence, and you're not my boss."

I grit my teeth as I look at him out of the corner of my eye. If it wasn't for the defenseless child in the back of my truck, I'd be tempted to drive us into a tree just to put myself out of my misery. Terry hasn't noticed her back there yet, and I need to try to keep it that way if there's any chance of me not losing every strand of sanity I have left.

I keep my mouth shut as I drive to avoid any more conversation. Terry finally stops shoving food down his throat, throwing his wrappers on the floor at his feet before blindly reaching for a bottle in the cupholder. It doesn't even register in my head until warm liquid is being spat all over my dashboard, droplets hitting my face in the process.

"What the hell, Terry?" I yell, nearly slamming on the brakes before I remember what's behind my seat.

"I forgot I pissed in the bottle, man. I thought it was tea." His piss is so dark it it's damn near brown so it's not far-fetched. I'm not sure his kidneys are even functioning if that's what it looks like.

I swipe at the liquid slowly dripping down my cheek and reach over, wiping the piss on Terry's mouth while keeping my eyes on the road. He opens his mouth to say something of a threatening manner I'm sure, but the look I pin him with has him cowering in his seat.

Good.

"You're paying to wash my truck, and cleaning it yourself," I say as I gesture to the urine coated dashboard and crumb covered floors.

"Hell no. The crumbs will disappear into the carpet eventually." He grinds his boot into the floorboard as if to prove his point and I wish more than anything I could drive us off a bridge and end it all right now.

"And the piss that's all over my dash?" I ask.

He grumbles as he turns in his seat like he's reaching for something in the back. The instant I see his fingers fumbling for the blanket covering Starlette, I panic. If he finds her back there I may truly kill him in his seat.

"Stop!" I yell, nearly driving us off the road as I snatch his wrist before he gets the chance to touch her.

"What the hell dude. Do you want me to clean it or not?" he argues.

"Just leave it, prick. I'll deal with it later."

The rest of the drive is silent as I fume and Terry picks at the grime under his nails with his teeth. I wouldn't be surprised if he has E. coli or Hepatitis, or whatever else you can get from being the most disgusting person on the planet.

I pull into the warehouse lot and park the truck, contemplating how I'm going to deal with my dilemma. It sits on a private acreage out of town on a dead-end road, the nearest house or business miles away.

"Go in and make sure everything is ready for me," I say as I toss him the keys. He grumbles under his breath but doesn't argue as he hops out of the truck. I quickly change out my license plate in case anyone saw something while we were taking care of Reed's car. It's unlikely but not impossible so I switch the plates out to be safe. I have a stash of them ready to go when the need arises, which is often.

We bought the warehouse five years back when Biggy first started utilizing my skills to this extent. It used to be an automotive factory but has since been renovated for my needs. To any normal person walking in, it wouldn't raise much suspicion as I have maintained its run-down gloomy interior keeping all of my business in the basement which has been soundproofed. Not that anyone would be able to get within a mile of this place without my knowledge. It's bugged with cameras everywhere.

Starting with Reed, I pull his body out of the truck, not caring when he thuds against the hard ground. He's fighting again, thrashing like a pissed off toddler and throwing any profanity he can think of at me. I roll my eyes before delivering a sharp kick to his ribs that has him curling into a fetal position. Lifting him up under his arms I drag him into the warehouse to the basement where Terry is waiting with more rope. He's foaming at the mouth like a rabid dog. I haphazardly shove Reed's body onto the chair letting Terry go to work restraining him properly. Terry isn't a skilled man, but I can't deny he knows how to tie a knot.

I make my way back out to the truck and pull out Reed's phone to look for anything that will tell me why his daughter was in his car. Pulling up his messages, the last one was sent from an unassigned number roughly twenty minutes before he left his house: Cape Motel Room 119.

My gut starts to churn. It doesn't look like he has any other messages of value, and no phone calls were made to, or from the unknown number. My guess is he's been sneaking around, but the fact that I haven't seen him with another woman in two weeks is strange. I'm about to pocket the phone again when something tells me to look through his photos.

There's several random pictures, some of which don't make any sense. There's one of a plate full of what appears to be dogshit that I think is supposed to be nachos. That's what this man considers to be photo worthy? There's also a handful of family photos that look ancient. Must have been when he actually cared about his family.

Scrolling through the rest of the images, they all change to pictures of Starlette and my heart sinks as anger rages through me. This sick bastard. My eyes go from the screen to the little girl, back to the screen. Every picture is of his daughter lying unconscious only partially clothed. Some are taken of him defiling her small body while she sleeps. It makes sense now why her room was the only other room besides the bathroom that had blinds. Guilt racks my brain as I realize he was probably hurting her while I was outside in my truck watching the house. I should've placed cameras in the house. I could've saved her. If Biggy would've just let me bug the place, she wouldn't have… he wouldn't have been able to… I feel sick.

I have a feeling she has no idea what he's been doing to her since she's unconscious in every single photo, and I now don't care how big of a mess

31

I make. He's going to die. I carefully lift Starlette out of the truck, her hair falling from her face as she dangles in my arms. She's a beautiful girl with dark black hair and pale skin speckled with golden freckles. Rage sizzles beneath my surface as I think about how her innocence has been stripped from her. How anyone can defile a child like that is beyond what I can fathom.

Carrying her into the basement, Terry has Reed strapped tightly to a chair, his ankles and wrists bound so tight to the wood I can see the skin turning purple.

"Um, what is that? Who is that?" Terry asks as his eyes collide with the girl in my arms. If I could've avoided him seeing her, I would have, but I wasn't going to leave her in the truck, especially not knowing how long she's going to be out. The fact that she hasn't woken up yet makes me even angrier as all the dots start to connect.

"The bastard had her in the back of his car when we stopped him. Looks like he drugged her."

I wasn't sure when I found her, and I was terrified that she might wake up on the way here, but her limp form tells me he did something to keep her out for a while. I lay her down on the floor, tucking my hoodie under her head. Terry starts towards her with a look in his eyes like she's prey that he's hunting.

"Stay far away from her Terry or I swear I will put a bullet between your eyes."

"What? I can't have fun with the mom, and now I can't have fun with the daughter? She was dropped right in our laps, dude! What, you think you can have her all to yourself and not share?" He seethes.

The thought of that makes bile rise in my throat, and each word out of his mouth is bringing him closer to death.

"No, I'm not touching her, and neither are you. Now we need to deal with him," I say, gesturing to Reed, his face caked in snot and blood. I walk over to him, his eyes wide as I get closer. No doubt his reality is really setting in at this point.

"Please, no. I swear I can get you the money! Don't hurt me," he pleads. I was just going to leave him with a couple broken bones and deep bruises as a warning for running off with Biggy's money. But now that I know what a sick pedophile he is, I'm going to enjoy killing him. Telling by his dilated pupils and bloodshot eyes that I couldn't see clearly in his car, he's high. No doubt with drugs he bought using the money he owed Biggy, too.

"Oh, I'm going to do more than that," I snarl.

"Please! I'll get you the money plus interest! Please don't kill me," he cries, his tears mixing with the blood dried on his cheeks.

"Well, Benny Boy, you shouldn't have screwed over my boss. He gave you a chance. You came to him with a need that you could no longer afford." Well, to Reed the cocaine was a need. Not something I'd consider an essential, but I'm not an addict. "When you didn't have the money, he offered you a deal. He gives you five grand, and you use those gambling skills of yours to turn it into profit."

I pull a knife from the table next to me enjoying when his eyes turn to saucers as I spin the blade between my fingers.

"Not only did you turn that five grand into twelve, but you ran away with it, pretending you lost it all."

Approaching his shaking body I slowly slice the knife across his cheek and watch as blood seeps from the wound. "Did you really think he wouldn't find out? He was testing you. Even if you'd lost it all, you still would have owed him that money plus interest."

I rip open his shirt, slicing the fabric with my blade to expose his heaving chest. Pointing the tip of my knife at his sternum, I dig in just enough to break the skin before dragging it down all the way to his belly button, each of his wails sending the blade slightly deeper into the subcutaneous tissue. He's lucky at the moment to have so much of it.

"But instead of paying him back, you decide to go and spend it all at the casino and on blow. From another dealer at that."

"Please," he begs, snot dripping down his face.

"Terry, get me the drill," I say, not looking away from Reed so I can bask in the fear that fills his face at the demand.

"Terry!" I yell, not hearing a response.

My eyes lift to the other side of the room where Terry is bent over Starlette, his hand roaming over her thighs while his other fumbles with his belt. Rage blinds my vision as I run across the room barreling Terry to the ground, his pants falling down past his hips. My fists connect with his jaw, and I can feel the skin of my knuckles cracking open as I hit him repeatedly.

"I-"

Punch.

"Told-"

Punch.

"You-"

Crunch.

"Not-"

Crunch.

"To-"

Punch.

"Touch-"

34

Crunch.

"Her!"

I don't know how long it takes for me to come down from my adrenaline high before my vision clears and I take in Terry beneath me. Or what is left of him. Blood has pooled on the floor around him, his face now unrecognizable. I drop the knife that was gripped in my hand I didn't even know I was holding. The stab marks covering Terry's upper body tell me I did more than just punch him. The knuckles on my left hand are steadily dripping blood, my arm now covered in a mixture of my own blood and Terry's. I can feel droplets dripping down my face.

A retching sound pulls me back to earth, and I turn to see Reed vomiting down his front. Looking back down at Terry, I can't say I blame him because I was beyond brutal, though I can't deny that it was cathartic. Terry had that coming for ages. I'm just thankful he finally gave me a good enough reason to get rid of him. Not sure how I'll explain this one to Biggy without getting myself killed in the process, but that's a problem for later.

Still shaking with rage, I stand noticing Reed's gaze fixed on something beside me. I follow his eyes to Starlette's body on the ground, Terry's blood only inches from touching her. I wipe my hands and arms on my pants as best I can and quickly lift her off the floor, moving her to the other side of the room. I will not allow a drop of his blood to touch her.

"Please don't hurt her," Reed wails from his chair.

In an instant I am across the room, my face inches from his.

"I'm not the one who she has to worry about hurting her, you sick fuck," I snarl, spit hitting his face.

I pull his phone from my back pocket, thankful it isn't broken from my rage fest. I pull up one of the less graphic photos of his daughter shoving it in his face.

"How long?"

As soon as his brain registers what he's looking at, his body racks with sobs. Too bad they're falling on empty ears.

"I asked how long!" Pulling the gun from the back of my waistband, I aim it directly at his kneecap and shoot, his screams echoing through the room.

"Scream all you want." I grab his hair in my fist and pull back, so he's forced to look at me. "This room is soundproof, and there's nothing for miles. Answer the question."

"Four years," he chokes out on a sob.

A growl rips from my chest as I grab the knife still caked in Terry's blood from the floor and walk back to Reed, stabbing it through his abdomen in a spot I know won't kill him. Yet. He screams, but it does nothing to ease the anger racing through me.

I am going to kill him, but he's going to give me answers first.

"You've been assaulting your daughter since she was eight. You sick bastard." I pull back before launching another punch to his already shattered nose. His eyes are starting to swell shut so I decide to remedy the problem. Pulling one of his eyelids out by the lashes, I saw through it with my blade, dropping the piece of skin to the floor. His body writhes against his restraints as he screams in agony.

"Where were you going tonight?" I ask.

"Nowhere. Just to work," he manages through his blubbering.

"Bullshit. Where?"

"I told you. Work." His lies aren't going to make his execution any easier, and I'm not sure how he hasn't realized that yet.

I pull his other eyelid out enough to slice it off as well before shoving it in his mouth.

"Eat it," I demand.

He wails but does as he's told before retching all over himself and my shoes.

"I was going to get the money to pay him back." He's referencing the money he owed Biggy and I'm pretty confident I know where this is going, but I want confirmation from his blood and vomit-soaked lips.

"Why was your daughter in the back of the car?"

No answer.

I grip his middle finger and push it back until it meets the top of his hand, his screams overpowering the sound of his bones crunching.

"Answer me."

When he doesn't reply in a timely manner, I grip his pointer and middle finger on his other hand and bend them backwards, feeling the bones give under the pressure.

"Okay. Okay. Okay."

I step back, twirling my knife as I wait for him to catch his breath enough to answer me.

"I needed the money to pay back your boss so he wouldn't come after me."

"What were you going to do with her?"

Silence.

I grip his left ear between my fingers before digging my blade into the flesh, sawing it off and dropping it to the floor now covered in his own puddle of blood.

"Please, I'm sorry. Just stop."

"Wrong answer," I say before plunging my blade into his thigh just far enough over to avoid his femoral artery. Can't have him bleeding out yet.

His screams lessen as he starts to pass out. I shove some smelling salts back under his nose to prevent him from succumbing to the pain, but I know my time is dwindling.

"What did you give her?"

"Rohypnol," he blubbers.

"How much?"

His answer is cries.

Walking over to my bag, I grab the drill and place it on the floor before kneeling and taking off his shoe. I line up the drill bit in the middle of his foot and press the trigger, watching as blood spurts out of the wound as the drill bit digs deeper into his flesh. Terry's restraints have him tied so tight his foot can't even move. His head starts to bob so I reach up delivering a sharp slap to both sides of his face.

"I don't think so. Wake up, buddy."

"She'll be out till morning," he whimpers, coughing up a mouthful of blood. His words are hard to decipher as he tries not to choke on his blood, vomit, and loose teeth.

"What were you doing with her? Who's number is this?" I ask as I shove his phone in his swollen bloodied face, the message thread pulled up. He doesn't have to look at it to know what it is.

"His name is Peter Simmons. He was going to give me fifteen grand."

"For what?" I growl.

"For one night."

My eyes travel back to the helpless girl knocked out on the floor, my gut wrenching at memories of my childhood being beaten 'til I was bruised. My torture was not the same, but I ache for her just the same. An innocent soul placed in the hands of evil.

Using Reed's phone, I send a quick text to Mr. Simmons. Guess I'll be paying him a visit tonight too. *Something came up with the wife. Be there as soon as I can with the girl.* Typing the message alone makes me want to hurl.

"Please. You can have her after. I just need the money."

This douche wad is dumber than I thought if he really thinks the money is going to matter from this point on, because the only way he's leaving this building is dead as I drag him back to my truck. Not to mention the fact that I wasn't going to kill him until I figured out what a sadistic pedophile he is, and he hasn't figured out that I'm not sick like him. The fact that he even offered that makes my rage grow, turning my blood to lava as if it wasn't already on fire.

"You won't be needing the money anymore." I crouch so I'm eye level with him, though I'm confident his vision is beyond clouded by the blood that has been pouring from where his eyelids used to be. I pull his pants down, exposing his pitiful dick.

"Is that why you drug your daughter?" I run the tip of my blade down the short length of his dick pausing at the base and digging the tip into his balls. "Because your dick is so puny that even your own wife doesn't want to touch you?"

He pukes again, not having the energy to crane his neck so it just falls out of his mouth, dripping down his chin.

"You got any tattoos, Benny Boy?"

He shakes his head back and forth slightly, his head hanging.

"It's okay. I know just the marking for you."

My patience is wearing thin, and the fun is dwindling away, but I want to accomplish a couple more things before he bleeds out. I take my knife to his chest feeling the skin give way to the tip of my blade as I slice. I pull back, baring my teeth in a sinister smile as I admire my work, the words Rapist Pedo carved into his skin.

Low whimpers are leaving his lips as he fades into unconsciousness. I crouch again, gripping his puny manhood in my fist as I saw my knife blade back and forth until the appendage is sliced clean off. Blood is pouring from the wound, and I know he'll be dead in a matter of minutes, but it feels fitting to kill him by ripping away the piece of himself he used to torture his daughter. I grip his jaw between my fingers, cringing as they slip through the vomit on his face, and I force his jaw open as I shove the flesh into his mouth.

"Choke on it, you sick fuck."

Poetic justice if you ask me. I know in the back of my mind I'm going to be in deep shit about all of this, but in the moment, I'm struggling to care. No amount of torture would be enough to make him pay, and death is a blessing he doesn't deserve.

Leaving him bleeding out in the chair, I clean myself off the best I can with rags and strip out of my blood soaked clothes before grabbing a clean pair of sweats and hoodie from my bag before picking Starlette up off the concrete and taking her out to the truck to lay her on the back bench seat. The last thing I want is to soil any part of her with blood. I drive her to the hospital, dropping her off in an alley by a side entrance before calling 911 and telling them to retrieve her for medical care. I break the burner phone and trash it after watching from a distance to make sure she's safely taken in for care.

Next stop is the motel. The last thing I needed was the pedophile running off, but I'm sure my text kept him waiting. I pull into the motel, taking in the surroundings. Reed was so classy he couldn't even prostitute his daughter off at a motel that wasn't crawling with crackheads and cockroaches. I slip on my gloves as I make my way towards Simmons's room. Luckily, I don't notice any security cameras.

I walk up to room 219, rapping my knuckles on the splintered wood. I hear muffled voices coming from a TV on the other side of the door before it's swinging open.

"About ti-" I shove my way through, slamming the door behind me and flipping the lock.

"Who are you? I didn't order room service," he asks, confidence seeping from his pores that appear as if he hasn't showered in days. He knows I'm not room service, and I know this motel doesn't even know what room service is. I do have a delivery, but it's going to be his heart on a plate, not eggs.

I take in his appearance. He's older, probably around 50, gray hair peppered throughout his once dark brown hair, rather scrawny, but tall. I can tell by his appearance and mannerisms that the fifteen thousand he told Reed he had never existed. I doubt he has fifty dollars to his name, just a sick twisted bastard who was looking for a victim, and poor Starlette was caught in the middle of two sick bastards' desperation.

"I'm the guy who's here to kill you," I say as I lift the remote from the dresser and blast the TV volume to the max. Granted, I have a feeling that even if the rooms next to us are occupied, the people in them are likely invested in something that involves a syringe.

He throws his arms up in defense as he backs away towards the bed.

41

"Look man, take whatever you want." The only thing he has worth taking is his life.

"Oh, I will. As soon as you answer some questions." The back of his legs come in contact with the bed, and he stumbles back onto the mattress, his eyes wide with fear. In seconds I'm at him, my knife blade held firmly to his jugular.

"You can try to scream, but this blade will be slicing through your vocal chords before you even have the chance."

"What do you want, man?" he asks, tears streaming down his face. Are all pedophiles this wimpy? He's a pathetic excuse of a man just like Reed.

"Why are you here tonight, Petey?"

"I'm sorry."

"For what?"

He doesn't answer right away, and my response is the blade pressing into his flesh, blood breaking through the skin and leaking down his neck.

"I know I'm disgusting. I promise I won't do it again. Just please don't kill me, man. I have a family." I kind of doubt that, but even if he does, they're better off without him.

"You know, you should've thought of that before you decided to buy a child for your sick pleasure. How many?"

"How many what?" he asks, his eyes darting between me and the door. He's an idiot if he thinks anybody is going to be busting that door down to save him.

"How many have you hurt?"

"I don't know."

Lies.

Lining the blade up with his dick through his pants, I start pushing down just getting through the fabric when he folds.

"Stop! Okay! Seven!"

Clucking my tongue, I grab the corner of the bed bug infested comforter, stuffing it into his mouth to muffle his impending screams.

I slice open his stained t-shirt quickly making seven deep clashes to his chest.

"This last one is for the little girl you were going to hurt tonight," I say as I plunge the knife into his abdomen, twisting it as he writhes, coughing blood up around the comforter. I pull out the knife and watch the blood pour from the wounds, the color draining from his face as he bleeds out. I grab his phone digging through it finding pictures of Starlette saved to his phone. Bile rises in my throat, but I swallow it down as I wipe his phone of every photo before shoving it in my coat to dispose of. That poor girl doesn't deserve those pictures being analyzed by a bunch of law enforcement goons. I pull a bag of cocaine from my pocket, planting it underneath the bed in a spot that makes it look like it was somewhat well-hidden. The area that this motel is in, it isn't hard to frame it as a drug deal gone wrong.

I turn down the TV slightly and leave his bloody body on the bed before heading out to my truck to go back to the warehouse. The drive there allows the reality of the situation to sink in. Biggy is going to lose his shit about Terry. I haven't decided how I'm going to spin it to him.

I take in the mess when I walk into the room where Terry's body is still lying in a pool of blood, hamburger where his head should be, Reed slumped over in the chair across the room, his limp dick still hanging from between his lips. I don't typically enjoy the gore accompanying this job, and I have to admit even I'm surprised by the extent of my torture tonight.

Torturing those who made a poor decision that got themselves into a hole they can't climb out of tugs at me because it's a position I've been familiar with. One that landed me in the role I'm in. A choice I made and am barely surviving. If it wasn't for my history, I likely would have suffered the same fate as those that I've tortured. At the hands of some other unfortunate soul that got sucked into Biggy's grasp. Benny Boy here was a rare case that is giving me enjoyment as I watch the blood that has drained from his body. People like him are the absolute scum of this planet, wasted oxygen that never deserved to live.

Between Terry's and Reed's body I've got a huge mess, and I sigh at the thought of not getting to lie down any time soon. I lay out the tarp I brought in from the truck and grunt as I step over the blood surrounding Terry and hoist his body over my shoulder nearly gagging when a chunk of brain matter falls to the cement with a plop.

Gross.

I should have just made him go with the damn tow. Though I have to admit I'm not disappointed that I've finally gotten rid of the dog shit stuck to my shoe. Good riddance, if you ask me, but I know Biggy won't. Not only is he not getting his money, but Terry is dead. This is not going to go well.

I lay Terry's mangled corpse on the tarp and roll him up before doing the same with Reed. I'm winded by the time I get both of their bodies into my covered truck bed. I power up the sprayer, watching the red evidence of my night spiraling around the drain in the floor before falling into the pipes beneath. I inspect the room ensuring that nothing is left uncleaned.

I drive to the junkyard, the sun now poking over the horizon, sleep pulling at my tired eyes. I pull into the gravel lot, stopping in front of the small brick building at the front of the lot. Lyonel, the guy who makes thousands off of his deal with Biggy to destroy my evidence, is propped up against the brick taking a pull from a cigarette, his eyes fixed on me through the windshield. I take a quick glance around. I don't see Reed's car; I hope I'm not too late.

I exit the truck, the gravel crunching under my boots as I make my way to Lyonel.

"What can I do for you?" he asks, breathing out a puff of smoke. I'm sure I still look like hell after the night I've had, and there's no doubt still blood on me but Lyonel shows no sign of giving a shit. He knows not to ask questions.

"The dark red Chevy shitbox that you brought in last night."

He nods giving acknowledgement.

"Has it been scrapped yet?"

"Not yet; it's out back. You need it for something?"

He tosses his cigarette to the ground, not caring to stomp out the burning embers.

"I just realized I had some extra… parts to the car. I wanted to make sure they were scrapped along with it."

His eyes fill with a knowing look.

"It's back by the compactor, but I wasn't planning on crushing it today."

"Well, you won't mind if I drop off the extra parts in the trunk and move up the time for discard, right?"

"I might be able to make that happen," he says, his eyebrows raised in challenge. I roll my eyes as I pull a wad of cash from my wallet and stuff it into his open palm. He's making a pretty penny as is from his deal with Biggy, but surprise, surprise he's a greedy prick. He takes a second to count it out with his dirty fingers.

"I can get it done tomorrow morning."

I groan as I turn on my heel and get in the truck following the dirt path back to the compactor. I pop the trunk of Reed's car and haul the tarp covered bodies from the bed of my truck, dropping them into the trunk of the car along with the gun that was in his console, and Simmons's phone that I destroyed.

I double check making sure I have Reed's phone in my pocket before slamming the trunk and climbing back into the truck. When I make my way back to the front of the junkyard, Lyonel is still perched against the brick, huffing on another cigarette. I hop out, pulling another handful of bills from my wallet and shove them at his chest.

"Get it done, now," I say over my shoulder as I climb back in the driver's seat, pinning him with a glare.

He throws down his cigarette, making his way down the gravel lot motioning for me to follow. I could offer him a lift in the truck but I'm not feeling generous. I watch with satisfaction as he lifts the car on a forklift, hoisting it into the compactor and smashing it into a metal cube, crushing Terry and Reed to bloody dust within it. The crushed metal falls to the ground with a thud, and I pin Lyonel with a *keep your mouth shut* look before peeling out of the junkyard, leaving him in the rearview as he puts another cigarette to his lips.

Chapter 4
Lawrence

———————— * ★ * ————————

I pull into the garage of the house and lay my head on the steering wheel, dying to shower off the filth. My truck needs a serious wash, too, but it's going to have to wait. I changed at the warehouse and wiped off as much as possible, but my body aches, and I feel disgusting. It's 10 a.m. and I assume Starlette is home from the hospital by now. I pull out Reed's phone—several missed texts and calls from his wife.

I pull up the text thread, and bile rises in my throat as I attach several of the images of Starlette. I need to make sure her mom wasn't a part of it because I think I may actually shatter if she has to lose both parents. I don't think she was aware, but I need to make sure. I press Send with a message that reads, *I'm sorry.*

Almost instantly she's calling, repeating the process when I don't answer. A voicemail comes in after the second failed attempt at an answer. This will tell me what I need to know, so I put it on speaker playing the message, relief flooding my veins when her voice is full of tears as she screams through the phone:

"You sick bastard. What have you done? What did you do to our little girl? I am going to make sure you rot in hell, you son of a bitch. You better make sure the cops find you before I do because I'll kill you myself."

Already done; sorry. I almost wish he was still alive so I could watch her torture him, her motherly wrath ripping him to shreds. But his body is compressed to sludge in a block of metal. I'm glad to know she wasn't in on it, but I will make sure that she and Starlette are taken care of.

I carry my aching body inside and fall onto the bed, too tired to move. Sleep starts to take over immediately, but my ringing phone pulls me out of the sleep threatening to take over my mind. I grumble, running my hand through my greasy hair as I sit up, pulling my phone from my pocket wishing I could crush this one like I did with my burner. I would do just about anything to avoid this conversation, but I need to get it over with.

"Yeah," I say, digging my fingers into my eyelids so hard I see stars.

"Did things go to plan? I haven't heard from Terry."

Welp.

"Terry's dead," I breathe out.

Silence fills the line and it's so loud it's almost deafening. I pull the phone away from my ear making sure the line is still connected.

"What did you just say?"

"Terry's dead."

"Okay. You're going to tell me every single thing that happened tonight and then I'm going to decide if you're going to die, too."

I sigh, hoping Biggy buys what I'm gonna tell him.

"I cut Reed's gas line, so he'd stop on the road before he got to work. Terry got out to drag him from the car and Reed pulled a gun from nowhere and shot him. Shot him in the head." I make sure to sound distressed like it hurts me. "He was dead before I even got out of the truck."

"How did he have a gun in the car?" He asks through gritted teeth. "You know to look into that!"

I can tell he's pissed but I don't know if he believes me. "The gun wasn't registered. I didn't know he had it. It wasn't in the house when I scoped the place out, so he must have kept it in his car."

I can hear his heavy breathing through the line and it's irritating that I can't see his face to decipher what he's thinking.

"What did you do with him?"

"I got rid of him with Reed. There was too much risk not to."

"What the hell, Lawrence? He was my brother! You dumped him like the pieces of shit we discard?"

"What do you mean, your brother? I thought that was just a term of endearment." Though Biggy and the term "endearment" have never belonged together. Frankly I had no idea if they were truly related or not, though he doesn't seem as mad as I'd expected for killing his brother.

My heart rate picks up as I wait for his response.

"No, Lawrence, you moron. Terry was my little brother."

Well shit. I guess that explains why they butt heads all the time and Terry got away with anything he did.

"Is that why he always called you Shotty?"

He hesitates like he's unsure if he wants to answer my question.

"Well, that is my name."

No fucking way that's his real name, but I can't help but ask.

"Your real name is Shotty?"

Again, he hesitates, anger clear in his voice.

"Yes. You got a problem with it?"

"No." I try to suppress a laugh. Someone's mother was unstable.

"You killed my fucking brother and now you're laughing at my name? You want a slow and painful death or a slower more painful death?"

I choose to stay silent. Clearly now is not the time for humor.

"And what do you mean you dumped them?" Biggy continues. "You weren't supposed to kill Reed."

I'm still not sure why he didn't want Reed dead anyway. He's had me kill people for much less than twelve grand, but then again there never seems to be a method to what this man does.

"I didn't have a choice. I just got so mad when he killed Terry, I saw red and I couldn't help myself. He needed to die for what he did. He was a pansy, and he would have cowered easily, but I'll be damned if he deserved one more breath of oxygen into his lungs. We both know he didn't have your money. He blew it as soon as he got it, and he has nothing of value to make up for it. Was it worth it to risk him running around snitching, giving you more to deal with?"

He's had enough on his plate lately and though it wouldn't be hard to wipe away whatever evidence someone like Benjamin Reed would've spouted, I know he realizes it was either that or wiping Reed out of existence. His reputation relies on that shit.

"What about his family?" Biggy asks, my pulse racing.

"What do you mean?"

"I mean you got rid of him; did you not think to use them as leverage?"

I grind my teeth so hard my jaw hurts. I have to reel in my temper if I want to sell this. "There was no point, Boss. They have a small basic house, nothing of value as far as belongings. His wife is a receptionist at a vet clinic, and he worked at a factory. There's a reason why he didn't have any money to keep buying coke from you."

Biggy usually avoids dragging women and kids into it, but he's crossed the line before, and I will not let him cross it now.

"You know as well as I do that bringing them into it creates more mess to clean and you weren't going to get that money back. Having him gone takes a load off your shoulders."

Actually, it's a load off of mine but I'll humor him to sell it.

"Shit!" I can hear the anguish in his voice, and I almost feel sympathy for him. Almost.

"I'm sorry, Boss. I know I'm at fault for missing the gun. I own up to that. If you want to kill me for that then so be it."

I'm not really fond of the idea of him killing me, especially now that Terry is gone, but I'm hoping that saying it keeps him from following through.

"I should."

I don't respond and listen to the silence on the line.

"But you're right. I'm going to trust that you cleaned up your mess?"

"As always. I set it up so Reed's presence won't be missed. They'll be looking for a ghost."

I still have some things to plant, so it works out how I want but I'll take care of it. All it will take is a quick talk with a couple certain officers downtown to paint Reed as a guy who disappeared on his family of his own free will, but I still try to plant evidence in case the wrong people go snooping.

"Something like this happens again, Lawrence, and you're going to wish you were dead. Don't make me regret trusting you."

I know exactly what he's threatening, and it makes me want to do to him what I did to Terry. Rot in prison with the psychos Biggy has on the inside, sleep in the dirt with Terry, or risk him going after my mother. None of the above.

"Won't happen again, Boss," I assure him.

The line goes dead and relief floods through my veins as I strip my clothes and turn on the shower, allowing the hot water to singe my skin as it washes my sins down the drain.

I wake up covered in sweat again, a strangled cry of my brother's name falling from my mouth. My eyes take in my surroundings to remind myself I'm not living that horror anymore. Not those horrors anyway. I throw off the covers and make my way to the kitchen where I pour myself a glass of whiskey. Not exactly the glass of water my body probably needs, but it's what it craves. It helps chase away the nightmares. The clock tells me I got the same three hours I always do.

They started when I was eight, when the abuse started, and haven't stopped since. My mom cheated on my dad when I was seven, and my brother Thomas was five. Dad had started working a lot and didn't pay Mom much attention anymore, so she found it somewhere else. Our life had been pretty typical before the affair. We'd go out for ice cream as a family, eat dinner together at the table, laugh together. We were happy. At least I thought we were.

Once Dad caught Mom cheating, everything changed. He started drinking excessively, constantly fighting with her for ruining our family. From the arguments I overheard, Mom wasn't the only one to blame. I guess behind closed doors they had been much unhappier than I knew. Not that it was hard to put on a show for a seven and five year old.

I remember starting to see the bruises on Mom that she tried to hide once Dad started going off the deep end. I still don't know if he was hurting her before the affair, but I know something in them both changed.

Dad had never laid a hand on us before. It wasn't until the night that Mom left him with two kids to raise on his own that his anger changed aim. She had grown tired of his abuse and the fighting, so she left. I don't know if it's true or not, but it makes me feel better to think that Mom never expected Dad to hurt his own kids which is why she left us behind. Little did she know.

I will never understand why she didn't take us with her. Why she vanished without ever coming back for us. I want to hate her for leaving, but as I've grown and as I witnessed Dad's abuse firsthand, I can't say I blame her either.

We didn't have any other family. Both of my parents had run off to get married when they were young and left their pasts behind. They never gave much detail, but from what I gathered, neither of them had gotten along with their parents. It was just us.

It wasn't so bad at first after Mom left. Dad would come home drunk, and we'd get a smack or two, mainly Thomas. But Dad always apologized the next day and told us how sorry he was, and how much he was struggling, but that he would get better for us. We learned pretty quickly that he wasn't sorry, and he would not get better. He would only get worse. Much worse.

As the years dragged on, the abuse only increased. Thomas got the majority of it, though I never understood why until Dad got mad one night and said my brother only reminded him of Mom. I guess looking more like my dad is the only thing that saved me.

As we got older, we tried to fight back, but it only made it worse. His abuse would just get harsher. When I'd try to stand up for Thomas or defend him against Dad, I'd get beat so bad I couldn't move without flinching for days. School wasn't an option after a while. Too many questions arose when the injuries became too obvious to hide easily. I didn't mind not going to school. I'd always felt that I was too smart for what they taught anyway. But the breaks from Dad were nice. Eventually,

Thomas stopped wanting my help, knowing it would only cause more pain. He'd take the bruises if it meant I stayed unscathed for the most part.

I thought about running away on several occasions, but I couldn't convince Thomas to come with me. I think a part of him was always convinced that Mom would come back for him. She never did.

When I was eighteen, I got a job at a small auto shop and worked as many hours as I could. I wasn't getting paid enough to save quickly, especially considering most of my paychecks went to feeding my brother and me, but it got me out of the house. Thomas wasn't allowed to leave. He tried sneaking out once and got a broken nose and ribs as a reward.

I came home from work one afternoon to a silent house. Well, nearly silent. I knew as soon as I stepped in the door that something was wrong. I could sense it in my bones. The only noise coming from my brother's room was muffled cursing. As I pushed open the door to his room, my mind went blank.

My dad was pacing back and forth, his hands tugging on his hair.

"What do I do? What did I do? I didn't mean it. He just makes me so mad."

He didn't even notice me standing in the doorway, weak in the knees as I stared at my brother's lifeless form on the carpet. His face was bloodied beyond recognition, his neck at a strange angle.

Walking towards Thomas, I dropped to the floor in front of him. I didn't bother to call 911 because I knew it was too late. My brother was gone. I felt for a pulse to make sure, but there was nothing there. His blown pupils stared into space. I let my head fall as I sobbed for my brother, both out of anger and out of relief. He was free. But he was also dead.

Suddenly my cries of anguish must have pulled my dad from his haze as he dropped down next to me, taking my shoulders in his blood-stained hands and shaking me.

"It was an accident, Lawrence. I didn't mean to. You have to help me clean this up. I know you don't want your dad to go to jail. They won't understand that it was an accident."

His breath reeked of alcohol, and I could tell by his pleading eyes that he was serious. He wanted me to help him cover up his murder of my brother. Rage overtook me as everything went red. I stormed out of the room, leaving my father on the floor. He was still in the same spot when I returned a minute later and pointed the barrel of his gun to his temple and pulled the trigger.

It should have bothered me as I watched his brain matter splatter onto Thomas's dead body. It should have bothered me that I was now staring at the only family I had left lifeless on the floor. But it didn't. One was in Heaven, the other in Hell. I only wished I had done it sooner. Then maybe Thomas would still be alive.

I knew I had to act quickly if I wanted my plan to have a chance of being believable. I scribbled a barely legible note to match my dad's handwriting, wiped down the gun, and put his fingerprints all over it before planting it next to him on the floor, his body splayed out as if he'd pulled the trigger on himself. A murder/suicide was the only way to spin this unless I wanted to rot behind bars for killing a man who didn't deserve to live after the suffering he'd caused.

I ran to the bathroom and threw on the shower. I tore off my clothes and soaked my body and hair. I didn't bother to dry myself off before throwing my blood stained clothes back on and dialing 911.

Several hours and questions later, I was released from the police station. I'd managed to pull it off. I had come home from work and gotten in the shower to clean off my day. When I heard the gunshot from the shower, I threw on my clothes and that's when I found the bodies in Thomas's room and called the police.

I explained the abuse that had occurred over the years and told them most of the truth. Dad's suicide note had said he was sorry, and he'd lived too long in this world. He couldn't live with what he'd done. Given the autopsy on Thomas that I knew would reveal several broken bones that never healed correctly, my story would check out. Plus the scars that riddled his body. I have several of my own that Dad took pleasure inflicting, but not as many as Thomas. Not to mention the tears I shed made it more believable. They were real, but not a single one was for my dad as the detectives drilled me with questions.

Since I was eighteen, they couldn't put me in the system, so I was on my own. I tried to support myself, but it was impossible. The house was taken away, and I was homeless. My mental state went to hell after I killed my dad. I was so scared that I was going to get caught, I couldn't think straight. After I lost my job, I got desperate. I took to dealing to make my money, to survive. Now I almost wish I had died in that room with my brother so my fate didn't end up the way it did.

Turns out I got involved with the wrong people, not the small fish in the sea, but the big ones, and Biggy caught wind of me. Turns out I was dealing in his territory. "Stealing from his profits." he'd said. He would've killed me, made me just another homeless troubled kid that the world wouldn't notice had gone missing, but after doing his research on me, he thought I could be of use. I don't know how he figured out I had killed my dad, but he did, and he held it over my head. That, and my mother. He said he knew where she was, and he had evidence that I killed my dad. He'd throw me in prison and go after my mom if I didn't do his bidding.

I should've known that I'd never do enough to earn my way out of his clutches. No sooner than I had released myself from the hands of one demon, I had found myself in the hands of another.

Chapter 5
Piper
Fifteen years later

It's only Tuesday and I already want to throw myself off a bridge. Work has been an absolute nightmare and coming to this café seems to be the only thing that offers me solace lately. It has as much to do with the eye candy sitting across the coffee shop as it does with the delicious chocolate croissants I'm taunted with every time I come in here. Both are mouthwatering and enticing.

I sigh as I put my car in park before grabbing my backpack from the back seat and hauling it over my shoulder. I order a large caramel latte and chocolate croissant from the unhappy barista, hoping that the caffeine magically erases the dark circles under my eyes and provides me with the will to work. I grab my coffee and sit at the table I've occupied every day for the past two weeks. The Creamy Pie, though unfortunately named, is actually a very nice, charming little café. It's a mom-and-pop shop but I seriously question how they settled on the name because pie isn't even something they sell. Maybe I don't want to know.

I settle into my chair, taking a sip of my hot coffee, hissing when it burns my tongue as I pull out my laptop and power it on. When I glance across the room, my eyes meet with his and I try to suppress the smile that naturally happens when I look at him. He's always sitting in the same spot across the room with a book in his hand.

He's a devilishly handsome man despite the fact that he's clearly older than I am. His dark brown hair is buzzed short on the sides, and just long enough on top to run your fingers through. Not that I've thought about that.

Gray has started to pepper his hair, and barely noticeable stubble decorates his defined jaw. I can see tattoos creeping out of his leather jacket, the top of one hand covered in ink, and by the looks of the black lines poking out just above the neckline of his t-shirt, I have a feeling the tattoos travel over most of his skin. Something about tattoos has a way of drawing me in, the curiosity of their story making me want to know more, what the story is behind them.

His dark eyes bore into mine, and I feel a strange pull to him, almost as if I know him, though I know I've never seen him before because I would absolutely not forget a face like that. He's taken no initiative to indicate that he's interested in me, and I don't want to come off as desperate. Instead, we just trade quick glances at each other, me turning my face down into my books to hide my smile and blush when he catches me looking his way.

I tear my eyes away from him as his eyes return to his book, blush from embarrassment creeping onto my cheeks at the fact that he didn't return my smile. Granted, he hasn't one time since I've been coming here, but he doesn't seem angry either, just distanced. Like he's drowning in his own mind and is going through the motions physically while his mind fights a battle nobody else can see.

I force myself to focus enough that I try to work on several of the things screaming at me from my to-do list: research, reports to my boss, some ridiculous training session. I just can't make myself care enough to do anything with them right now. An hour has passed and I accomplished half of a task. I pack up my bag, tossing my empty cup into the trash before making eye contact with the gorgeous man again as he watches me walk out the door.

I'm about to unlock my door when I hear someone behind me. My heart rate spikes slightly when I turn to see a scrawny young guy a few feet away from me. He's dressed in skinny jeans that are hanging on for dear life on his upper thighs, the belt on his pants clearly being used as a decoration rather than for its intended function. He looks like he's about twenty years old with a fraternity sweatshirt clinging to his torso, and though I wouldn't really call him ugly, he's definitely not my type. I noticed him in the café at the table next to mine, but could hardly even acknowledge his presence when I was too busy drooling over the guy across the room.

"You know, my couch would look a lot better with a pretty little thing like you on it. Would you want to hang on Friday? We can Netflix and chill," he says as he slides his hands in his pockets, making his jeans drop even lower.

At this point I'm not sure why he's even wearing pants. The cool winter air has to be freezing his cheeks. He's got a smug grin on his face like I haven't eaten in three days, and he's just offered me a royal feast. Like he thinks his offer is so enticing there's no way I'm going to say no. This is why I hate dating anymore because I'm convinced chivalry has literally ceased to exist. It has burned to the ground, the ashes evaporating into the wind. I'm trying to enjoy my twenties and this is what flirting has become for people my age.

"Actually, I'm busy Friday, but thanks for the offer," I say as kindly as I can, trying not to let my face show that his offer was repulsive. I unlock my car and toss my bag in the back seat hoping he leaves me alone, but instead he leans against the driver's door blocking my ability to leave.

"That's cool. How about you give me your number and we can hook up later." He winks at me, and I want to throw up, the action giving me flashbacks of my frat boy stage freshman year of college. There's a reason frat guys have a bad reputation, and this dude definitely isn't helping the case. I glance around the lot, cursing myself for parking near the back. We can't be seen from the lobby of the café at this angle, and there's nobody else in the parking lot.

"You know, I don't think that's a good idea. I appreciate it though."

His body stiffens and his face drops slightly, his eyes raking up and down my body, sending goosebumps down my spine. And not the good kind.

I've backed up to the point that I'm next to the trunk of my car which to any normal person would indicate that I'm uncomfortable, but douche face over here doesn't seem to be picking up on the hint as he steps in closer to me.

"And why is it a bad idea, hotcakes?"

Hotcakes? Ew. "You know, I actually have somewhere to be, and I have a boyfriend so I'm not available," I say, my voice stern as I walk around him, grabbing the handle to the driver's door. He doesn't even let me open it before he's stepping into my arm, breaking the hold I had on the door. Asshole.

"Are you sure about that?" he asks. I'm about two seconds from kicking this guy in the dick. Take a hint, buddy.

"Mmmhmm," I say, my lips pulled in a tight smile.

"Here's the thing, I don't particularly like being told no, and most women don't have the audacity to say no. So, let's just start over. Give me your number, and you can come over to my place on Saturday."

I have a hard time believing he's not used to hearing no. His sagging pants, overwhelming stench of pot, and lack of respect for boundaries screams charmer.

He's pressing his body into mine, turning so I'm pinned against the car door. Anger is rising to the surface at his persistent behavior, but I'm trying not to cause a confrontation. I will stab him with my keys if I have to though.

"I really have to go. I have class," I lie as I reach behind me, fumbling for the door handle. Still, he's not backing up, his hand reaching out to grip my arm.

"Don't touch me," I hiss. His grip tightens, the fabric from my shirt digging into my skin.

"I said get off me!" I yell. "I'm a p–"

It's that moment I'm about to rear back to punch him with my free arm, but hands are fisting him by the back of his shirt before I have a chance. In an instant the guy's body is pressed against the pavement, his cheek digging into the cold ground.

"She said not to touch her, you dickhead."

My mind races to catch up with my eyes as I take in what I'm seeing.

The hot book guy from the café has Frat Boy pinned to the ground, his knee digging into his back while he pulls his head up by his hair a few inches before slamming it down into the pavement, holding his face firmly against the ground, his wiggling form no match for the strength pushing down on him.

"You don't know–" His sentence is cut short as his head is pushed harder into the ground.

"I know enough." His knee digs into Frat Boy's back even harder causing him to cough as he fights to breathe in air.

"I'm going to let you up, and you're going to take your sorry ass back to whatever hole you came from, and if I see you coming around her again, I'm going to beat your skull in."

He climbs off the guy who pulls himself to a standing position, the textured pavement imprinted on his bruised cheek. That was definitely hotter than it should have been. I need to get laid.

He coughs again, shooting daggers at me before turning away towards the front of the lot.

"I didn't know it was your pussy, man," he says over his shoulder. Dick.

"Psycho," he mumbles before he's far enough out of range to not hear the curses coming from his battered face.

Staring at the man beside me, he looks murderous as he watches the guy stalk off and for a moment I'm concerned he's going to follow the guy and finish through with his threat. I know I should be scared that I'm now standing alone with a guy much more menacing, but I'm not.

Finally, his eyes turn to me, and I'm nearly breathless when I see him up close. He's gorgeous. Easily the finest specimen of a man I've ever seen, and I envy whoever he has at home. He's older, but not too old. I'd guess he's about 38, but he's aged like fine wine.

"Are you okay?" he asks, his eyes roaming over my body—but not in a creepy way; in a protective way like he's assessing for injuries douche canoe may have caused.

I'm aching, but not in a bad way, and not in a place I should be after I was cornered by a psycho desperate to get his dick wet. My tongue feels like sandpaper stuck to the roof of my mouth. Tingles skate down my spine, good ones this time as his eyes drink me in. I swear I see the corners of his mouth turn up slightly in a smile, but it happens so quickly I'm convinced I imagined it.

"Yeah, I'm fine." I focus my eyes on anything other than him because I know I look like an idiot ogling him like a teenage girl.

"He's just an asshole who thinks he's entitled to whatever he wants," I say, staring at my shoes.

"There's a lot of those."

He turns to walk away, and I stutter as I call after him: "I uh, thank you…"

"Lawrence," he says, turning his head to reply even though he's still walking away.

"Can I buy you a coffee? As a thank you?"

He pauses briefly before replying: "That's not necessary. It wasn't a big deal. I saw a problem and I fixed it."

He continues walking back towards the café, and the words spill from my mouth like vomit.

"I've seen you in there a lot," I call after him. Instantly I'm mentally scolding myself because now I just seem creepy and desperate when he's clearly not interested.

At first, I think he's just going to ignore me, but he turns and walks a few steps closer, though he's still several feet away.

"Yeah. I come in here on my breaks. It's a calming environment for me."

I shift back and forth on my feet from nerves and I'm questioning if I'm actually 13 instead of a grown woman.

"What do you do for work?"

Seriously woman? Back off. No way in hell is he going to be interested in you if you keep pushing him.

He pauses as if he's contemplating his answer. "I'm an independent contractor of sorts." Awkward silence fills the air for longer than I'm comfortable with, but he's not walking away.

"I've wanted to talk to you several times," I admit, rubbing my hand down my opposite arm, the cold air starting to get to me. It's not freezing, but it is too chilly to be having a full blown conversation with the breeze adding to the windchill. He watches the movement, but he doesn't say anything, though I see a vein ticking in his jaw like he wants to.

He walks closer, leaning against the hood of my car but leaving a respectable amount of space between us, presumably to keep me from feeling threatened.

"Why?" He asks.

"Why what? Why haven't I talked to you?"

"That and what have you wanted to talk to me about?"

I fidget with the sleeve of my thick sweater, and I can feel a blush creeping up my neck. I hate myself for reacting this way around him, unable to figure out why I feel so drawn to him.

"I don't know. Anything really," I admit. "What books you like to read, your go-to coffee order. Whatever would spark a conversation with you. But you're intimidating."

His eyes narrow, slight wrinkles appearing beside them as he smirks at me, and I swear I melt on the spot. He is too damn attractive for his own good and he knows it.

He crosses his arms across his chest. "I'm intimidating?"

"Yes. You give off this whole dominant 'Don't screw with me' vibe, and I didn't want to end up on the concrete like buttwad did." I motion to the pavement near my feet where Lawrence held the guy down threatening to beat in his skull if he showed his face again.

He chuckles and it's a beautiful sound that I want to hear again. My stomach flutters at the fact that I'm the one who made him laugh.

"Buttwad?" he asks, amused.

"Yeah, I like to come up with as many names for insults as I can. It's like a game to me." I shrug.

"I wouldn't dare mess up a face as pretty as yours. And honestly, I think I only helped buttwad's face." There's humor in his tone when he repeats my nickname for the guy, but the good mood is pulled from him as soon as he pulls his ringing phone from his pocket.

"I have to go," he says before turning on his heel and heading for the front of the lot.

"And you should wear a coat next time. You're too pretty to freeze to death."

He glances over his shoulder at me before climbing in his truck and I just have a gut feeling that this man is going to be my ruin.

Chapter 6
Lawrence

———————— ⋆ ★ ⋆ ————————

I'm sipping on my burnt cappuccino when a flash of black hair and pale skin draws my eyes up. She looks around as if she's looking for something, or someone, and I feel a pang of jealousy before her eyes lock on mine. Not that I have a reason to be jealous, I don't even know her name, but I am anyway. I try to keep my face neutral, but I feel my mouth pull slightly on the corners. Damn it.

I return my eyes back to the book, not reading a single word, but keeping my focus on the page so I don't look at her again. A few minutes later, the chair across from me scratches against the floor, and I don't have to look up to know who it is. I can sense her. It's like this weird pull to her that I can't explain or understand.

"This seat taken?" she asks, not waiting for me to answer before she sits down anyway.

"Be my guest," I gesture to the seat, though she's already made herself comfortable leaning back in the chair, legs crossed.

She's unbearably gorgeous, her dark hair a dramatic contrast against her milky pale skin. Her eyes are a deep brown, and looking at them feels like she's seeing straight through to my cold soul. I hate it. And I hate that I want to keep staring at her, so I stare at the book in my hands instead.

"I had a feeling you'd be here reading."

I quickly glance up at her long enough to notice she heeded my advice and wore a coat today before returning my eyes back to my book. When I don't respond she continues.

"I mean you're always sitting at this table reading that book, but it never looks like you get very far. At this point I'm convinced you're a slow reader or you're stalking me," she says with a flirty tone. "You a cop or something?"

I lift my eyes, staring directly at her with a straight face. "I'm not a slow reader, and I'm definitely not a cop."

Her expression drops, a look of fear plastered to her face, and I hate that my dick jerks in my jeans at the sight.

"I've just had trouble getting into this book. I don't like not finishing something once I've started."

"I get it; I don't like not finishing books either," she replies, kicking her foot up and down as she stares at me.

I don't even have to look up to know because I can feel her eyes boring into me like she knows all of my secrets already.

"You read?" I ask, surprise evident on my face.

"Yeah, I read," she says, her full pink lips pulling into a smile. God those lips. I bet they'd feel amaz–Lawrence, stop it. She's like half your age.

"What do you read?" I ask.

Her face blushes as she fidgets in her chair, pinning me with a serious face.

"Honestly?"

I raise my eyebrows in challenge because why wouldn't I be asking honestly?

"I read smut," she admits, her eyes looking down as she answers.

"What is smut?" I ask genuinely, taking another sip of my now room temp cappuccino. The normal barista, Cammie, is gone today, so the new kid made my drink, and it sucks even more than it usually does. It's espresso and steamed milk, kid.

"Basically, porn but in book form."

I choke on my drink, caught off guard by her response.

She smiles and laughs, clearly embarrassed by my response, and I almost feel bad about it, but she's too cute.

"What?" she asks, twirling her thumbs, her gaze shifting from the floor to me. She's shy.

"Nothing," I lie. It's a good thing I'm sitting in the corner because my cock is straining against my zipper at the thought of her getting off while she reads one of her dirty books.

"You should try one sometime. I could loan you one of mine," she says playfully.

Absolutely not. She would never get it back.

"That's okay."

"You're not much of a talker, are you?" she asks as she adjusts the bookbag on the back of her chair as it starts to fall.

I snort. "I can be when I want to be."

"So, you just don't want to talk to me then."

False, but she didn't ask it like a question, so I just stare at her without offering a reply.

"You're peculiar," she says as she leans forward, planting one arm and the table, the other hand propping under her chin.

"Peculiar? What are you, 75? Who says that?"

She looks at me offended. "I'm 23 and an educated woman, that's who," she huffs.

So, she's 16 years younger than me. Down, Lawrence. Shit.

I close my book, placing it on the table, and pull up my long sleeves. I'm getting hot and it's not due to the temperature in this coffee house.

Her eyes shoot to my arm, the scars causing my tattoos to look warped. I'm not embarrassed by it, but I'm not surprised she's focused on it. When she realizes I've caught her, her eyes shoot back to mine, and I can see the questions sitting on the tip of her tongue. I could be a smartass about it, but I don't want her asking questions I can't answer so I keep my mouth shut.

"I don't think being peculiar is a bad thing. It's better than being predictable or desperate like the majority of my generation." She's not wrong.

"Who says you're not predictable?"

Emotion flashes across her features quickly, but it's gone before I have the chance to decipher it.

"I'm not," she defends.

"Really? So, you don't come here to study because you have no social life and you're desperate for some exposure to the world around you? You don't leave here hating your life because you're questioning why you're still miserable at 23 years old because you never allowed yourself to experience fun and now you're busting your ass to get a degree simply because you want to impress yourself? Oh, and you're single because you're too hard to please." I want to punch myself for being such a dick to her.

Her face remains blank, but she doesn't reply.

"Predictable," I say, leaning back in my chair and crossing my arms across my chest feeling anything but victorious.

"Actually, I choose not to have a social life because I have yet to find anyone my age who is enjoyable to be around for longer than six minutes, and I prefer the company of myself over idiots. I partied harder than I care to admit in my early college years, though I don't remember much of it because I was blacked out for the majority of it. I'm not miserable; I'm ambitious. Hence why I'm torturing myself with getting a master's degree."

She's feisty when she comes out of her shell.

"And for the record, I'm single because the men in my books hold my standards to a level–" she eyes me up and down "--no man will be able to achieve," she says with a devious smirk.

Is she challenging me? That's a challenge I'd love to win.

"What's your name, Little Miss Predictable?" I ask, feeling the need to know. Curse this stupid café for not being as simple as Starbucks and writing orders on the cups instead of names.

"Enjoy your reading," she says, and next thing I know, before I have the chance to reply, she's grabbing her bag and sauntering off, my traitorous eyes going straight to her ass as she walks away.

I growl as I swipe the cup off the table and down the rest of my crapuccino. She's stubborn, and I hate that I enjoy it. I could easily figure out her name if I wanted to, but something about not knowing is alluring.

The fact that she didn't stay to study makes me think I went too far. She always comes in here to work. I don't regret intervening yesterday because the wank stain (I'm playing her game now), was harassing her, but it drew her attention to me and it's attention I can't allow. Even if I wanted to entertain it, I can't.

I'm lounging on the couch scrolling through the channels on TV, everything either depressing or stupid. After my encounter with Miss

Feisty yesterday, I've been itching to see her again, but I know it's a bad idea, which is exactly why I'm not sitting at the café like I have been every day for months. Not seeing her feels like I'm having withdrawals, which pisses me off because I don't know why I'm so intrigued by her. It's like an involuntary pull to her, an invisible string tethering me to her and trying to reel me in closer no matter how much I fight it.

The doorbell rings and I'm far too giddy about the Amazon package sitting on my doorstep. I rip it open and grab out the books. Both of them have nearly naked men on the front covers, and if I wasn't so confident in my masculinity, I would be ashamed. I grab the first one and eagerly open to the first page as I plop back down on the couch, curious to see what that girl is into.

This is the first day in weeks that Biggy hasn't had me doing his bidding. After Terry died, things were tense for a while. But as he started relying on me for more, I became more valuable to him by unintentionally throwing myself into work to try and forget about the asshole who was assaulting his daughter. My father was an asshole, but he never touched us kids like that, and I had a hard time getting past what was done to that little girl. Over the past few years I've become Biggy's right-hand man, my skills at ridding him of his problems making me too important to get rid of. I've come to realize that I will never pay off my imaginary debt to him because he's holding onto me like a leech, sucking every ounce of life from my body.

But I know I'm also to blame because I've come to develop this sick sense of loyalty to the guy. I know I've got problems and I would not lose an ounce of sleep if the guy dropped dead tomorrow. But after fighting it for so long, I knew I would never get out. I learned to accept my fate. I wasn't willing to risk my mother's life. While I will admit there were a few times I contemplated calling Biggy on his bluff to see if he actually had information on my mother, something in me kept me from doing that. Maybe I don't want to know; maybe I'm so sick I like being his enforcer.

Regardless, something has kept me here. He could have killed me any time–or at least he's said he could– but he took me in instead. I'm not saying I'm a good person in any sense, but this job has let me hurt those like my father, like little Starlette's father. People who don't care how their choices affect those around them. People whose deaths make the world a better place.

Maybe I have daddy issues; hell if I know. It's like I have this sick sense of belonging. I know I'm good at my job, and I know he needs me. I will never forgive myself for all the blood on my hands, but I've been taken care of in a sense. He pays me enough to have a decent life, and he butts out of my personal time for the most part. Though, I've always had a feeling that he'd lose his shit if he found out I was ever with someone for more than a casual fuck.

I wouldn't wish my life on anyone else, but it's more than I had after Mom left and Dad grew to hate us like dirt on the floor.

That's why I can't shake the thoughts of the girl who keeps invading my mind. She looked at me, and it was like the life I was void of was suddenly breathed back into my body. She awakened something that I didn't know still existed, and it makes me uncomfortable because it's been so long since I've felt anything.

I groan and toss the book on the table and lay back on the couch, shutting my eyes, willing my body to succumb to sleep that I desperately need. Minutes go by and all I can see behind my eyes are images of her. What ifs about her being alone at the café right now. What if that twat waffle comes back and corners her again? What if someone else makes a move on her and asks her out? Not that I should care. She can do what she wants. You don't even know her. Stop thinking like a stalker, Lawrence.

Next thing I know I'm growling as I throw myself to my feet and rip my jacket from the arm of the couch, throwing it on and slipping on my shoes before I'm out the door grumbling to myself as I climb in my truck. I turn over the engine and gun it for The Creamy Pie. Goddamnit, Lawrence.

I lecture myself the entire drive, but that invisible string refuses to fray even a little bit. I can see her through the large front windows as I pull into a spot right in front of the door. I make my way inside and force my eyes not to glance at her as I get to the counter and place my order, thankful that Cammie is back so at least I know my coffee won't taste like piss.

I grab my coffee and make my way to the same place I always do, thankful that nobody was dumb enough to sit there. I notice the newspaper that the old man two tables over is reading. The headline on the front reads, *Overdose cases on the rise across the city.* It makes me tense because it's another problem I'm more than likely going to get roped into. If someone is lacing drugs, it's not us, but it puts our reputation at risk.

I'm reading something on my phone when I sense her walk up to the table.

"You're sitting at the exact same spot you always do," she says. "So, I'm not the only predictable one."

Still, I refuse to look at her because I know that string will just pull me closer, and I'm still dumb enough to think I can snap it. I need to snap it. Burn it.

"It's a seat preference. There's shade in this spot." While it is tucked away from the sun rays that blast through the large windows, it also gives me a perfect view of her, but I keep that part to myself.

"Okay, and I'm sure this isn't a cappuccino with extra foam," she says, grabbing my hot coffee cup and waving it in front of my face which is still pointed down at my phone.

Relenting, I look up at her as she brings the cup to her lips, taking a sip of my drink. I can't help but smirk when she cringes either at the temperature or the taste. Either way, it's cute. She sets the cup back down on the table with force to make a point, causing liquid to splash up through the small drinking hole. I stare at her lovingly. My stare seems to get under her skin slightly as she fidgets where she stands.

"Like I said, guess we're both a tad predictable. But only one of us is a twat waffle." She's ballsy calling me names considering she saw me threaten a man right in front of her, and she knows nothing about me, like the fact that I kill people. I admire that.

I lean back in my chair, crossing my arms over my chest and allow my gaze to roam over her body quickly before returning back to her eyes. By the look on her face, I know she caught the action.

Good.

"You're right," I admit.

"About what?" she asks, mimicking my pose with her arms now crossed over her chest.

"That I'm a twat waffle." I bite my lip as I try not to laugh at the insult she chose.

"So, you acknowledge it, but you don't apologize for it," she states, shifting back and forth on her feet as I continue to stare at her.

"No, because that would be predictable, and something a nice guy would say. I'm not predictable, nor a nice guy," I say both hoping that the statement pushes her away and pulls her in closer.

She rolls her eyes and turns on her heel to leave, clearly over my bullshit. I should let her and watch the string snap, but my brain is more than a little screwed up.

"You were right by the way," I call after her.

She turns, staying a few feet away. "About the fact that you're a douche nozzle? Yeah, we established that," she scoffs.

She's lucky she's too young for me because I want nothing more than to spank that attitude out of her system. The thought makes my cock jerk in my pants, and I curse myself for driving here.

"No, about your books," I say, holding up the book I brought with me so she can read the title. Though the half naked man on the cover is enough to tell her what it is. Her jaw drops when she realizes what I'm holding. I may or may not have looked her up on Goodreads to see what she liked and bought a couple of them.

"They are much better reading material than what I usually read. This girl is a freak," I say, flipping through the pages enjoying the way her face flushes. I've surprised her and it makes me feel things I shouldn't.

"Definitely a fictional woman," I say, closing the book and grabbing my coffee, taking a sip. It's when the hot liquid hits my tongue and I see the pink lip marks on my cup from her lip-gloss that I remember her lips were on this cup mere minutes ago, and I hold back the moan that wants to escape at the thought. That's the closest I'll get to kissing her, so I savor it as I down the scorching liquid, keeping my eyes pinned to hers as she stares in awe, pulling her bottom lip in between her teeth. I want it to be my teeth biting on her lip.

"Not necessarily," she finally says, shrugging her shoulders, her eyes on the ground as a slight grin graces her face. Her dimples make an appearance, and I hate myself for focusing on how cute they are. Please don't tell me she's hinting at what I think she is because my dick is already crying behind my zipper, and this book has given my imagination far too much to work with as is.

She pulls the chair out across from me finally giving in to the conversation and plops down, crossing her leg over her other thigh.

"Let me guess, you think all women are pillow princesses who put in zero effort and lay there moaning like a porn star. You think it's impossible to find a real woman who knows what she wants and wants to please her partner just as much as she wants to be pleased herself?"

I quirk an eyebrow at her, surprised by her words.

"You don't think a woman like that can exist because every woman who was dumb enough to sleep with you was nothing but a warm hole," she states, a look of victory on her face. I swear this woman is going to kill me without even trying.

"You are bold, aren't you?" I ask.

"No, I just know what I want." Her eyes dart between the table and her shoe as it bobs back and forth on her foot as she bounces her knee.

"Which is what, exactly?" I pry, leaning in placing my elbows on the table and staring at her until she looks at me. Apparently, my brain and my mouth are on different pages because I'm supposed to be telling her to leave, not entertaining her. She remains silent for a beat like she's considering her answer before she leans in, placing her elbow on the table and getting close enough that I can smell the cherry lip gloss coating her plump lips tipped up in a devious smile. I note the light freckles dusting her natural face–mostly high on her cheekbones, and a few sprinkled on her nose. Her eyes alone have the ability to bring me to my knees, my soul nearly falling into the chocolate caramel pools. Whoever said brown eyes weren't as pretty clearly never had the privilege of staring into hers.

Brown eyes don't get the recognition they deserve. Blue and green are nice and all, but staring into hers, it's like they pull me in. Like I could easily drown in them as they sparkle back at me.

"I want you to stop playing coy and take me out to dinner," she says before she leans back in her chair, putting too much space between us and not enough at the same time.

I open my mouth to speak but she continues, cutting off any response I had on my tongue: "No. Either I'm insane or you are interested but you're refusing to acknowledge it. If you hate talking to me then I won't speak to you again. In fact, I'll find another coffee shop to get my worldly exposure, but I don't think you want that."

I admire her guts to go for what she wants, but I don't miss the hesitation on her face, her fear of my rejection.

"It's not a lack of interest sweetheart," I say honestly. "Believe me, attraction is not an issue," I add, taking extra time to drink in her body before bringing my eyes back up to hers.

"So, what is?" she asks, defeat evident in her tone.

Everything.

"Honey, you're 16 years younger than me. That kind of thing is frowned upon." Not to mention the fact that my lifestyle doesn't exactly accommodate the whole dating thing, but she won't get to figure that out.

"So, you care what other people think of you?" she questions, pinning me with a doubting glare. "I don't buy that," she continues. "Next."

She's persistent, I give her that. And it's really unfortunate for me.

"It's just not a good idea. You should be dating guys your own age. I'm not good for you and you would definitely not be good for me."

That statement could not be more truthful.

"Are you just going to throw an excuse out for every answer I give you?"

I stare at her, not giving her the answer she's looking for.

"Right okay. Enjoy your porn," she scoffs, grabbing her bag from the floor and walking out to her car, my eyes following her the entire way, my brain battling with my body not to chase after her.

———

I groan and wipe my hand down my tired face as I wait for the microwave to beep, signaling that my pathetic TV dinner is done cooking so I can stuff my face with useless calories. I couldn't sleep so eating was the next best thing to curb my anxiety.

I can't stop picturing the way she looked as she walked away from me. The hurt seeping from her retreating form as the confidence disappeared. The way my body raged, wanting to chase after her and not let her go. The way I wanted to rush to her and give her exactly what she was wanting from me despite the fact that I've never had the desire to approach any woman in over 10 years. I still don't even know her name, and I can't rid myself of her. It's like she's wormed her way into my psyche so deep that carving out my own brain wouldn't do the trick.

My world is dangerous, and the last thing I need is her getting involved in something she doesn't need to be. The lack of ability to stop thinking about her has me needing a reminder of why I can never have her. Frankly, I've been enjoying the break from beating people senseless in a concrete room of screams and pleas, but I can't trust myself to sit here and not think about her, because I know I'll end up going to her.

I pull my cell from my pants pocket, pressing send and speaking as soon as the line connects.

"You got any work for me?" I ask eagerly.

"Bored already?" Biggy asks, amusement in his tone. It's only been two days free of my typical work. Apparently, people are getting smarter and learning not to screw with Biggy as his reputation only continues to grow.

"Just asking," I reply casually, though my muscles are tense with the need for something other than thoughts of the dark-haired girl plaguing my mind.

"Frederick is doing a job for me tonight. You can help him."

I suppress a grunt at the mention of Frederick, the only other man Biggy trusts to follow through on punishing anyone who messes with him. Granted, he doesn't get nearly as many assignments as I do because I'm better at it than he'll ever be, but if I ever make something more of myself than this-or I end up dead- then he has someone else somewhat capable.

The microwave beeps, and I don't even bother getting out the plastic tray of hot garbage. My appetite is craving something else. Something that I want to sink my teeth into so deep the marks will never heal, just like the way she's weaseling her way into me.

"Fine. Send me the details."

I end the call and head for my room to pack a duffel for the job.

———————

"What did this one do?" I ask Frederick as I circle the man bound and gagged to the chair in front of me. He's a gangly man, sweat plastering his dirty blonde hair to his forehead as he seethes at me from behind the rag in his mouth. His thin white t-shirt is dirty and clings loosely to his thin frame. I'm easily twice the size of him, but his mind must be telling him he has a fighting chance as he follows me with his eyes.

He's going to be fun to break.

"Quinton here ratted out information on one of our dealers, got him killed. He owed our boss some money, so he was letting Quinton deal off some of his debt. Turns out he was just a rat, getting inside information for his boss." Frederick says, toying with the knife in his hands.

"Oh shit," I say, a smile gracing my face at the knowledge that this man royally screwed up. We've got a couple gangs that are decent competition, though we've surpassed them in the past few years. Whoever it was is ballsy enough to think that they can overtake us, and sending in a rat was a bad choice on their part. This shit stain in front of me is about to find out why.

"Who'd they kill?" I ask, though I don't really care.

"Jeffrey. Korbin found him with a bullet between his eyes, meant to be a threat to Biggy, no doubt."

Well, whoever this guy works for is a moron. Jeffrey was a newbie, and Biggy won't lose a drop of sweat over his death, but he won't let the threat go regardless.

"And I found this on him when I brought him in." Frederick dangles a plastic baggy with white powder between his fingers.

"The idiot was partaking in our product, too. He's a rat and a thief," I snort at the irony.

"Our product is better, isn't it?" He's fighting the restraints, and his dilated pupils tell me he's also high as a kite. Smart move. Might help with what he's about to endure.

I crouch down so I'm eye level with him and slide my knife between his lips and the fabric over his mouth, pulling until it rips through the gag.

"So, are you gonna cooperate and grant yourself an easy death, or are you gonna make this harder than it needs to be?"

He snarls, exposing his near rotted teeth before rearing back and spitting in my face. Great, now I gotta get tested.

"Well, I guess we're going with the latter. You wanna show him how this is gonna work?" I sneer as I use my sleeve to wipe the spit from my face. Fine by me because it means more fun for us.

"My pleasure," Frederick says as he takes his knife and rips through the fabric of Quinton's shirt exposing his pale heaving chest. He places the tip of the blade near his armpit. He's not pressing hard enough to draw blood, but enough to elicit warning.

"Who sent you to get information?"

"Fuck you," he spits.

Frederick's lips curl up in a devious grin as he pushes the tip of the blade in just enough to slice the skin, trailing the blade from his armpit down to his ribs. Blood leaks from the wound and trails down his body and onto the floor. It's superficial, but we've got a ways to go so he can't bleed out yet.

"Here's the thing, Q. You're dying regardless. Your boss doesn't give a shit about you or he wouldn't have put you in this position. So, the quicker you give us what we want, the easier this will be for you. You still wanna fight this?" I ask as I walk towards him and slide on a pair of latex gloves.

"I'm not telling you anything," he says, though the way his eyes are bugging as I approach him tells me he's nervous. "And my name's fucking Quinton, not Q, bitch."

Good.

Starting at his shoulder, I trail my finger down until it hits the start of the flesh wound Frederick gave him. I press my finger into the wound, enjoying when he grunts through gritted teeth trying to hide his pain. I dig my finger into the nail and drag it down the wound, feeling muscle tear as blood now pours from his side and pools on the concrete beneath him. He writhes in pain, but I gotta give the guy credit for keeping as composed as he is.

"We'll ask again, Q. Whose rat are you?" Frederick asks, leaning down so he's inches from Quinton's pained face. His answer is silence just before the sound of flesh hitting flesh and bones cracking as Frederick punches him in the face repeatedly.

Frederick gets off on his torture, and by the look on his face as he smiles at his busted, bloody knuckles, I'm almost afraid he's going to jack off right here.

"Son of a bitch!" Quinton yells, spitting one of his teeth onto the concrete. He was already missing a few anyway, so he won't miss them.

"That I am. My mama was a lot of things, including a bitch. Thankfully she's six feet deep." Frederick chuckles as he eyes me and waits for me to continue. I've never been fond of the torture like he is, but I welcome the distraction when it presents itself. Anything less than enthusiasm would have him running to Biggy claiming I'm not a true player, and I don't need someone messing it up for me after all these years busting my ass to stay on his good side.

Grabbing a knife from my back pocket, I quickly slam it into Quinton's thigh, making sure to aim far enough over to avoid his femoral artery. His screams fill the room and I hate to admit how much I enjoy it. He grits his teeth, veins popping in his jaw, and I have the urge to slice through them and watch the blood pour from his face.

"It's not too late to cooperate, Q," Frederick says and he paces in front of him, Quinton's eyes tracking him trying to anticipate his next move.

"What's it matter? I'm dead anyway. My boss would've done more damage than you two could ever do to me."

Frederick busts into maniacal laughter before going silent. The change in demeanor is eerie, and frankly I'm glad I'm not in Quinton's position because I'd probably be pissing myself. Frederick is far from stable, and I don't think Quinton wants to see just how far he is.

Before I can even process what's happening, Frederick is storming up to Quinton and pressing his thumb into Quinton's eye. His screams are loud, but the squelching coming from the injury is far louder, and I put my hand over my mouth to prevent myself from hurling.

Quinton, however, slumps over, vomit spewing from his mouth and down his torso, the pain taking its toll on him.

"You wanna bet on that?" Frederick says, a smile on his lips.

The only sounds coming from Quinton are pained cries, music to Frederick's ears.

He is a pitiful sight. His body is covered in blood, piss, and vomit. The knife wound on his side has started clotting slightly, though blood still drips from it. His face is battered and bruised beyond recognition. The one eye that Frederick let him keep is swollen to the point that I'm not sure he can see out of it at all.

"Who's your boss, Q?" I ask calmly, waiting for the answer that I'm sure is on the tip of his tongue.

"Is it Lloyd?"

There's only two big rings that it could be unless someone small was stupid enough to think they could overtake Biggy's spot.

"P-Please," he whimpers. Wrong answer. Lifting up my foot, I kick it right into his chest knocking his restrained body, and chair to the ground. A slight grunt leaves his lips, but I knocked the wind out of him. I glance at Frederick and a glimmer of something passes in his eyes before I can tell what it is. But it doesn't matter because in the next second he's undoing his pants and pissing all over Quinton's face.

"Choke on it, bitch," he says as Quinton coughs, blood and urine spewing from his lips.

"Must be bleeding internally there bud," I say as I squat next to him, nearly holding my breath to keep from inhaling the putrid scent of him. "How long do you think it will be till you bleed to death?"

As if he got a second wind, his body flails back and forth fighting against the restraints, pained moans and screams coming from his mouth.

"Fuck you, fuck you, fuck you, fuck you," he says, though the last one is barely audible as he breaks into a sob.

"I wouldn't grant you that privilege even if you begged."

Images of the black-haired beauty from the café flood my mind, and I growl, the need to see her invading my senses. The distraction that Quinton was supposed to provide has dissipated, and now I'm bored, frustrated that even in this moment, I can't vanquish her from my head.

I grab a large pair of wire cutters from my bag before squatting again next to Quinton and placing his middle finger between the blades before clamping down, severing the digit from his hand. He wails, and I place his ring finger in the blades, removing it as well.

"There. Now you can be Spiderman," I say.

"Please. F-F-Fuck. I'll tell you. Just stop," Quinton pleads.

"I'm listening," I say, waiting for his answer. When he takes too long, I place my boot on his severed hand and apply pressure, watching as he writhes in pain, blood spewing from where his missing fingers should be.

"The Snipers!" he screams. "The Snipers hired me!"

I had my suspicions, especially given how Jeffrey was killed, but he just confirmed it. The Snipers are our biggest competition in the drug trade. They used to deal primarily with heroin, but have expanded, trying to grow and gain more power. Biggy's reputation and worth has surpassed them in the past few years so it was just a matter of time before they tried something stupid.

"What did they hire you to do exactly?" Quinton is weak and I know I don't have much left in him before he croaks. He lasted longer than I gave him credit for.

"They told me to get in with your crew and swap his product to sell on the streets." I grind my teeth, anger radiating from me. I know the answer to this question before I ask it, but I hadn't even considered it until now.

"Swap it with what?"

"They gave me coke laced with fentanyl," he cries.

The overdose cases had skyrocketed over the past two months, and it was hurting our reputation. While we always sell clean product, The Snipers have been known to cut in shit like drain cleaner and baby powder. Then there's the scum drug pushers cutting in Mexican fentanyl like they want to kill their clients.

Don't get me wrong, I'm a part of the drug trade, but it began out of desperation. I did what I had to do to survive and keep my mother alive. But to purposely lace a drug intent on killing is beyond evil, though I'm not surprised that something man made by pharmaceutical companies is being utilized for nothing more than evil and destruction. If it was possible to wipe out the entire drug trade, I'd do it in a heartbeat because I know firsthand how a drug can turn someone into something they never planned on becoming. A person with so much potential can be reduced to the shell of a human, dependent on their next fix.

"Thanks, Q. Nice knowing you." And with that I swipe my handgun from my pocket and shoot him in the head granting him the death he so desperately wanted.

Chapter 7
Lawrence

— ⋆ ★ ⋆ —

I step into the steaming shower, letting the hot water cascade over my aching muscles, red swirling around the drain as the water rids me of Quinton's caked blood. I'm getting too old for this shit. After disposing of the body, I immediately missed the distraction. Back home, my mind is flooded with images of her, and I can't understand how she got her hooks in me.

Not once in my life have I even thought twice about a woman who I found attractive. Hell, I didn't even think twice about the women I screwed and left before they could wake up the next morning. I was never proud of being the guy that got his dick wet and left before morning, but sex was an easy distraction and I couldn't afford anything more than casual sex. Not that any of my hookups were ever interesting enough to make me want more anyway.

I haven't even kissed this girl and it's like the universe is magnetizing us. What pisses me off the most is that I want so much more than to sleep with her. Oh, I absolutely want to sleep with her, but the desire to properly date her and treat her like a queen is unfathomable. And I don't date.

I drop my head and let the water run off. I really need a haircut. Before I get in the mindset to berate myself for what I'm doing, I fist my throbbing dick in my hand and pump slowly. I close my eyes, letting images of her invade my senses. I can still smell the cherry gloss on her lips. The reminder of her mouth on my coffee cup pulls a grunt from my chest. I wish I could taste her. All of her.

I lean against the shower wall, supporting myself with my forearm while I stroke myself with the other. I'm cursing myself for not knowing her name so I can hear it coming from my lips. I pump myself faster, remembering the way her eyes bore into me like she could see every single one of my secrets, her midnight hair cascading around her shoulders, a beautiful contrast to her pale skin. Her beauty is ethereal, like she doesn't belong here because she's so perfect.

I imagine her dark hair wrapped around my fist as she sucks my cock, staring up at me through her thick lashes. She's made it clear how she feels, and it drives me insane that I can't do anything about it. Forget the fact that she's sixteen years younger than me–not that stamina would be an issue–and I can't endanger her. I promised myself I wouldn't get attached to anyone, and as much as I would love to indulge in her, I know I wouldn't be capable of sneaking out on her the next day.

The thought makes my cock jerk in my palm. The thought of having her for a night, leaving marks on her beautiful skin while she screams my name in pleasure. The sound in my head alone is divine. Thoughts of her begging for more as I taste her, lashing my tongue against her clit as she rides my face.

Streams of cum coat my hand, mixing with drops of water as I pump out my release. I grit my teeth but can't help grinning. If she can make me come like that without even being in the room, I can only imagine how good it would be to actually feel her.

I rinse off my disgrace before turning off the shower and stepping out, mumbling to myself. Nothing is going to make me forget about her, though masturbating to the thought of her definitely won't help. I sigh as I slide on my sweats and slide into bed before picking up my book from the nightstand and flipping open to the bookmark. This girl has not only invaded my thoughts but my life. I'm reading romance before bed, and I like it. What kind of freaky witch magic does she do?

There's a lot of things I should be doing. Not going into this horrifically named café is one of them. But instead of listening to the voice in my head telling me that I'm a stalker, an idiot, and a creep, I order my usual and take a seat at my normal table.

A quick glance around the room tells me that she isn't here yet, so I read another chapter to pass the time. Thirty minutes later I find myself anxious and paranoid by the fact that she isn't here. I got here later than I usually do which makes it even weirder that she hasn't shown up. It is a regular thing for her, just like it is for me. I like to think I'm the reason she hasn't stopped coming here at the same time, but that's likely just the cockiness in me.

My mind reels with the reminder of the last time I saw her walking away irritated and hurt that I wouldn't give her what she wanted. I curse myself for it, thinking that maybe she's resorted not to coming anymore to avoid me. I should be happy about that, but I'm not. I lecture myself before acquiescing to the idea that she may just have been busy today. You know, living a normal life like a 23-year-old should.

The next day I'm sitting at my table, unashamed as I immerse myself in the last half of the smut book Dicked Down and Dirty I got from her list online. No wonder women don't watch porn like men. This shit is crazy and so much better.

Sensing her, I lift my eyes from the page, her black hair catching my eye across the room. She plops her bag down at her feet, sitting down before pulling out her laptop and propping it open in front of her. I'm willing her soul snatching eyes to look at me, and I'm filled with disappointment when she won't. I don't know how I know, but I know she senses me just like I sense her.

Her focus is honed in on her laptop, oblivious to her surroundings, and willingly oblivious to me. I stand up to leave, knowing I need to walk away. This girl isn't healthy for me. As I walk across the room towards the entrance, her eyes finally meet mine, and I swear my heart stutters before it shatters. I can see the hurt in her eyes, and it physically pains me. Though I don't know if she's upset because of me or something else. Either way I don't like it.

Against my better judgment–actually, who am I kidding, I don't have any with her–I make my way over to her table. I keep a few feet away from her and try not to let it kill my ego when she looks away, turning her focus back on her laptop.

"Having coffee withdrawals?" I ask, though I know it sounds stupid as it leaves my mouth. I'm just looking for excuses to talk to her and we both know it.

"Something like that," she says, not even sparing me a glance. I shift on my feet, awkwardly gritting my teeth.

"I'm sorry," I say.

"For what?" she asks, her tone full of hurt and anger.

Well, I guess that answers my question.

"You know what," I reply. Apparently, I can't be a grownup and use my words. Likely because I know as soon as I open my mouth, I'll want to say a million things I definitely should not say. Telling her, "I'm sorry for being so attracted to you that it hurts. I'm sorry that I want to take you out and treat you like a queen, but I can't do either of those things because I'm part of a drug cartel and my boss will likely kill both of us if he knows I'm involved with someone, and I'm a terrible person who has killed repeatedly and I don't even know your name, but I have the desire to hear you screaming mine in bed" isn't exactly a good idea.

She stares at me for a moment, and for a second, I freak out, worried that I may have said all of that out loud instead of in my head.

"For humiliating me when I tried to be confident?" She eyes me up and down. "I was fine before, and I'm fine now." She straightens in her chair before turning her eyes back on her laptop. She's got fire for sure. Add it to the list of reasons why I can't stop myself from liking her.

"Well, I didn't see you, so I was hoping I didn't upset you."

You idiot, Lawrence. Not only is it obvious that I did in fact upset her, but I also just willingly admitted that I was looking for her yesterday. Damnit. I grip the top of the chair across from her and fight the urge to sit down.

She closes her laptop partly and crosses her hands on the table as she looks at me.

"You give yourself too much credit, Lawrence." Even when she's upset, it sounds glorious coming from her pretty mouth. "You aren't interested. I'm not your type. I get it. Like you said, I should be wasting my time on guys my age. I'll work on that." She smirks in a *screw you* kind of way before pulling her laptop open again and typing on the keyboard, her fingers pressing so hard I'm worried she might break it. Either her homework is *really* taking a toll on her, or she's really pissed off at me.

It pisses me off that she's talking so poorly of herself as if she's not enough for me. I firmly pull out the chair and sit down, ignoring her scoff when she realizes I'm taking the seat. I reach across the small table and close her laptop before propping my elbows on the table and leaning in. She opens her mouth to yell at me, but I don't give her the chance.

"Sweetheart, I already told you, attraction is not an issue. You are undoubtedly the most gorgeous woman I've ever seen. I was telling the truth when I said you should be dating guys your age and not me, because once something is mine, it will never be anyone else's. I'm possessive and I don't like sharing. I have a busy, complicated schedule and I couldn't give you the relationship I want–or that you deserve."

She swallows almost as if she's nervous before clearing her throat.

"What's so complicated about your job? Do you not get days off or something? If you're an independent contractor, aren't you like your own boss?"

She's asking questions I don't want to answer because I don't want to lie to her, so I avoid it instead.

"Like I said, it's complicated. But like I also said, I'm possessive, and I don't think I'm your type."

I have no idea if I'm her type or not. For both our sakes, I need her to hate the idea of being with someone so...well, me.

"So, you'd treat me like a possession? Like you own me?" I read her expression, expecting to see disgust, but I don't. I see intrigue.

"If I was with you, you would be mine. I'd have no problem giving you everything you asked of me," apart from telling her what I do for work "but I'd be trying not to rip the eyes out of the skull of any man who thought to look at you. I would treat you like a queen, but yes, I would own you," I say, leaning back in the chair and crossing my arms over my chest.

"Well, I'm guessing a guy who looks like you isn't celibate, so why are you single?" she asks.

"I haven't fucked a woman in over ten years. I told you, once I get my hands on what I want, it's mine. Permanently. I don't take that shit lightly. Even if I wanted to take you out, I wouldn't be able to let you go. You'd be stuck, and your leash would be short. You seem like a woman who likes her freedom, not like the type of woman who likes to be restrained and kept."

Her eyebrow raises in challenge, like I couldn't have said a bigger lie, and I can't deny that my cock jerks behind my zipper.

"Maybe I'd like the restraints," she teases. I'm fighting not to bust in my pants because of it. This woman does not know red flags when she sees them. She's staring me down as I try to discreetly adjust myself. Though not discreetly enough apparently as her eyes track my movements.

She should be running for the hills, but instead she's staring daggers into my soul with her sparkling brown eyes.

"Are you always this difficult?" I ask.

"Wouldn't you like to know." She smirks as she puts her laptop in her bag. She's playing with me.

"I'm tired of playing games with you. I've made it clear where I stand. You are nothing but mixed signals, and for someone your age, you're sure acting like the guys my age. See you around, porno," she snorts as she turns to leave, her statement loud enough that several people are eyeing me around the café.

This is exactly why she can't be mine because she'd be getting punished for that. I try not to think about that fact as I let it sink in that I have absolutely screwed myself.

I'm not proud to admit it, but I follow her home. I tell myself it's to make sure she gets there safely, but I know I'm lying to myself to make me feel better. I want to know where she lives. Where she feels safe. Where she lets herself think about me even when she knows she shouldn't.

I make sure to climb in my truck only after she is pulling out of the café. I may be a stalker, but I didn't want her to know that. I have had to speed through a few red lights to keep her in my sight which grants me the finger from an old woman who looks like she is seconds from death. Sorry, not sorry, Granny.

As she pulls into her apartment complex, I park across the street among several other cars in a strip of businesses. As she climbs out of her car, I almost wonder if she can sense me there. She closes her car door and looks around the complex as if she is unsure about something. I know she can't see me, but I will admit, seeing the slight fear on her face makes me hard.

I watch as she carefully makes her way inside the complex, watching over her shoulder for a boogeyman to pop out. The day will come, but not today.

I am relieved yet agitated when I see her from her kitchen window, her apartment facing the street. How convenient for me. Of course all of her blinds are open. Is she inviting a pervert to stare at her? I mean me, but she doesn't know what other kinds of creeps could be lurking. I can see her staring out the window, looking down into the lot still as if she is looking for something, or someone.

The next few days pass in a blur as Biggy throws more jobs my way, pleased at my enthusiasm to take my mind off of the one thing I need to stop thinking about. Each day I make the time to stop by the café hoping to lay eyes on the black-haired beauty, but she is never there. The first couple days I figured she was butthurt and didn't want to see me. The third day I got angry because she didn't seem like the type to give up so easily. She found comfort in that café, and she shouldn't let a shit stain like me take that from her.

Today is the fourth day and I'm worried. I still don't know her name, but I know where she lives, convincing myself it is necessary just in case something ever happens. There is no reason for me to find out where she lives other than the fact that I'm grossly obsessed with what I can't have.

I promised myself I wouldn't do anything with my knowledge of her living situation, and I've stuck to my guns in that aspect. But today, my worry has me pushing away all sense of rationality as I stare at the chair that she should be sitting in, instead occupied by a 70-year-old decrepit man in a business suit who clearly hates his wife too much to retire.

I try to reason that she's just pissed at me and is avoiding me, which is probably the case since I've been a dick and rejecting her every advance. But after four days, my mind needs to know. I need to know that she's okay because the tiniest chance that she's not has my stomach fighting knots and my blood boiling.

Twenty minutes later and several mental lectures later, I'm parked across the street from her apartment complex, concealing myself amongst the other cars in this dental office parking lot. She knows me, and I can't risk being seen in her complex. I shut off the engine and feel relief when I see a light turn off and another turn on in her apartment. She doesn't seem to care about privacy which irks me.

At least I know she's in there so I should just drive away. But I don't know for sure if she has a roommate, and the thought that it could be someone else in there bothers the hell out of me. So, I decide, like the rational man I am, to wait it out. I don't have an assignment tonight. My first free Friday night in a while has me wishing I was spending it with her, but this will have to suffice.

I see a younger guy in a black car pull into the complex. I don't think much of it until he doesn't get out of the car and I get this nagging feeling in my stomach. He's not here for her. I'm just irrational.

Half an hour later, the lights in her apartment all go out and I'm watching her walk out of the complex, her eyes darting around the lot, her arm crossed over her chest, rubbing her other arm through her coat jacket. She looks nervous, but she also looks stunning. Like ridiculously unimaginably gorgeous. It makes me want to conceal her away from anyone else with eyes because nobody deserves to see her. Am I drooling?

Her coat is unbuttoned down the front, allowing view of her tight fitted skinny jeans and dark green blouse, and I don't have to be up close to know that it makes her eyes pop like glitter. It's nearly freezing outside. Her hair falls in loose bouncy curls over one shoulder, stray strands blowing in the slight breeze. Her long legs are steady in her heeled boots. I want to know what she's dressed up for, and my stomach churns at the thoughts of where she could be going.

As the thought crosses my mind, the guy gets out of the black car parked on the far end of the lot. Fury bubbles in my chest as he approaches her and laces his arm around her lower back ushering her to his car. His hand is far too close to where it shouldn't be, and I imagine cutting it off at the wrist. The thought brings a smirk to my lips.

She has a boyfriend? No. There's no way she would've been pursuing me the way she was if she had a boyfriend. I can sniff out cheaters, and she's too good for that. She gets what she wants and gets rid of what she doesn't. So, it has to be new. First date maybe. She pulls her coat tight around her, not returning his touch. As I watch his hand snake down to her ass, I decide he's too handsy for a first date. Though he looks like an absolute douche with his slicked back blonde hair, curls gathered at the nape of his neck and his white button down. He looks prepubescent, far too young for her even though he's likely only a couple years younger. I snort as the thought crosses my mind. Hypocrite. She's also clearly taller than him in her heels. Shorty probably has trouble reaching the gas pedal. I hope he has a booster seat to see over the steering wheel.

She doesn't appear to be very comfortable as she slinks down into the passenger seat. Twatknuckle didn't even open the door for her.

I notice my hands are white knuckling the steering wheel and I have to tell myself I'm overreacting. I told her no. She's allowed to date. I told her to. But it still feels wrong. I know she has needs, but I want to be the one quenching her thirst. Images of him touching her, feeling her, tasting her, it sends me over the edge as I bash my knuckles into my dashboard. I don't feel the sting as the skin breaks and blood trickles down my hand.

His car pulls out of the parking lot, and I don't hesitate as I turn over the engine. Go home, Lawrence. Let it go. Let it go.

As his car drives down the road and threatens to turn the corner out of sight, I remember I'm not the rational type and I follow them. Let's see what kind of date this shit stain has planned for the goddess sitting next to him. Movies? Dinner? A stroll through the park? I don't know what young people are into now. Whatever it is, I guarantee it's not good enough for her. Not because she wouldn't think it's good enough, but because I know she deserves the world on a platter, and he can't give it to her.

Twelve minutes and seventeen seconds later–yes, I counted–we're driving through the local college campus. I get why she stays away from campus for studying when I see the girls on the sidewalks pretending to not be freezing their asses off as they walk around in their mini skirts and dresses, boobs on full display, and faces caked with makeup as if they're auditioning for a Sephora ad. Heaven forbid any of their skin be covered to conserve body heat.

He pulls into the lot of Sterling, right off campus, and I park several rows behind him, but in a spot that still gives me a clear view. Sterling is a decent restaurant, but not the quality she deserves. I watch as he gets out of the car, waiting at the driver's side for her to get out as well. This guy clearly has no date etiquette. She still appears uncomfortable as she makes her way over to him, keeping herself a good foot away from him as they make their way to the restaurant. I can't help but wonder if she's only doing this to prove a point to herself after my rejection. Yeah, I have a big ego, I'm aware.

Every fiber in my body is fighting the urge to storm after her and haul her over my shoulder to carry her out and take her on a proper date. I can't storm the restaurant without raising suspicions, so I have to sit here helpless and watch this play out. I know she's a grown woman who can take care of herself, but I can't help keeping myself planted where I am and wait for her to leave.

As the seconds tick by, worst case scenarios start playing through my mind. I swear I'm about to blow everything to keep this date from going any further. But I can't screw this all up, and she's a big girl. She'll be okay. But will I?

My thumbs tap the steering wheel, every muscle in my body tight, my eyes fixated on the door of the restaurant. I can practically hear the seconds ticking in my head. After thirty minutes, my resolve crumbles and I make my way into the restaurant crossing all of my fingers that she doesn't see me. I make my way to the bar after triple checking that they aren't sitting anywhere near it.

I order a whiskey, keeping my head down as I scan the restaurant before finally laying my eyes on her across the room. Her back is to me thankfully, her unfortunate choice for a date sitting across from her. I stay firmly on my stool watching their interaction.

I watch for an hour noting that she doesn't laugh at anything he says once. Instead, I see the tension radiating off her shoulders. There hasn't been one point where she relaxed and seemed comfortable. Though I can't hear their conversation, I think it's safe to say they have no chemistry.

Ten minutes later she gets up to go to the bathroom, and my blood sizzles when I see their waitress approach the table flashing a flirty smile his way as she leans closer to him. Instead of doing what a sane man with a woman as beautiful as his date would do, he scribbles his number down on a napkin and hands it to the batty-eyed waitress before running his hand down her arm, clearly reciprocating her interest. I'm two seconds from beating the guy's face in and taking his seat when I notice her standing feet away from her date, anger lacing her features. She saw the whole thing. I should feel bad, but instead I feel relief.

She's frozen in place as she watches her date ogle another woman. I watch the scene unfold and can feel the anger and pain radiating from her as she crosses her arms across her chest, walking over to their table and pushing past the slutty waitress before she grabs her purse and coat from her chair.

Tweedle Dumb yells after her, and I feel a spark of pride as she turns around throwing both middle fingers up in the air in response.

"Bitch!" he calls out. This motherfucker has a death wish.

I can still clearly see her from my stool at the bar as she stands just outside the front door, her phone illuminating the night air, and I hope she's ordering a car home. She's obviously not getting a ride back from Tiny Dick and I can't just show up to the rescue without her thinking I'm a psycho stalker. Which I'm totally not for the record. I feel more stressed now than I have in years, and I kill people for a living.

I slam a wad of cash on the bar top for my tab and creep towards the front of the restaurant, but staying out of view. I can see her sitting on a bench outside, her shoulders shaking. She's crying. That bastard has no idea all of the ways I'm imagining killing him right now. I itch to pile her into my truck and kiss away her tears, but I know it would ruin everything.

In this moment I decide she's going to be a more permanent part of my life than either of us thought so I can keep shit like this from happening. She's become a leech on my soul that I can't pry off. Though if I'm being honest with myself, I don't think I want to feel the absence of her. Something tells me it would be like living in a darkness unlike anything I want to experience.

A car pulls up next to her and I feel relief as she climbs into the back seat, shutting herself into safety away from the man who was too stupid to keep what he had. I make my way to my truck, but not before slashing the tires of Dick Weed's car. I'd love to stay and watch him find that little problem, but my priority is elsewhere.

I make my way to my girl's apartment to make sure she's home safe before I head home and drown in the thoughts taking over my broken mind, keeping the sleep at bay as I figure out my next move.

Chapter 8

Piper

I sink down into the tub letting the scorching hot water singe my skin. Something about the burn is soothing as my aches disappear. If only the water could work its magic like that on my brain and release me from the aches and pains dwelling inside. Tonight was an utter disaster, and frankly I know I can only blame myself for the catastrophe that is my "dating" life.

I didn't even want to go out with Cory. I was trying to prove a point to myself. Well, point proven, Piper: you're an idiot. I groan as I sink further into the water until my chin touches the surface, the loose strands of my hair that have fallen from my bun float on the water. Cory has been interested in me for weeks after a mutual friend introduced us. I played oblivious for a while because I didn't have the energy to entertain his fuckboy attitude. I'd rather be snuggling up next to Lawrence on a date, but that plan clearly isn't working in my favor.

Honestly, I haven't even dated much in the past few years. Every relationship I had in my younger years ended up being a waste of time, and my life has been too busy to really care enough to want to get to know anyone of the male species for my enjoyment. Until I saw Lawrence. My work situation complicates things with him, and he has made it more than clear that I have no chance in hell at bagging him, and I haven't been laid in so long my vibrator has started taking Viagra to keep up with me.

So, when Cory texted and asked me out yesterday, despite the sirens screaming at me in the back of my pea brain not to go out with the 23-year-old heathen, I said yes. I know a bad seed when I see one and I knew

Cory wouldn't treat me like a treasure, or even an equal for that matter. Honestly, if I expected anything, it was a lackluster date before I brought him back here and had a quick fuck that had him running for it as soon as the condom came off. But at least it would have been a date. Some effort on my part, and sex with something other than purple silicone.

I at least thought the man would have the decency to engage in real conversation and take an interest in my life. Instead, he only talked about himself, not bothering to leave out the details of how many girls he's slept with in the past month. Then he had the audacity to call me a bitch when I left after seeing him eye-fuck our waitress. I should have just called an Uber the instant he pulled up to the restaurant and told me he forgot his wallet, but no, Piper has to prove her point that she can date like a big girl. Yeah, right. I hope he had to wash dishes or mop the floors to pay the bill.

I don't even know why I cried after seeing him with the red-haired bimbo at our table. I felt like an idiot sobbing on the curb looking like some heartbroken teenager when I wasn't even sad about Cory. But all I could think about was what a failure I am. I can't get Lawrence, the only guy I've had an interest in for years, despite going against my nerves and being bold enough to show him what I want. Now I can't even have a successful date with a guy who's been interested in me for weeks? Way to go, Piper. You've still got it.

I sip on my glass of wine until the water goes warm. Something about a bath that isn't the stinging temperature of molten lava isn't appealing to me. Downing the rest of what's in my glass, I wrap the towel around my body, not caring to dry off first. Droplets of water fall to the floor all the way to the kitchen where I pour myself another generous glass of wine before heading back to the bedroom to drown my depressive thoughts in Cheez-Its and The Vampire Diaries. Don't judge me.

I peel back the curtain and check the window again. I know what I'll find, but my heart sinks at the sight anyway. He's not here. I know Lawrence has been watching me. I noticed him one afternoon while I was deep-cleaning the kitchen. Scrubbing down the windows, I saw him park his truck across the street. The windows are tinted too dark for me to see it was him, but I know it was. I've seen him get out of the exact same truck multiple times at the café.

I've noticed the truck parked across the street a few times in total, just sitting there until he eventually drives off. He never gets out or comes to my apartment. He just lingers. That fact should have me sleeping with a gun under my pillow and getting a restraining order, but it doesn't. He's alluring. I've never felt like I was in danger with him. If anything, I've felt safer with him. I know, that's exactly how true crime episodes start and I'm the idiot woman who was too infatuated with a man to see his red flags.

But I can't help it. Something about me is so drawn to him, like there's nothing I can do to erase him from my mind or diminish my need to be near him. I don't mind that he watches me. I like it. But it doesn't make it any less frustrating that I can't figure him out. He denies every advance I make on him, seems interested but refuses to allow himself to indulge in it, but he stalks me? I don't get it.

I'll admit, I've had the urge once or twice to "accidentally" walk past the window naked just to see what would happen. I have a bad habit of keeping blinds open, but I don't want to give some perv who isn't him a show.

If I had the balls, I would storm into the café and demand he tell me why he's watching me if he isn't interested in me, but I'm scared.

And not of what I should be.

I should be scared that he will corner me and kill me. But instead, I'm scared he'd stop watching. My heart was giddy this evening when I left the apartment to meet Cory in the parking lot and saw Lawrence's truck across the street. I hoped seeing Cory's hand on my body would give him the incentive he needed to storm up and claim me, but that didn't happen. From what I could tell, he didn't follow us either, and I didn't see his truck when I came home. Maybe seeing me with another guy scared him away from me. I guess we'll find out.

Why wouldn't it? What man, especially a guy of his age, would want to play with a girl who's dating around? And it's not because I want to. In fact, I'd much rather not date at all than try to prove a point to myself after how tonight went. What frustrates me the most is that I can't even figure out why I want him so badly. He is the last person I should want, even with Cory in the mix.

At first, I thought maybe it was just pure attraction. Then I thought maybe it was because he was denying me and I was making it a game to prove I could get him. But it's more than that. It's like nothing I do can shake him. It's like he's weaseled his way into everything about my life and he hasn't even tried. My mind can't escape him. Even when I know I shouldn't be thinking about him, my thoughts are on nothing but him.

What it would be like to be his. How he'd feel. How he'd claim me so no one else could. I can't stop wanting to seek him out. I walk out of my apartment and my stomach drops when I don't see him in his truck waiting for me. Watching. Even though my brain tells me he's a bad idea and I need to run for the hills, I want nothing more than to run towards him. He could break my heart. Ruin me. Kill me. But I still want him.

It just happened and it pisses me off as much as it intrigues me. It feels like that moment when you walk into a haunted house and you're just waiting for the monster to jump out with a chainsaw to chase you, but the thrill is too intoxicating to turn around. Lawrence is the man with a chainsaw, and I'm too intrigued not to turn the corner.

After three episodes of The Vampire Diaries, two more glasses of wine, and a generous cry, I've decided that I need to let it all go. I need to stop trying to pursue someone who obviously doesn't want me. And if he shows up to watch me again, I'll confront him about it. I'm too old to be playing these stupid games, and I'm mad at myself for entertaining it so long.

I feel like Elena in this show drenched with teenage drama. Wanting a man who I know is bad for me. She fights her feelings for Damon because it's easier than admitting that they shouldn't work. Can't work. He's the mysterious, alluring, dangerous bad guy. She knows she shouldn't want him, but yet she does. They find comfort in each other even when it doesn't make sense to find a sense of safety in the one person you know you shouldn't. Oh my god, am I a TV cliche?

But I've seen this show twelve times through. I know how it ends. I know how epic their inevitable love becomes despite the toxicity. But this is real life. I don't have two blood sucking vampires falling in love with me while the entire world revolves around my life. Lawrence isn't fighting to win my heart. He's pushing me away while I fight to make my heart not want his.

I should know by now not to waste my time on someone who isn't willing to dedicate time to me. As intriguing and unforgivingly attractive Lawrence is, he's eating at me far too much. I don't desire to get to know people, but for some reason I've wanted nothing more than to get to know him, and I'm done. He can stay in his mysterious bubble all alone. But I'm not giving up my comfort spot at the café. That place is my safe space, and while he's invaded everything else, he doesn't get to take that from me. He doesn't get to win.

Chapter 9
Lawrence

— ⋆ ★ ⋆ —

Walking in the brightly lit café, my eyes immediately find her as she leans over a notebook, scribbling something. I go to the counter and order my daily flavorless cappuccino before walking over to her as I contemplate following through. I thought about it all night as I'm sure the bags under my eyes convey, but I only kept picturing the hurt she felt from Cunt Nugget's betrayal. I vowed I would keep her safe, and not being able to keep her in my range isn't going to cut it anymore.

My restraint is dwindling. While I didn't want to subject her to the mess that is myself, I sure as hell don't want her with anyone else. I'm aware of what a hypocrite and psychopath that makes me. If I can't have her, I'll make sure nobody else can. But it doesn't matter because I've decided I *can* have her. I *will* have her. Assuming she doesn't hate me enough to reject me after all the times I've rejected her. If she punches me in the nuts as soon as I walk up, I guess I'll know.

"Is this seat taken?" I ask as I pull out the chair across from her, grinding my teeth as the metal scrapes the floor.

"Would you care even if it was?" she asks, slamming her notebook closed, not even glancing up at me–and honestly it would probably hurt less if she did punch me in the balls.

"Not particularly," I admit.

"What do you want, Lawrence? I'm studying." She hasn't looked at me once, and I ignore both the sting and the urge to force her eyes to mine.

"I want to take you out for dinner."

That gets her attention as her eyes snap to mine, confusion and anger etched on her face. "What?" she asks.

"You heard me. I want to take you out. So do you want to pick where we go, or shall I?" I'll admit the idea of her picking the destination is unsettling because that's not her responsibility, but I also have no idea what she likes. She better not be one of those vegan picky eaters.

"Yes, I heard you, but I'm confused. You said–"

"I know what I said. I'm still an asshole, I'm still too old for you, and I'm still controlling."

"So, what made you change your mind?" The words come out before I have any chance to think twice.

"Let's just say I don't want other people touching what's mine." She leans back in her chair eyeing me up and down as she crosses her arms across her bulky blue sweater, a slight smirk gracing her lips that I so desperately want to kiss.

"So, you reject me repeatedly, and suddenly I'm yours now?" She sounds offended, but the blush covering her skin speaks to the contrary. I love that she's unable to hide it even if she tries. Being pale must suck.

"Well, you seemed pretty insistent about knowing what you wanted, so unless that's changed, I'm following through on that. Now, have you changed your mind? Say the words, and I'll leave you alone permanently."

Not actually, but I won't have to anyway.

"No, I haven't changed my mind but–"

"But it's on my terms," I say, interrupting whatever argument she had.

"Your terms?" She rolls her eyes. Troublemaker wants to be punished. "Which are?"

"We go out to dinner. You decide if we go out again. If you say no, I leave you alone and you go about your life. You say yes and we give it a trial run." There's a lot more to my terms than she's getting from me, but that's irrelevant. What I do without her knowledge if she says no is beside the point.

She laughs. "A trial run? Have you never dated before?"

"I don't want to date you in the traditional sense. If we do this, I'm all in. I'm going to show you what it means to be with me. I need to know if you can handle it before it goes too far."

"You make it sound like you're some sort of psychopath."

If only she knew.

"Well, it's up to you if you want to find out," I say. The lack of control I have over this whole situation has my entire body itching with fire. I don't want to give her a choice, but I know I have to play this carefully if I want my way.

"Okay," she says just above a whisper.

"Okay?" I ask, double checking that I actually heard her right.

"Okay." She shrugs, a smile pulling at her glossy lips.

"One other condition," I say, stepping away from the table. "You tell me your name."

She smiles, and I hate how it brings a smile to my lips without consent.

"I don't think you've earned that yet. Pick the right place for dinner and we'll discuss it." She's being playful, and it makes me happy that I'm the cause for something other than hurt.

"I'll pick you up at 7 on Thursday. If you have study plans, cancel them. If you have something for work, call off." I am already turning to leave. I don't care that it's a school night for her. She's spending the evening with me.

"You don't know where I live," she shouts after me. I turn my head over my shoulder and smirk at her.

"I'll find it."

"Make it 7:30," she tacks on. She thinks she has control over this. It's cute. I'll give it to her for now.

It really should concern her that I didn't ask for her address. A sane woman would be running in the opposite direction, but she doesn't seem like the sane type which makes my jeans far too tight. I swore I'd stay away from her for her safety, but I have a feeling it might have been for mine.

"Please. I'll get the money. Just let me go." Snot and tears run down his battered face as he begs for mercy. Biggy texted this morning with this assignment. Johnny, the 31-year-old blabbering man tied to the chair in front of me flaked on his payment for a bag of pills that Biggy gave him to distribute. Idiot stole pills for himself and then tried to tell Biggy that he couldn't sell them, thinking the guy wouldn't be smart enough to count them.

That's one of the things that makes Biggy so intimidating. He makes people think they're safe and waits to strike.

There was one time this guy, Timmy I think, was overcharging and skimming. Taking a bite of the profits for himself thinking Biggy wouldn't care. So one day Biggy catches wind of it, calls in Timmy...no, Todd.

Yeah his name was Todd. Anyway, Biggy calls him in, says he understands it. He expects Todd to take a cut for himself. It's like a waiter getting a tip for his work. No need to worry Todd.

So he left with a pep in his step, wanting to celebrate. He pulled one over on Biggy without consequence. He doesn't think to look over his shoulder for someone like me. Biggy isn't out to get him. He's safe. Todd's walking home later that night with some sleaze with long legs that he picked up at the club, itching to find a dark place to screw her brains out while they're both high, and I don't mean on life. When his eyes spot mine, I give him a little wave, but he isn't nervous. He's not scared. An hour later his date is traipsing around looking for another fix while Todd's swimming in the Willamette with the fish.

Biggy did the same thing to Johnny here, telling him it was okay that he couldn't sell the pills and he could try again later. Then he puts me on the guy's tail to punish him, because of course Biggy can't ever do any of the dirty work himself. The old man likes to sit on his throne of money and watch his problems get taken care of by his peasants.

"You know, usually I would drag this out and lie to you. But I'm feeling generous, so I'll be honest. My boss is pretty insistent I teach you a lesson. While I'm sure he'd prefer I just kill you to avoid this incident happening again, I'll let you choose."

I circle around him, building up his nerves as I trace my finger across the brass knuckles on my hand. While I don't think stealing a couple of pills is equal to a death sentence, Biggy is getting harder and harder to please. I'm not sure if it's because of his age or the fact that he's become bigger than all of his competition, but the fact still stands.

My skills for getting rid of bodies has only improved over the years, and to him, any amount of betrayal is enough to make someone disappear.

Though it's making my life more and more inconvenient, Biggy doesn't give a shit. I'm stuck under his shoe, and while I've done more than enough to end my sentence, he's not letting up. I'm not sure he ever will, and if it weren't for my interest in my girl, I'd probably be at the point of just ending it for myself. An eternity of nothing would be better than being his puppet.

"Let's play a game of *would you rather*, Johnny." I chuckle at my immaturity. "Would you rather I break all of your fingers, or kill you?"

"What the fuck kind of choice is that?" he cries, anger in his words. He knows he's screwed either way. Pain is inevitable. Isn't that the quote of my life? In Johnny's position, in love, in anything—pain is inevitable.

"You took too long," I say as I reach from behind him and grip his left ring and pinky finger, pulling them back until they reach the back of his hand. The cracking of the bones is drowned out by his hoarse screams. He writhes in pain, kicking and screaming as I continue with each finger on his left hand before taking a hammer and slamming it on four of the fingers on his right hand, smashing them into the arm of the chair. I push his smashed fingers down to his palm, leaving his thumb unharmed which means he's now giving me a thumbs up while he continues to scream in agony.

"Consider that my leniency to you. Don't let my generosity go unnoticed, Johnny. Mess with Biggy again and next time, you will wish you would've chosen death today," I say in his face before I connect squarely with his nose, knocking him unconscious. I load his flimsy form in my truck before dropping him off in the dumpy alley I found him in. He'll be in pain for a while, but he's not dead. If anybody were to pass by him, they'd just assume he's an alcoholic or druggie sleeping one off. And they wouldn't be wrong.

Laying in bed, I can't stop my mind from racing about my date. I don't know how I'm going to make this work. So many things can go wrong. But more importantly, I find myself worrying about the possibility that she may hate the date and choose not to continue. Though she'd still be a fixture in my life, it would only be from a distance without her knowledge and that thought kills me more than it should. It's what I have now, and it's just not enough. I am a man of my word, and I would let her walk away. I'd keep an eye on her for her safety, but I would exit her life in every other sense. To her, I would cease to exist. No more Creamy Pie for me. Ha.

But I have also promised myself that I won't be someone I'm not to get her to stay. Some things will be kept from her for obvious reasons, but otherwise I will not change to keep her close. I can't be transparent about what I do, but I will show her what it will be like to be mine. If she chooses to stay, I want her to know what she's getting. Well, minus the danger she's in by associating with me. I've already planned out my response should Biggy find out. He's never cared about what I do in my down time so long as I get his jobs done, but I'm not willing to risk her life should he find out and suddenly find himself interested in my personal life. I want her to make the decision wisely, but I also know I won't be letting go if she makes the decision to be with me.

The next day when I don't see her in the café, I worry that I scared her away with the address thing. After the second day, I'm pretty sure she's probably let realization set in and is staying away from me. Smart girl. When Thursday rolls around, she still hasn't made an appearance, but my check-ins assure me she has been tucked away in her apartment.

115

It feels juvenile, wanting to look nice for a woman who is probably avoiding me, but I want to anyway which is why I'm running my fingers through my overgrown hair in the reflection of the glass door as I pull on the handle and step into Manicures and Manes.

"Well, well, well. I was starting to think you'd found someone new," Cheryl says as she finishes sweeping the hair from her station floor into the vacuum in the wall.

"I could never replace you, sweetheart. Nobody is trusted with my locks but you," I say as she approaches and pulls me in for a hug before pulling back and looking me over.

"Damn straight. Now get in that chair and let me fix this mess," she says as she pulls a cape from her cabinet to drape over my shoulders.

Call me a pussy for coming to a fancy salon for my haircuts, but Cheryl has been cutting my hair for years, and I'll probably cry like a baby when she retires. She's getting older, and I know standing on her feet all day kills her, and it does nothing good for her arthritis, but she needs the money for the great grandkids that she's had custody of for years. She hasn't had an easy life, but you'd never know it by the smile that she never stops wearing. She's the grandma I never had.

"So..." She hands me a glass bottle of water from the fridge and clasps the cape around my neck. "The usual?" she asks.

"I was thinking we'd spice it up a little this time. Let's take a little more off the top."

She raises her eyebrows at me in the mirror and I know exactly where this is going.

"Mmm, and who is the young lady you're spicing it up for?"

"Who says it's for a woman? Can't I just want to look nice?" I ask as she starts shaving the sides of my head, the buzzer whirring in my ear.

"You can, but I'm not stupid. Don't worry, I'll get you back to looking handsome in no time."

I roll my eyes at her, and she catches it in the mirror, swatting me upside the head. It would piss me off if it was anyone else, but she gets away with it.

"Okay fine, it's for a girl. Not that it matters because I don't think she's interested in me anymore anyway."

"Anymore?" she presses. Cheryl knows vague details of my life, but she's never pressed me for more than I am willing to give.

"I think I let her chase me a little too long."

"Son, you never let a woman chase you. That's how you lose the good ones."

"I know. Why do you think I'm trying to look good so I can show up at her place and plead forgiveness?"

"It's gonna take more than a haircut for that," she snorts as she puts her scissors to my hair.

"Oh yeah, and what's your advice, grandma? She doesn't like flowers."

"You're brave when I've got a blade to your head," she chuckles.

"And shall I remind you, I was happily married for forty years to the love of my life before he died. I have some knowledge on the topic."

Her husband Chester passed away five years ago from aggressive lung cancer. She has always talked about that man like he was the best thing to happen to her.

"Chocolates are always a good way to go. Can't go wrong with a good orgasm either. That is what usually got Chester out of the doghouse."

Ew. Cheryl and orgasms are two things I do not need to be picturing together.

Twenty minutes later I'm shoving a tip in Cheryl's hand that, as always, she insists is far too generous, but I make her take it anyway, closing her fingers around the cash as I hug her delicate frame.

"Don't come back unless you get the girl." She winks before ushering me out the door.

———————

I contemplated even showing up here because if she has decided to be smart and stay away from the psychopath that is myself, it needs to stay that way. But I showed up anyway. If she slams the door in my face, I'll take that as my answer, but I'm not giving up my chance to treat her tonight.

7:30 on the dot, my knuckles rap on her apartment door and I half expect to be greeted by the barrel of a gun. Wouldn't be the first time. I hear shuffling on the other side, and my heart hammers as she opens the door, eyebrows raised like she's surprised. Her hair is pinned in curls up against her head, her face glowing, free of makeup because she doesn't need it, and a robe draped around her. She's gorgeous. A few seconds tick by before she stands to the side.

"You got a haircut," she says.

I tilt my head and grin at her. That would be the first thing she notices.

"Um, sorry. You can come in. I just have to finish my hair and throw on some clothes. Don't mind the clutter," she says as she hurries off down the hallway. I quickly glance around the space, noting that it's almost completely clean save a few dishes in the kitchen sink and a couple pairs of shoes thrown under the coffee table. It's small but cozy. The kitchen and living space are one open room. Colorful decorations occupy the white walls making it feel welcoming yet simple. Almost like one of those model homes.

"Take your time," I say. She could have come on the date wearing a paper bag, and I still would've thought she was stunning. A few minutes pass before she's peeking her head around the hall and poking an earring through her ear, her curls falling down both shoulders.

"I know this is our first date, but you should know that if you are taking me to an Italian restaurant, I'm out."

I stand there speechless when she smiles.

"Does the silence indicate Italian?" she asks.

"What? Oh, no I'm just surprised." She disappears down the hallway again turning on what I know is the bedroom light, presumably to get dressed.

"About what?" She calls out.

She comes walking out into the living room, and I can't help it as my jaw falls and my eyes drink her in. She's wearing a wine-red silk dress that falls mid-thigh, tights underneath with black ankle boots. The neckline accentuates her chest in a modest but attractive way, draping just low enough to show some cleavage. She reaches for her long black pea coat and throws it over her arm as she stares at me waiting for an answer.

"I show up at your apartment without you giving me the address, and you're not even fazed? You pushed back the time, and you're not even ready. You invite me in like you trust me and leave me in your living room unattended. Do you not have any self-preservation skills?"

"Okay, well, first of all, if this is going to work, then you better learn now that you have to add half an hour to whatever time I give you. I will never be on time. Accept it."

Did she just demand I accept it? I suppress a growl at my desire to spank her ass for that. Make her demand more of that instead. I don't like giving up control, but giving it to her is quite the turn on.

"I invited you in because these walls are thin as hell, and my neighbor Gladys would hear it if you did anything I didn't want you to." She winks at me, and I know what she's hinting at. My restraint is already snapping into nonexistence as she tests my limit.

"She's like a grandma to me and would come in to beat your ass with her cane. Not to mention that you've been stalking me at the café, and you know where I live, so if you wanted to kill me, I think you'd have done it by now unless you're just incredibly patient. And I didn't ask about the address because I figured you'd avoid the question anyway. What's that?"

She points to the small velvet box in my hand, and I hold up the box feeling stupid for getting her fancy chocolate instead of flowers like a normal man. I'm too old for this shit. I have no idea what I'm doing. She snatches and rips open the box without hesitation, looking at the French truffles before looking up at me.

"You got me chocolates? Most guys would bring flowers. Well, or nothing for that matter. I'm not a flower girl, but chocolates?" She brings one to her mouth and takes a bite, closing her eyes and moaning as she chews. I audibly groan now because I don't even want to go to dinner at this point. Fuck leaving this apartment.

"Holy shit. These are incredible. You should know I am a chocolate whore. Except the ones with fruit filling. But these? These are divine. When's the wedding?" She chuckles as she finishes the truffle, and I step closer, wiping the corner of her mouth with my thumb and bringing it to my mouth to suck off the small amount of chocolate. A blush creeps up her chest as she clears her throat.

"Set the date and I'll be there," I say, not dropping eye contact.

"How's this weekend for you?" she asks, gaining her composure as she places the chocolates on the small coffee table.

"I'll clear my schedule," I say.

"If the ring is ugly, the wedding is off."

I think I love this woman. I am so screwed.

"You're not worried about testing out the merchandise before you buy? I don't do returns." She eyes me up and down in a flirtatious challenge, her mouth pulling at the corners as she suppresses a smile. She is so much trouble for me.

"Typically, yes," I say, raking my gaze down her body before settling back on her sparkling eyes. "But in this case, I have a feeling the merchandise will be nothing but beyond satisfactory," I supply.

"'Beyond satisfactory'? Is that what you'll write in my Amazon review? Zip me?" she asks as she turns, exposing her bare back, the zipper dangerously low. She knows exactly what she's doing. Is she trying to stay in this apartment? Because I can hear her breath hitch as my fingers brush her buttery skin, my dick straining behind my slacks. I respect her too much to deny her a proper date, but my mind is not going to be on dinner. I gently tug the zipper up as she pulls her hair over her shoulder out of the way.

"So, no Italian, but what about seafood?"

She turns to face me, a grimace on her face, and my heart sinks. I know this woman's address but can't decipher her taste in food. Fuck me.

"You don't like seafood either do you? Please don't tell me you're vegan." She gives me a mischievous grin and my mouth turns down into a frown as my heart sinks before she barks out a laugh.

121

"I'm just messing with you. I'm a slut for some salmon." With that she's throwing open the apartment door and staring at me from the hallway.

"You coming, or am I going to be whoring it up by myself with the fish tonight?"

"You think you're funny, don't you?" I say as I join her in the hallway.

"I know I'm hilarious, yes."

————————

Dinner is a disaster and it's barely started. Purely because I keep fumbling over my words and looking like a dipshit. Everything about her is mesmerizing, and I've been evasive to a lot of her questions.

"So you said you're an independent contractor. What does that involve?" she asks.

"It's a security job of sorts." Not totally a lie.

"Security? So you're like a private bodyguard or something? Oh my gosh! Do you work for celebrities? Do I have competition with Taylor Swift?"

I can't help but snort at her sarcasm as she tears off a piece of bread and shoves it in her mouth

"I deal with people, but not celebrities. Believe me, sweetheart, you have no competition." It isn't the answer she wants and she rolls her eyes, but I don't elaborate and she doesn't keep pushing.

She's started to get the hint, but I can tell she's slightly irritated that I'm so closed off. As much as I need to keep her safe from my world, I refuse to lie to her. And I haven't. I've just been careful with my words. She hasn't explicitly asked what I do yet, but I have a feeling the question is coming eventually. All she knows is what I mentioned briefly before at the café, which is that I'm an independent contractor, but I don't know how long that answer will suffice.

The waiter approaches the table barely granting me a glance as he smiles at her and eyes her as if I'm in his seat, and she's on the menu.

"Good evening. What can I interest you in tonight?" he asks as he eyes her flirtatiously, paying far too much attention to her chest. I grind my teeth before interrupting any chance she has to answer. I can smell his putrid douchebag personality from across the table.

"She'll have the crusted salmon with seared vegetables, and I'll have the Cajun seafood platter. We will take a bottle of Malbec as well. Thanks. And I advise that you not ogle my girl like that again if you know what's good for you."

The idiot catches my drift and walks off with a dirty look.

"Well, that was kind of hot."

"Wait. What?" I ask, surprised yet relieved she doesn't seem angry I ordered for her. Though I probably would've done it anyway even if she didn't want me to.

"You. I mean, you weren't lying about the controlling thing, but it's kind of attractive. Geez, that sounds so toxic."

I choose not to reply because I can already tell this woman is going to be the death of me, and we haven't even had our entrees.

She answers all of my questions about her life, and I enjoy listening to her answers.

"Why teaching?"

"I don't know honestly," she shrugs.

"At first I picked it for my undergrad because it seemed easy, but then I found out I really enjoyed it. But the whole elementary level thing wasn't for me. I couldn't do the snotty noses and attitudes so that's why I'm getting my master's, so I can teach at a college level."

I break off a piece of bread and slather it in butter. I get lost in asking about her life, wanting to know as much as I can.

"So you had a good childhood then?" I ask, genuinely curious how hers differed from mine.

"Um, yeah. I mean my parents didn't have much, but my mom did her best to give me a fun childhood experience. Even in the summers when we couldn't afford to go on vacations, she'd try to come up with as many activities as she could to keep me entertained." A little smile came across her face as she focused on the tablecloth and I could tell she was immersed in a memory.

"Where did you go just then?" I ask. Her eyes shoot to mine like she doesn't think I'd notice.

"Oh," she chuckles. "It just made me think about the summer before sixth grade. I had become obsessed with the water and had begged to go to the beach, but we couldn't afford it and my mom was not about to risk me catching a disease from the bacteria-infested waters of our public pool. So she made a homemade slip and slide in the back yard with trash bags she taped together, soap, and the garden hose. I was covered in bruises by the end of the day from all the dirt and rocks under the slide, and I had a burn so bad she thought I'd gotten sun poisoning, but I didn't care. It was a lasting memory."

She's enrapturing, and I can't take my eyes off her. I try to learn everything about her, and I take every crumb she gives.

"What about your dad? Are you two close?"

Her face falls and I realize I have struck a nerve.

"No, we're not." The sparkle leaves her eyes at the mention of her dad, and as much as I want to pry, I don't push it. Luckily the food comes in time to save me from my bad question, and she doesn't hesitate to dig into it. I move the conversation in other directions asking her about hobbies and her classes. I relax as I see her shoulders release the tension that was produced when I brought up her dad, and the glitter in her eyes slowly comes back. I get it; I don't want to talk about my old man either.

I take a sip of my wine as she finishes off the last bite of her crusted salmon. She wasn't kidding when she said she has a lustful relationship with the fish. The hunk of dead fish had me jealous as she tried to refrain from drooling, the sight of the plate set in front of her bringing lust to her eyes. I can only hope I get to be the reason for that flicker soon.

"I take it you enjoyed it?" I ask, eyeing her empty plate.

A flicker of embarrassment crosses her face. "Oh, um yeah, I did. Thank you for dinner. It was delicious. I don't have much in the way of a grocery budget these days, so delicacies like this don't happen often." She avoids looking at me like she's ashamed to admit it.

"Well, I'm glad I can treat you. It won't be the last time if I have anything to say about it. But since you liked it so much, does that mean I earned knowing your name?"

She eyes me cautiously before the waiter returns to the table, paying attention to not look in her direction. Smart.

"Will there be any dessert tonight?" he asks.

"No, thank you. He'll be eating dessert at home," she remarks.

I choke on my sip of wine as she eyes me from across the table, a grin on her face. What the fuck? I take the check from the waiter as I cough, struggling to catch my breath. As shocking as it is, it's nice to see her shell crack.

Her innuendo nearly kills me as I reach for my wallet, pulling out my card and placing it in the small black book. She's bold, but I can tell behind that mask, she's still nervous. She's still feeling this out. She's pushing her limits of comfortability, but I don't know why.

"If I didn't know any better, sweetheart, I'd say you were trying to get in my pants tonight," I say.

"Maybe that's exactly what I'm trying to do." She winks at me, but I can see her nerves shining through. She's pushing too hard too fast, trying to see what all of this is in one night.

"Sweetheart, I think we should hold off on that."

The smile on her face drops slightly, disappointment and embarrassment lacing her features before her mask slips back in place. I can't seem to do any of this right, damn it.

Silence fills the air even as I slide her coat on her shoulders, running my hand down her back as I guide her out to my truck. She tries to open the passenger door, but I slam it shut, gripping her arm, and spinning her to face me as I pin her body to the door. She inhales, and I lace my fingers through her silky black hair, gripping tightly and angling her head to give my mouth access to her throat. I glide my nose up her skin, inhaling her scent. I can feel her pulse hammering under her skin. She smells intoxicating, and I take the opportunity to nip at her skin, a hiss coming from her sweet lips.

I pepper gentle kisses down her neck before sucking on the skin above her collarbone hard enough to mark her skin. The moans coming from her parted lips have me fighting every urge to rip off her dress and fuck her right here in the parking lot. I pull back. Her eyes remain closed for a breath before they flutter open and focus on my lips. As much as I would love to take her lips in a kiss, I refrain, my cock battling my pants. Keeping my hand in her hair, I tilt her head to make her look at me.

"I don't know how many times I have to tell you that attraction is not a problem. Believe me, I have imagined every way that I want to take you, to feel you wrapped around me, every way that I want to claim you and consume you. The ways I want to worship you."

A squeak slips past her lips, and I can't suppress the chuckle that leaves my lips.

"So then why won't you take me home and show me?" she asks quietly. I groan because I want to so so bad.

"I want to. But for both our sakes, I need to know that you're serious before that happens. You need to know the kind of person I am before you decide, because like I told you before, once I sink into that pussy of yours, you're mine. Nobody else will be allowed to touch you. In fact, nobody else will be able to look at you without consequences. I don't give up or share what's mine, and until you're sure you can handle that, I won't pursue that part of things with you because I have a feeling that once I get a taste of you, I'm done for. I want so much more than to fuck you, sweetheart. I want to give you the world on a platter which still won't be enough."

She goes to open her mouth to speak but I interrupt her: "As much as you might want to say that you know, you don't. Not yet. I could see your nerves in the restaurant. If you want to give this a trial run, we can, but don't try diving in headfirst to try and prove a point. I'm a patient man when I want to be." I don't want to be with her, but I will do anything to make her mine at this point.

I place a quick but gentle kiss on her cheek.

"You really know how to charm the ladies, don't you?"

"Just you, baby," I wink as I open her door and help her in. "Just let me treat you for now. I want to date you. I want to show you what I have to offer." I want more than that but I'm not going to overwhelm her. If I had it my way, I'd put a ring on her finger tonight and force her to be mine. But then she wouldn't truly be mine. She'd be devoted to getting away from me. Maybe not immediately, but soon enough she'd be running away from me, not to me.

I climb in the driver's seat and fire up the engine, blasting the heat to warm up her shivering body.

"So, are you going to ask for my number? I know you're old and all, but texting is the thing now."

I growl because I want to spank her raw for that comment. But instead, I settle for what I can do and lean across the console taking her head in my hands and kissing her. She opens her lips allowing my tongue access, and I eagerly take it. Her hand slides into my hair, and I moan as her nails scrape my scalp. She's kissing me hungrily and I know if I don't stop this, we aren't making it back to her apartment and my resolve will crumble completely.

I pull back, and she whimpers at the loss. I place a gentle kiss on her lips before nipping on her bottom lip and returning to my seat before pulling out of the parking lot. I can't help but chuckle as she throws herself back in her seat and sinks down with a huff, crossing her arms across her chest like a teenager.

"You're a tease. I take it back. You can't have my number or my name. Though I'm sure if you want it bad enough, you'll get it."

"It's okay. I know where you live, baby."

"Creeper."

I glance over and see the smile she's trying to hide unsuccessfully. She likes the chase whether she wants to admit it or not.

Chapter 10
Piper

As soon as I shut the apartment door, closing Lawrence off on the other side, I throw myself on the couch and curse myself. I loved the date. So much that I didn't want it to end. I invited him in, but he insisted he go home and let me sit on things for a bit to figure out how I feel.

The problem is I don't know. I mean I know that he was amazing and beyond respectful. Most guys would jump at the opportunity to screw on the first date, but he didn't. And he made sure to know it wasn't because he didn't want to, but because he wants to do this right. But another part of me can't get over how evasive he is about his life.

He never just didn't give me an answer, but I could tell he was careful with what he said which makes me question what was the truth, what can I trust? I'm not exactly the post girl for truth or trust myself. He said he was a security guard of sorts that deals with people, like he's a cop or a private bodyguard, which he isn't. How do I know if any of this is real or just some sick joke? And who am I to even ask that question? Maybe he just likes playing with me, thinking I'm just some naive young girl desperate for attention.

He asked so many questions about me though. And he seemed genuinely interested in what I had to say. I didn't let him push me on things I wasn't ready to share though. Like my dad. He wasn't exactly forthcoming about his job, either. I could see him absorbing everything I said even if he knew we were both keeping secrets.

I have bad trust issues, but I still didn't get bad vibes from him. He may be a bit controlling, but I honestly enjoyed it. His face when the waiter was hitting on me nearly crippled me. For a second, I thought he was going to lunge across the table and beat the guy senseless. I also never thought I'd find it attractive to have a guy order for me, but it was.

And he seemed genuinely interested in my life. He asked about my upbringing which I kept brief. As much as I love my mom, I don't like bringing up my childhood. We talked about my ambitions and my favorite books. He even wanted to talk about my favorite shows and snacks. It never got boring or dull, and I think it was the first date I've been on that a guy hasn't gotten on their phone while listening to me talk.

I want more. Something tells me that even if I wanted to walk away for my own safety or sanity, I wouldn't be able to. The pull to him only got stronger after tonight. I hate that I decided he couldn't have my number, but it's probably a good thing because my swooning ass would probably be texting him ten minutes post date asking for date number two.

I slip out of my shoes and go to the bathroom to start a hot shower. This apartment is nice, but getting hot water takes an eternity. Leaving the water on, I go to the bedroom and take the pins out of my hair, letting the side pieces fall as I shake out my hair before pulling it up in a bun on top of my head and reaching for the zipper on my dress. I notice the curtain on my bedroom window is open slightly, and all of my modesty and sanity fly out of it. I can't check for his truck because I don't want him to know I'm looking for him, but I can feel it in my gut that he's watching. Good.

I walk closer to the window, playing oblivious to the fact that the curtain is open as I finish pulling the zipper down my back. I turn away from the window and slowly let each strap fall off my shoulders as the dress falls down my body to the floor exposing my peaked nipples.

Goosebumps erupt on my skin. I can feel his eyes on me as if he were in the room with me. Overexposing my entire back side with a deep bend, I slowly take off my tights, leaving me in nothing but my red lace panties that I wore on the off chance that he did see me naked tonight.

A part of me is glad that he turned down my advance for sex because I want to savor the chase until then, but that doesn't mean I won't enjoy taunting him, too. He wants to be a tease; I can play that game. There's an ache between my legs, and I know I won't be able to sleep without easing it. A smirk comes to my face as I reach for the purple vibrator in my bedside drawer, holding it up as if I'm inspecting it to see if it's charged. I want him to see I'll be getting off tonight whether he's in here or not.

I turn to the window and laugh to myself as I pull the curtains closed. I hope he enjoyed the show because that's all he gets. I grab my robe off the bed and slip it on, tying it around the waist as I grab a towel from the closet and head for the bathroom, placing the vibrator on the counter, steam fogging up the room.

My hands reach for the tie on my robe when a loud knock on my door scares the shit out of me. A scream breaks free as I clutch my chest. The pounding gets louder as I cautiously approach the door. On the way, I grab a knife from the kitchen, shaking as I get closer.

"What do you think you're doing, young man? It is too late for that kind of ruckus," I hear Gladys shout in the hallway.

"It's none of your concern." I recognize his voice immediately, and my fear melts. It's not a serial killer.

"I beg your pardon, but that young lady in there is my concern, and with knocking like that I don't feel like you've got good intentions."

Leaning against the front door, I listen for his response.

132

"Baby, open this fucking door right now before I kick it down," Lawrence shouts from the other side of the door. For a second, I think about letting him stay there with a closed door in his face, but I have a feeling I won't like the consequences of that option. I'm not sure I'll like the consequences of opening the door either, but I'm intrigued enough to find out.

"That's it, young man. I'm calling the cops."

At that, I throw open the door.

"It's okay, Gladys. He's not dangerous. No need for the police."

I look at Lawrence, and my knees nearly buckle. He's furious, and the look in his eyes has me questioning my statement about him not being dangerous. The ache between my legs only intensifies as he pushes me back before slamming the door, ripping the knife I forgot I was holding from my hand and tossing it on the kitchen floor. My instincts should have me kicking and screaming, trying to get away from him as he stares me down, anger radiating from his body, but my feet are stuck, and my throat is bone dry, unable to formulate any words as he stalks towards me.

"You're in so much trouble, sweetheart," he growls.

Chapter 11
Lawrence

I slam the door behind us, leaving Gladys in the hallway. She can call the cops. There will be screams coming from this apartment, but not the bad kind. I grab the knife from her trembling hand and toss in on the floor in the kitchen. I really gotta work on self-defense with this girl if that's how she would hold up against an intruder.

"You're in so much trouble, sweetheart," I growl as she stands and stares at me, terror and intrigue seeping from her. She should be scared.

"In what universe do you think it's acceptable to undress like that in front of the window? If anyone else sees what's mine, I'll have to kill them. Do you really want to be the reason for someone's death, baby? You think it's funny to tease me like that? I rejected your proposal to come in tonight because I was trying to be a respectful gentleman, but now I don't care. Fuck being respectful."

She doesn't reply as she stands there, planted in place. I walk closer until I'm inches from her and can practically hear her pulse hammering beneath her skin that I'm all too eager to taste.

"I was going to give you a choice, but you just made the decision for yourself, and now I'm going to take what's mine."

She stutters as she searches for words, but nothing comes from her mouth except a whimper. Plenty will be coming from that pretty mouth soon enough.

"What? You're not scared now, are you baby? You had your chance to run, and you ran in the wrong direction. You're supposed to run away from the devil, not towards him. Did you really expect to play that game and win? No baby, I always win."

I can see the thoughts reeling behind her eyes. She played a dangerous game, not really thinking about her opponent. The rational part of my brain should be asking questions, like how she knew I was watching her outside and if this is the first time she's seen me out there. It's very possible this is the first she's seen me and was watching me leave after our date. She would likely argue she had no idea I was there, but I could sense it. She knew and she wanted me to see.

The rational part of my brain should also have won the argument that I should not be standing exactly where I'm at right now, but clearly that part of my brain isn't working properly. I mean how could it when this woman was playing a game of strip tease in her window giving any perv besides me the chance to ogle her. Absolutely not.

Without warning, I scoop her up, my hands gripping tightly under her thighs. Instinctively her arms wrap around my neck, her legs around my waist, and a little whimper leaves her lips. I can feel the warmth and wetness between her legs through my shirt where her robe has ridden up, and it pulls a growl from my throat.

"Already so wet for me baby, and I haven't even started."

She pulls back to look in my eyes, mischief in hers as a slight smirk graces her lips. "I thought you said we should wait."

She worries on her bottom lip, and I can tell, even in this moment, she's scared of my rejection. I'm about to remedy that, because this girl is more than enough, more than I could ever hope to deserve, and I hate that there's any ounce of doubt in her mind.

"I did. But that was before you decided to test me, and my self-control was already hanging on by a thread. I also said I was letting you make the choice about what happens going forward, but that's not the case anymore."

I carry her to the bathroom, steam filling the room and spilling into the hallway, and set her on the bathroom counter. She's staring at me trying to anticipate my next move. I lean down, trailing my tongue up the side of her neck. She bends to give me better access and sighs as I make my way to her ear and nip on it before whispering, "You don't get to make that choice anymore. I'm making it for you. No trial run, no considering how you feel. You're mine from here on out."

I don't give her time to respond before my lips are on hers. She kisses me back fiercely like she's scared it's going to end. She opens up letting my tongue in to swirl with hers. One of her hands holds herself steady on the counter while the other snakes around to grip my neck. Her nails scratch my scalp, and I groan.

"Please," she pulls back enough to whimper.

I kiss her again, pulling her bottom lip with my teeth and bite hard enough to sting. She jumps and pulls back, putting her fingers to her lip, a drop of red blood staining her fingertip when she pulls it back. Her eyes dart from the blood to me, and at first, I think she's going to run, tell me to leave. Not that she'd get far. Instead, she smiles and sticks her tongue out to lick off the rest of the blood. Yup, this girl is going to kill me, and I'll be all too eager to let her.

She grips my shirt to pull me back to her, but I don't move. She frowns, and I fight to smile in response.

"I told you there were going to be rules."

Confusion laces her features as I reach for the purple silicone toy sitting beside her on the counter. She smirks thinking I'm going to use it on her. Wrong. Quickly, I grip both ends of the toy and snap it in half.

Her eyes widen like saucers as she gapes at me.

"That was my most expensive one! Also, kind of terrifying how easily you broke that," she argues as she watches me drop the pieces into the garbage can.

"Rule number one: I said once you were mine, nobody else touches you. I should add that nothing touches you except me. That includes these useless toys of yours."

She leans back, balancing both hands on the counter behind her as she looks me up and down. Her lips curve up when she notices the bulge behind my pants before lifting back up to meet my eyes.

"Well, does that include me?" she asks teasingly as she reaches for the tie on her robe before slowly letting it fall to either side of her, exposing her naked body save her red lace underwear. I grit my teeth as she traces a finger down her abdomen, beads of sweat gathering on her body from the hot shower still running. Her water bill is gonna be astronomical. She continues down until the tips of her fingers are playing with the waistband on her panties, her eyes not leaving mine.

Just as she goes to dip her fingers into her panties, I grip her wrist in my hand, pulling it away.

"That includes you, unless I give you permission. No one touches you, brings you pleasure except me. You won't like the consequences if I find out you're touching yourself without my permission, baby."

She rips her hand from my grip and jumps off the counter, her hands roving up and then down my chest, tugging the shirt from my pants and running her fingers underneath my shirt, feeling my sweat-soaked skin.

"Looks like I owe you another shirt. Oops," she giggles, slipping my jacket off my shoulders before taking my shirt off and raking her nails down my chest hard enough to sting. I barely register the sting over the arousal killing me behind my zipper. She traces her fingers over the tattoos covering my arms, paying attention to the areas that are scarred over, raising the ink off my skin. I expect her to ask me questions, but she doesn't. Instead she presses soft kisses to my scars, taking her time like she's admiring them.

"You are really looking to cause trouble, aren't you?" I ask as she continues to explore my skin with her soft fingers.

"Maybe I'm just trying to finally get you inside me," she teases. I stare into her eyes looking for any sense of nervousness. As much as I want to feel her, I will not force her to do something she doesn't really want. There's nothing but desire staring back at me.

I grip her legs again, lifting her and pressing hard enough with my fingers to leave bruises. She's not the only one leaving marks tonight. I place her back on the counter as her hands feverishly reach for my pants, trying to undo them. I swat her hands away, chuckling when she pouts like a child.

"As much as I'd love to sink inside of you baby, I want the dessert I was promised." Her eyes light up as I sink to my knees in front of her. I hook my fingers in the sides of her underwear, and she lifts to let me pull them down, but I rip them from her instead, shoving them in my back pocket.

She hisses at the action that is already leaving red welts on her thighs, but the sparkle in her eyes tells me she liked it.

"What is it with you ruining my st–?"

Her argument is cut short as I force her thighs apart and bury my face in her warmth. I bite her inner thigh before running my tongue over her clit and lapping up the wetness already leaking from her. She's fucking nirvana. She gasps and bucks against me, both of her hands latching onto my hair.

I pull her clit into my mouth and bite lightly. A scream erupts from her throat before I reach up with one hand and massage her breast in my hand. I said there would be screams coming from this apartment, and I was right.

"You taste so fucking sweet," I say before covering her with my mouth again. I lick up and down her slit, savoring all of her, and I know it will never be enough.

"Lawrence." My name sounds heavenly coming from her mouth, and I want to hear it on repeat. I suck her clit into my mouth again, swirling my tongue over it. I feel her muscles tighten the same time her grip on my hair tightens. Her thighs try to close from her impending orgasm, and I force them wider, lapping at her until she's screaming out her release on my face.

"Stop. Stop. It's too much!"

She doesn't make the rules. I don't stop as she tries to push me away unsuccessfully. I lick at her until her muscles relax and she gives in, her sensitive clit throbbing as she approaches another orgasm.

"Oh. Fuck. Don't stop. Don't stop. I'm gonna–" She throws her body backwards as another orgasm takes over her body. I catch her lower back with one of my hands to keep her from hitting the faucet. Her second release floods my mouth and I take every drop before finally relenting and pulling away, her body slack on the counter.

Her eyes remain closed for a few moments before finally opening to look at me, satisfaction lacing her features.

"That was, I mean I've never... Twice. At least not in a row and not without the help from a toy." I can't help but grin. She slaps at my shoulder as she smirks back at me, and in this moment, I know I would die for this woman. I will give everything I have to keep her.

She grips my face in her hands and pulls me up to kiss me. I can feel her wetness on my face, but it doesn't detour her as she kisses me fiercely, moaning as she licks at my lips tasting herself. My cock twitches in my pants, making me painfully aware how badly I want–no, *need* her.

I stand fully and unbuckle my pants, dropping them and my boxers to the ground and kicking them to the side. I follow her gaze as she stares at my dick and smirk as she looks back and forth between it and my eyes, her mouth gaping.

"Nope. No fucking way is that happening. Are you kidding? You're bigger than any of my toys. You'd snap me in half!"

I can't help but laugh as she babbles. She jumps off the counter and throws her hands up in defeat, backing away towards the door, but I'm quicker and lift her, carrying her to the shower, carefully stepping over the edge before putting her on her feet. The water pelts our skin and I hiss at the temperature.

"What is it with women and their scalding hot water? Do you think the only way to clean yourself is to singe the skin off your body or something?"

She chuckles as I reach for the body wash and the cloth hanging on the wall.

"Maybe we're just trying to burn off the man's touch," she says playfully, testing her limits. Gripping the soap and cloth in one hand, I spin her around and she gasps as I smack her ass, the water making the sound echo even louder throughout the room.

"Do you just like pushing me? Because believe me, baby, I'll have so much fun punishing you if you wanna keep testing me." I grin at the red handprint already forming on her skin and rub my hand over the mark to soothe the burning skin. She turns to look at me over her shoulder and smiles.

"Maybe I like getting punished."

I slam the soap and cloth down before landing another sharp blow to her other ass cheek causing her to jump and yelp.

"Keep going, baby. I can do this all night," I say before spinning her around to face me. I grip the back of her neck and pull her to me, devouring her mouth, groaning as she lets me in, tasting me with her tongue. Her hands travel over my back, her nails leaving more marks before her hand slowly trails down and grips my dick. I moan in pleasure as she strokes me up and down, moaning into my mouth. She pulls my bottom lip into her mouth, biting down hard enough to draw blood. I step back and she follows, darting her tongue out to lick the drop of blood off my lip.

"On your knees," I demand. She hesitates only for a second before doing as I say. I position us so the spray is on my back, and not hitting her. She looks up at me through her wet lashes as I grip my dick in my fist, pumping up and down. I wasn't planning on going this far, but my restraint is on zero at this point.

"Now, baby." I drop my hands to my side, balling them in fists as she leans forward, trailing her tongue up my thigh, stopping as she gets to my throbbing cock. She grips me firmly in her hand before licking my shaft from the bottom to the tip, swirling around the head of my dick. I groan as her mouth envelopes me, the feeling beyond euphoric. She goes halfway down before sliding back up to the tip and sucking. I look down and she's staring right back at me, the look in her eyes nearly enough to send me over the edge. I grip the side of the shower wall with one hand and place the other on the back of her head, encouraging her deeper. She gives in and goes deeper, trying to take all of me before I hit the back of her throat and she gags, pulling back for air. Embarrassment laces her features, as if I'm disappointed that she couldn't take all of me.

"It's okay, baby. You feel so good." I place my hand to her cheek and rub my thumb over her skin, her eyes fluttering closed for a moment before she opens them and leans forward again, taking me into her mouth. She flattens her tongue on the bottom of my shaft and focuses on the underside of the tip. She moans, and the vibration has my knees weak. She sucks on my tip again before sliding down my shaft. I feel her throat relax as she takes more of me, and I slide down her throat.

"Oh shit. You gotta quit baby, or I'm not gonna be able to stop." I look down and she stares up at me as she pulls off my shaft with a pop just long enough to smile at me before going back for more gripping me with one hand and pumping as she sucks the rest of me with her mouth.

I grip her head as my orgasm barrels through me and I spill my release into her mouth. She happily takes every drop, swallowing all of it before finally pulling away and staring at me from her knees.

"That was better than any dessert the restaurant could have offered," she teases, and I sigh as she stands, my knees weak. It's been years since I've been with a woman, and I've never come like that with anyone before.

"I'm not going to survive you," I groan as I grab the body wash and cloth again, dumping the soap onto the cloth and lathering it as I take my time washing each part of her body. She stands under the spray of the water letting the soap wash off as she takes the cloth from me and returns the gesture, washing my body, chuckling when she gets to my dick, already half hard again.

142

"What, you have a five-minute recoup time, too?"

I smirk at her and shrug. "It's been a while. Give me a couple times and I won't even need five minutes. I won't ever be satiated with you."

I rinse off before the water finally starts to get cold, and I see goosebumps forming on her skin. I shut off the water and help her out of the shower, wrapping a towel around her and using my shirt to dry myself off.

"I could've gotten you a towel," she scowls.

She dries off before slipping her robe back on and stands in the doorway staring at me with her soul snatching eyes.

"Do you have anywhere you need to be tonight?" she questions.

Even if I did, I would cancel it.

"What did you have in mind?" I ask, one eyebrow raised as I reach for my pants from the floor. She steps up to me, swatting the pants to the floor.

"I was thinking maybe you might wanna see my bedroom."

Yup. My night is free. Briefly my heart hurts at thinking about not being able to do this with her every waking moment, but I swat it away quickly.

"Lead the way, baby."

Chapter 12
Piper

I lead him back to my bedroom, glad that I decided to clean yesterday, so my floor isn't littered with dirty laundry. I tend to be a clean freak anyway, but I have been getting lazy with laundry lately. He closes the door behind him, and I turn to face him, enjoying the view of his naked body. He is glorious.

His arms are large and toned, covered in tattoos trailing up to his neck that I want to trace with my tongue, his thighs deliciously muscular. I noticed several scars decorating his skin, and the closer I look, the more I see. Bruises and scratches on his knuckles and arms. I know I'm stupid for not asking, but I'm not sure I want to know. His abdomen is toned, but not ripped. He carries a little more weight there, but it's honestly hot. He's the perfect balance between toned and dad bod. A vision quickly ripples across my brain picturing him as a dad, and I shut that thought down immediately.

His dick bobs, fully erect again. The thing is massive. I'm honestly impressed with myself for even being able to take most of him in my mouth, his size incredibly discouraging for someone like me who hasn't had sex in ages. I'd be lying if I said I wasn't terrified about my ability to take him, but I don't care. I need him inside of me.

"What are you thinking about over there, baby? I can see the thoughts racing."

I break out of my thoughts, my eyes focusing back on him as he stalks towards me until my legs hit the foot of the bed and I stumble, falling to the mattress, his frame towering over me.

The words leave my mouth involuntarily before I can even think to filter it.

"Just wondering if you know how to use that weapon of yours as well as you use your mouth," I gasp, my own words shocking me as an evil grin takes over his face. I shouldn't have said that. He leans down, and I use my feet to propel myself up the bed towards the pillows, his body staying inches above mine as he follows.

"Are you sure you wanna find out?" he asks. Before I can answer, he's taking my mouth in his, tangling his tongue with mine. I moan into his mouth as he uses one hand to pull open my robe, my nipples pebbling when the cool air hits my skin. Goosebumps erupt all over my body as he kisses my neck, biting and sucking on the skin.

I'm gonna have so many marks on my body tomorrow, and frankly I can't wait to look in the mirror and remember what each one was from.

He slides down my body, taking a nipple into his mouth and lashes his tongue over it before switching to the other one.

He peers up at me, my breath coming in pants as I grow desperate.

"I cannot get enough of you," he growls before trailing kisses down my abdomen and taking my clit into his mouth. I buck against him and moan, his tongue swirling over my clit. He shoves a finger inside me, keeping his mouth on my clit. He adds another, stretching me before curling them up just right so that he hits that sensitive spot inside of me and I feel an orgasm cresting again. I grip his hair, pulling him as close as I can get, but just as I feel my orgasm coming, he pulls away, leaving me panting and wanting.

"No," I whine.

He chuckles as he climbs back up my body and places a kiss on my lips.

145

"You're gonna have to learn some patience, baby."

Before I can protest, he's slamming inside of me in one thrust. I scream out, the burn from him stretching me feeling almost too much to handle. I push my hands against his shoulders, needing the pain to subside. He doesn't move, just stays buried inside of me as he lets me accommodate his massive size. I'm pretty sure he just ripped me in half.

"Such a good girl, taking all of me," he says as he rubs his thumb along my cheek before pulling at my bottom lip. I lean up, taking his thumb into my mouth and sucking before popping off. The burning subsides, and he looks at me like he's waiting for me to give him permission to move.

"It's okay," I say, sensing his question. He pulls out halfway before sinking back in and picking up a rhythm that has me moaning. He feels so good, his dick hitting that spot inside of me with each thrust. I grip his back, raking my nails down his skin, and he winces as I dig my nails in deep. I saw the marks on his abdomen in the shower, and the sight alone made me needy. I love marking him.

He pulls out and flips me to my stomach, lifting my ass in the air as he pulls me back to him and sinks into me with one thrust again. But there is no pain this time, only pleasure. It fills me so full, and this position allows him even deeper, but it's euphoric.

"Look at me," he growls as he grips my hair in his fist and pulls, my eyes finding his over my shoulder.

"You feel amazing. I want you looking at me when I come inside you."

I nearly melt into the mattress.

He releases my hair and reaches around my stomach and circles my clit with his fingers, sending me over the edge.

"Don't you dare look away," he demands. And if he hadn't, my head would be falling as the orgasm takes over my body. He continues to thrust before he grunts out his release, my eyes not leaving his.

His body goes still as he spills himself inside of me, not pulling out for several moments. I feel his come spill down my thighs when he pulls out. I let myself fall to the mattress as he falls beside me on the bed.

"Question answered. You can definitely use your dick as well as your mouth. I'm also on the pill by the way, and I'm clean," I joke as I look over at him. He's too attractive for his own good, and I know I'm screwed. He smiles before climbing off the bed and going back to the bathroom before returning with his boxers and a wet cloth.

He tenderly wipes me clean, and my mind can't help but admit that I've fallen for the guy taking care of me. I don't know exactly when or how it happened, but it did.

"I wouldn't have pulled out even if you weren't on the pill, and I haven't had sex in years so I'm clean, too."

Is it possible to get knocked up from that comment alone? Because I think it just happened.

"I hope you were serious about keeping this going. I don't want a trial run. I want you completely," I admit, and he stares at me longingly.

"I'm glad you came to that conclusion, baby, but I wasn't kidding when I said you didn't have a choice. You've ruined me, and there was no other option. But I'm glad you're mine willingly," he chuckles.

He wipes himself off with the cloth before tossing it in the laundry hamper and sitting on the edge of the bed as I pull on a pair of underwear and t-shirt.

"Where's your phone?" I ask as a realization hits me. He goes to the bathroom and returns with his pants, pulling his phone from the back pocket and handing it to me curiously. I love that he didn't ask why or say I couldn't have it. He just handed it to me willingly.

I pull up the contacts and type in my name and number.

"I guess it's time you finally know my name. That way I can hear you moaning it next time." I wink at him as I hit save and pass him his phone back.

He takes the phone, scanning over my contact. His face visibly pales and my heart sinks. Something is wrong.

"Did I do something? Did I just make this too serious? I'm sorry, I just thought–"

"No, no I'm sorry. You did nothing wrong I promise," he smiles, though it doesn't reach his eyes as he rubs his thumb across my cheek.

"It's late, baby. You should get some sleep."

I don't miss the way he says *I* should get some sleep instead of *we* should get some sleep. I guess that answers my question about him staying over. I pull back the covers and climb into bed facing away from him. I can feel his eyes on my back, but if I look at him, I won't be able to hide my hurt. He screws me, and when I give him my name and number, he tenses like I asked him to marry me.

I feel the bed dip behind me and then I feel the warmth of his skin as he slides up next to me, nuzzling his nose against my head.

"Are you staying?" I ask, still facing the wall.

"I'm staying," he says, though his body still feels tense, and the tone of his voice still makes me think something happened that I missed. There's more to his words, but I just don't know what. And just like that I'm building my walls back up, though it's hard with his body touching mine. He gives me a sense of belonging, of need that I don't want to feel because as much as I want to deny it, if he walks away, I'll be left in shambles on the floor trying to piece together a puzzle with missing pieces.

Chapter 13
Lawrence

———— • ★ • ————

I curse myself as I slip out of the bed, her sleeping form resting peacefully under the covers, her dark hair falling in tangled waves over the pillow. Star. I breathe a sigh of relief when she doesn't wake, but also hate that she's going to wake up alone feeling like I used her for sex. I didn't sleep at all last night, my mind too busy to let me rest, but I couldn't leave her yet as much as I knew I needed to.

I just need some time to gather myself and figure out what to do now. I knew my soul felt an unnatural pull to her, like the universe was unwillingly tying me to her, feeling a familiarity that I couldn't understand. I just couldn't figure out why, and I wasn't complaining. Until now. I am so royally screwed. I mean it has to be the same girl, right?

I have nobody to blame but myself either for going this long without knowing her name. I'm so idiotic that I thought the lack of knowledge was enjoyable, adding to the chase. If I would've known it was her, I never would have let it get this far. I never would've even entertained the idea. It was bad enough that she's more than a decade younger than me, but now that I know she's the reason I've started checking victim's phones and making it my mission to rid the world of any pedophile that comes into my path, I feel sick.

I slip on my clothes and allow myself to admire her for a few seconds from the doorway before slipping out the front and clicking the door shut behind me. As if she was waiting for my exit, Gladys pokes her head out of the door, her old woman eyes glaring at me like a child.

"She's a good girl, that one. You treat her right or I'll be finding somewhere much darker to keep this cane." She glances at my ass before waving her cane at me.

"I know." I shrug as I continue down the hallway. I can't even argue because I deserve her threat and so much worse.

I kill people for a living, and I've never felt an ounce of guilt like what is festering in my gut. I type out a message and hit send before I stop any rationality and storm back in there, climbing back in her bed.

The second I'm in my truck, I pull out of the parking lot, not wanting to risk her waking up and looking for me. I barely make it five minutes down the road before my phone rings. My heart thuds in my throat as I answer without looking, hoping it's Star, but knowing I shouldn't be anywhere near her.

"I have a job for you tonight. You good for a late pickup?"

Not Star.

"Would I have a choice even if I wasn't?"

"No, but I thought I'd be considerate and make you feel like you had a choice," he chuckles, and I want to choke him through the phone. I'm so sick of being tied to this bastard, but after last night, I welcome the distraction. I do my best thinking when I'm breaking bones. Unfortunate for the guy in my chair tonight.

"I'll send you the address. Be there to take care of it at 11 tonight. You're on this one alone."

I don't have a chance to respond before the line goes dead. Not that I had a response. I'm thankful I won't have to work with any idiots so I can focus. I didn't even bother to ask what this guy did because frankly I don't care, and Biggy will fill me in before tonight anyway. I just need to feel bones breaking and screams filling the room.

I take my time in the shower remembering what it was like to be in Star's last night. In her shower, in her. I would've gladly drowned in her, basking in the feeling of having her. I've been spending the last four hours trying to convince myself I need to disappear on her. Break any connection she felt before there's a chance for more than what I've already given.

But I also know deep down that nothing I do will work. I was never going to be able to leave her alone even if she'd decided to walk away from me. I knew I was going to always be a part of her life, even if it only meant from a distance. She didn't put her last name in her contact on my phone, but my brain immediately made the connection.

I'd kept an eye on Starlette up until she turned 18. I made myself stop eventually, and I couldn't even tell you why. After her mom rejected my last payment and made it clear I was no longer wanted, I just felt too invasive keeping myself in her world, even from a distance. Her mom didn't know much, just what I let her know, which was that there was someone out there responsible for killing her husband that was providing her with money to help support her daughter. If I hadn't given her that information, she likely never would've stopped looking for him herself, intent on killing him for what he did to their little girl. Now I guess I should've kept watching, and I wouldn't be in this incredibly screwed up situation.

I don't feel guilty for falling for her. I don't feel guilty for sleeping with her. I feel guilty for bringing her into my world, which is dangerous enough, not knowing that I had a connection to her I would never be able to break. And I don't know how to act like nothing has changed. It hasn't for her, but for me, my possessiveness of her has only grown since I read her name on my screen. She was already in danger if Biggy found out about us, but he cannot know who she is. The chances of him connecting the dots are slim to none, but he's far from stupid, so I'm not risking it.

I shut off the water and grab the towel from the hook, drying off before wrapping it around my waist and cursing under my breath when the only message on my phone is Biggy telling me about tonight's job. Nothing from Star. I rub my hand down my face and sigh as exhaustion racks my body. I make my way to the kitchen and pour a mug of two-day old coffee, sipping on the stale liquid when a thought crosses my mind. I don't know how I had been too stupid to realize it before now. Star, as she labeled herself in my phone, is 23. My Starlette would be older than that by now. Thinking about the timeline, she would have to be closer to 28 by now.

My heart starts to thud as questions run through my mind. It's all too coincidental. Finding her just a town over from where I found that little girl, jet black hair and pale white skin, a name all too rare to not be the same girl. They're both in their twenties, but not the same age. Is there really a chance they're not the same woman? No. It just doesn't make sense. I can feel it in my bones that they are the same girl, I just don't know why she'd say she's 23 if she's not.

I don't have time to lose myself in the questions as I look at the clock and realize I only have a few hours to get everything ready before leaving. The idiot I've gotta pick up–Biggy only gave me his first name, Dante– lives two hours away, and I want to be early.

I couldn't help the evil grin that graced my face when I read Biggy's message about what Dante did to earn his punishment tonight. He stabbed one of our own on a deal gone sideways which means he dies tonight, and that's exactly what I need.

I pocket my phone and pack up all my supplies before piling them in the truck and starting the trek to Garden Springs where Dante lives.

———————

It's ten at night, but the amount of streetlights illuminates the neighborhood well. This nimrod lives in a ritzy part of town which makes my job harder. This isn't an easy in and out job. Apparently, Biggy has had someone on Dante's tail for a week already, watching him. But I have to break in and take care of the asshole without drawing attention or being caught on any of the doorbell cameras that I know are inevitably on the neighbor's houses. I don't drive down Dante's road, knowing it's too risky to have my truck caught close to the scene.

Thankfully, Dante's house is in the back row of houses which sits in front of an open field which is clearly going to be used for another subdivision with all the construction gear parked throughout. I park my truck on the far side of the field away from Dante's house and pull on my gloves. There aren't any streetlights to expose my truck, and it's far enough away that any cameras on the back of houses wouldn't be able to pick up anything of value.

We have plenty of pull with local law enforcement that I don't think it would be any issue anyway, but being two hours from home, I don't want to risk it.

I pull up my hood, shadows covering my face in the oversized hoodie and make my way across the field. Dante's is one of two houses that has an incomplete fence around the property. There's a gap just big enough to squeeze through between his backyard and the neighbor's fence.

I shove my duffels, one full, and one empty, then myself through the gap and groan when a dog next door starts yapping through the wood.

Sounds like a chihuahua from the high-pitched yelping. Those things are better equipped for being footballs than "dogs."

I scan the backyard and snort. It's void of anything. No pool, grill, fire pit, string lights, nothing. I knew this guy lived alone, but dude. He lives in a family friendly neighborhood. You'd think he'd have something. The grass has also not been cut in a while, coming up to my ankles over my shoes. I bet the HOA loves this guy. Biggy said he thought the guy knew he was in deep shit and had been hiding away.

I pick up my bags and look for cameras and only spot a small one above the back sliding door. As I get closer, I realize it's not even a legitimate security camera. It's a stupid stick on WIFI camera. It's not lighting up and upon closer inspection, it's not even connected. It hangs slightly off the siding, one of the wires frayed and broken.

That makes it easy. The house is nearly pitch black when I peer in through the glass doors. The only light I see is being cast from upstairs. I open my bag and pull out the crowbar, ready to jimmy the door open. I grab the door handle and can't believe when it gives. This idiot knows he's got people on his tail, and he has a broken camera on top of an unlocked door?

He's up to something. The ease of the entire situation has the hair rising on the back of my neck. I open the door just enough to step in before closing it behind me. I stand there listening for any noise but come up empty. It's totally silent. I grab my phone from the back of my jeans and shine the flashlight around the room. There's a large flatscreen hanging on the far wall by the staircase, an oversized sectional separating the living room and kitchen, and a scattering of half empty chip bags on the kitchen island.

I set the duffles on the floor and grab my gun, spinning on the silencer. I hope I don't have to use it considering I'd like to have some more fun with the guy than that, but I'm prepared regardless. The bottom floor only has the hallway leading to the front door, a bathroom, and a door that leads to the basement. It looked creepy as hell down there, so my bet is that Dante is hiding upstairs.

Keeping the gun pointed in front of me, I make my way up the stairs, thankful that they don't creak beneath my weight. I still hear nothing as I get to the top, the light illuminating more the closer I get. Once on the second floor, I scan the space. There's a hallway to my right with four doors, the light peeking from the cracked door on the end while the others remain closed. To my left there's a railed landing that overlooks the living room and kitchen.

He knows someone is here. I'm not stupid enough to think he's in the one room with a light on, but apparently, he thinks he's smarter than me. I slowly creep up to the first room, twisting the knob and kicking the door open, my gun ready to fire if necessary. My eyes scan the room, but there's nobody in here. It's a small office space with a desk against the far wall and boxes scattered all over the floor.

I move down the hall to the next room on the opposite side of the hall and smirk as I hear slight shuffling behind the door. I'm not sure what his plan is, but it wouldn't surprise me if he has a gun and tries to shoot me through the wood. I go to the end of the hall and shove open the door of the room with the light on to illuminate the hallway and make him think I've entered that room instead. Going back to the door I know he's behind; I quickly kick the door in with force hoping I'm right about his position.

The answering grunt and clattering on the other side tells me I was right. I step into the room flipping on the light as Dante scrambles on his ass to scoot away from me and reach for the gun that fell out of his grip when the door hit him.

I point the silencer at his shin, shooting a bullet straight through his leg. Surprisingly, the guy seethes through clenched teeth, not letting a scream past his lips. He's much younger than I expected. Maybe early twenties at the most.

"Who the fuck are you?" he asks, his hands cradling the bullet wound, blood seeping through his fingers.

"That's not important," I answer, not feeling interested in entertaining conversation.

"Well, you're not the same guy who's been watching me for a week, so who are you?"

"Clearly someone better at my job if you knew someone was watching you."

This is why I don't trust anyone else to do anything in this job because you can't rely on anyone but yourself. Biggy has gotten careless lately letting people do jobs they shouldn't be doing.

"I know you're gonna kill me, so just get it over with."

Oh, well now, that's no fun.

"What makes you think I'm gonna kill you?"

"I'm not an idiot, and I knew I was dead the minute I stabbed the guy."

So, he has been hiding and clearly doesn't have much will to live which makes this boring for me.

I slip my gun in my back waistband and grip him by his upper arm, hauling him out of the room and down the stairs, blood dripping onto the floors. Thankfully, he has good enough taste to have hardwood floors instead of carpet. That would've been a bitch to clean.

Dante grunts in pain as I drag him down the stairs to his creepy basement, his injured leg hitting each step, blood still spilling from the wound. If it isn't already haunted, it will be in about ten minutes. I survey the room and see there's nothing down here. The concrete floors are cracked and crumbling. Cobwebs hang from the splintered wooden beams supporting the ceiling. The dull light flickers making the space all that more ominous as the corners of the room remain dark. It looks like they filmed a damn horror movie down here.

"Damn, Dante. As nice of a house you got, and you couldn't spring for a finished basement?" He mumbles something under his breath as I toss him to the concrete. I pat him down checking again to make sure the room is empty of anything he can find as a weapon before turning and retreating for the stairs.

"If you're smart, you'll stay where you're at."

Again, he mumbles under his breath, and I turn just in time to see him holding up his middle finger in salute as I make my way up the stairs. I snort and head to the living room to grab my duffel. I'm not in the mood to clean up what I'm about to do, but it's my only option unless I drag him back to the warehouse. If I hadn't shot him, I probably could've framed it as a suicide, but that's not an option now.

I grumble to myself as I make my way back down to the basement, pleasantly surprised that Dante hasn't moved. My mind drifts to my girl, and even being hours away from her, when I should solely be focused on this job, I can't stop thinking about her. I have questions, and I want answers.

"So, how is this gonna go, huh? Shot to the head? Slit my throat? Suffocation?" he asks like he doesn't have a concern in the world, the breaths he's breathing are going to be his last.

"Dismemberment," I mutter as I fish the tools and tarps out of my magical Mary Poppins bag. I swear I can fit anything in it.

"Oh, hell no, man. I'll kill myself before I die like that." He's shuffling around on the floor trying to stand up. I squat in front of him and pin him with my stare.

"What's the matter, Dante? Suddenly you care about dying? Don't worry. I'm not in the mood, so I'll do you the courtesy of killing you before I rip your limbs off. But dismemberment is inevitable to smuggle you out of here."

"You're messed up, man," he cries as he stands unsteadily, leaning against the concrete wall.

"You have no idea," I reply. If only he knew just how fucked up in the head I really was.

I take the biggest tarp, laying it out on the floor to catch a majority of the blood as Dante stares at me from across the room.

"If you knew we were coming after you, why didn't you run?" I ask, curiosity getting the best of me.

"I'm tired of running," he says, sliding down to the floor. There's a tone of defeat and exhaustion in his voice, and I can't help but prod.

"Running from what?"

"Everything. Life," he sighs, his head falling to one side as he stares at the floor beneath him.

"Your life really that rough you don't even care about dying?" Something in my gut is telling me to press him on this and I don't know why I care.

"Fuck it. It's not like it matters now so sure, I'll indulge you. My life is a shit show. Has been since I was six. My mom abandoned me on my dad's doorstep, not giving a shit that he was a druggie with no ambitions in life. God only knows where she went. She's probably dead now for all I know."

I stop what I'm doing and sit on the floor, suddenly intent on hearing this guy's story.

"Deadbeat didn't care day to day if I ate or starved. Most of the time I was nonexistent, until he decided I was worth more than that. The pervert started molesting me when I was nine. I started drinking at twelve, doing hard drugs at thirteen. Decided I'd had enough and ran from home. But I realized pretty damn quick the world was cruel even outside the doors of my 'home.' I started dealing and got involved with the wrong group of people. I was so high every day I don't even remember most of my teenage years. I got sober but couldn't shake the guys I'd fallen in with. That's why I still deal. Or did, I guess. They won't give a shit when I go missing. Not a soul on this planet is going to care or notice for that matter. I was always meant for death. It was just a matter of when."

The look on his face has my gut churning. I believe every word.

"How old are you, Dante?" He finally looks up, his eyes meeting mine, and I can see the defeat in his stare. He really doesn't care that he's about to die.

"Twenty," he mutters.

"Who's house is this?" At this point I know it's not his.

"I don't know. I staked out the neighborhood and saw it was up for sale. I busted in and have been staying here. I knew someone would find me eventually. I just didn't know if it would be someone coming to kill me, the family coming to get the rest of their shit, or a realtor."

I growl, irritated that I wasn't informed he was staying in a house up for sale. Pretty pertinent information, but that explains why there isn't much in the house.

"A guy your age should be doing something with his life. Going to college, trade school, working to save up money. You seriously have no ambitions?" I ask, suddenly caring far too much about this kid. And I know it's because I see so much of myself in him.

"There's no point. I was screwed from the beginning, forced into a life that didn't want me. I couldn't have gone to college even if I wanted to." His voice trails off at the end, pain etched in his words. I can see this kid has so much potential and he is just ready to die. He was dealt a shit hand, and I know all too well what that is like. I know I can't kill him.

I stuff my supplies back in my duffel and stand, hoisting it over my shoulder.

"Stay here," I instruct as I retreat back up the stairs. The only acknowledgement I get is a "Yeah, whatever" from behind me before I close the door. The basement stairs are incredibly creaky, so I know I'll hear him if he tries to leave. Though he'd have to have an incredible pain tolerance to do anything on his shattered leg. I know this has a chance of backfiring on me, but I can't end this kid's life.

Keeping my latex gloves on, I head up the stairs to clean the blood off the floors. I've become all too familiar with cleaning up my messes, but at least this is much easier than I had anticipated. I pull the cleaning supplies from my bag and make quick work of cleaning up the puddle in the room where I had shot Dante, in addition to the spots down the stairs towards the basement. I also grab his pistol and shove it in my bag.

Ten minutes later, I check the path with a blacklight to make sure I haven't missed anything before heading back to the basement. I open the door and make my way down the creaking steps, my heart stopping when I hit the last one.

Dante is sprawled out on the floor, blood pooling around his body, my gun lying next to his head. My hands fly to the back of my pants, feeling the empty space. It must have slipped out when I was packing up the bag. How did I not notice that?

I swallow, the bile rising in my throat as I approach his limp body. Shot himself straight through the skull. In one side and out the other. I feel sick as I look at him. My heart hurts knowing this kid had so much he could've done in this life but couldn't see past the shit hand life dealt him in this messed up game of poker. I know it hurts more because this could've been me.

Frankly, Dante was stronger than I was for getting out, while I've stayed stuck on the leash wrapped around my neck like a noose. I'm too cowardly to off myself, though the thought has crossed my mind more than a few times. Or had before Star.

I sigh as I drop my duffel and unload all my supplies again. I roll out the tarp and eye my saw. I can't tear him apart anymore. I think the act would physically make me hurl, and he deserves better than that. I pick up his lifeless body and lay him on the tarp, rolling him up before wrapping his body in a blanket as well.

"You were gonna get out of here, kid. You just couldn't wait ten minutes?" I can hear the agitation and hurt in my voice that I couldn't save him. The second kid I couldn't save.

Half an hour later I'm leaving through the back door, Dante's body over one shoulder, my duffels over the other. I cleaned up the basement and did a double check to make sure everything was clear. It was like nothing had ever happened. I hope Dante doesn't haunt the poor souls who buy the place.

I hadn't wanted to risk being seen with a body-sized tarp flung over my shoulder, but it felt too wrong to follow through on my plan to dismember him.

I shut the sliding door behind me, darkness blanketing the backyard. I squint through the night, making my way to the gap in the fence. I wince as I toss Dante over the fence, then my duffels. He's lanky, but the tarp and blanket make him too big to fit through the gap. I shove myself through before grunting and picking them up again to make it back to the truck.

I sigh, my muscles aching as I climb into the driver's seat, Dante in the truck bed. I glance at the clock on the dash and see it's almost three am at his point. I sigh as I pull out my phone and call Lyonel to let him know he has an early morning delivery. He picks up on the fourth ring.

"It's three in the damn morning. What do you want?"

I roll my eyes knowing this is about to cost me.

"I have a package that needs taken care of," I tell him. "I'm two hours out of town, but I'll be there to drop it off. I need it done tonight."

"You want me at your disposal in two hours, you're gonna make it worth my time, boy."

I suppress the curse sitting at the tip of my tongue.

"I don't care what it costs, just get it done," I argue.

"Five grand."

"Fine," I reply through gritted teeth.

Three hours later I'm climbing into the steaming shower, groaning when the water doesn't ease the ache in my muscles or my brain. I hurled the minute I got home. I felt sick at myself for getting rid of Dante that way, but there was no other way to do it. Biggy would be expecting his disposal, and as far as he's going to know, it went exactly to plan. He will never know I was going to let that kid free in the hopes he'd turn his life around.

The kid who's body is now liquified in a cube of metal. The thought passes through my brain that if I wouldn't have been a coward and just ended it like Dante did, I wouldn't be in the position I am now. In love with a girl who I have no right to love. Putting her in danger in a life I haven't tried hard enough to escape. I wanted to protect her and now I've dragged her into the life she needed saving from all those years ago.

I haven't heard from Star all day, and I know it's because of how I left. If I was a good man, I would leave her alone. I would let her be heartbroken over my behavior and leave her to pick up the pieces. But I'm not a good man, and Star will never be whole because I own a piece, and I'm not giving it back.

Chapter 14

Piper

It's been five days since Lawrence left me in my bed. All I got was a text: *Something came up with work. I didn't want to wake you. You looked so beautiful. Thank you for last night.*

I never replied because who does that? He screwed me and then left early in the morning, sneaking out like it was a dirty little secret. I'm still mad at the situation, mainly mad at myself for the fact that I'm so obsessed with him when I know I shouldn't be. Which is probably why I'm mentally lecturing myself as I sit in my usual spot at The Creamy Pie, staring at the two cups in front of me as I wait for him to show up.

He'd texted me last night and asked if I'd meet him here this afternoon during my down time. When I didn't reply, content on fighting myself and not caving at his invitation, he told me if I said no, he'd be waiting for me at my apartment, and I knew he was telling the truth. I could feel that as bad as my obsession was, his stemmed even deeper, to a dangerous level. That should scare me, but it doesn't.

The bell on the front door startles me out of my thoughts, and I can't help but grin as Lawrence enters, his eyes finding mine instantly as he approaches. Damn you, body, for betraying me. You're supposed to be mad.

"Hi, baby," he says with a smile, though I can tell there's something on his mind. My thighs instinctively clench at his words, at his presence. My body is a traitor. He sits in the seat across from me, and I slide his cup towards him. He glances at it before looking back at me, one eyebrow raised like I'm crazy.

"This is not a cappuccino," he says as he frowns at the whipped cream piled on top of the mocha blended drink. What an observation, Sherlock.

"Just try it," I urge as I take a drink from my cup, trying to hide the disgust on my face as the cappuccino hits my tongue and invades my tastebuds. How he drinks these all the time is beyond me. He reluctantly takes the straw between his lips and takes a drink of the sugary concoction. A slight smirk curls his lips, and I can't help but feel satisfied with myself.

"Good, isn't it?" I ask triumphantly as he takes another drink. He rolls his eyes at me.

"It's not terrible, but I can feel a cavity forming already from all the sugar. But I'll chug this whole thing if it keeps that look on your face."

I can feel a blush creeping across my cheeks, and I avert my gaze to the table. This man makes me cave so damn easily. He pushes the drink to the side, eyeing me.

"You hate it."

"I don't," he replies. Maybe not, but he's not going to drink it.

"Well, it's a good thing this is yours, and that's mine," I say as I snatch the drink from across the table and slide his towards him.

He happily takes a swig of his cappuccino. "Is that butterscotch?" he asks as he smacks his tongue.

"Two pumps of toffee nut. Not too sweet, but it doesn't taste like that burnt shit you usually get."

"I happen to like the shit I drink," he says.

No, he doesn't, he just doesn't like change. He settles back in his seat, crossing his arms as he stares at me.

"Why do I feel like there's a question looming?" I ask.

"Is Star really your name?"

166

I breathe a sigh of relief. I don't know what I was expecting, but it wasn't that.

"No. I mean it's a nickname. My dad gave it to me as a kid and it stuck with me. I always loved it. My real name is Piper, but that's what everyone calls me, and I'd rather hear Star coming from your lips."

He seems to ponder my answer for a moment before continuing.

"You haven't talked about your family much," he says, leaning forward with his elbows on the table. I can smell him, and it's intoxicating. He smells like mahogany and leather. Memories of the other night in my apartment flash through my mind and I bite my lower lip at the reminder of what he felt like. He reaches across the table, pulling my lip free and I'm almost certain I audibly moan at the action. A grin tugs at his mouth, but he doesn't say anything, just waits for an answer.

I clear my throat and lean back in my chair, staring out the window instead of at him.

"I just don't have much to talk about. I grew up an only child. My mom always wanted more kids, but she couldn't have more after I was born. Complications during childbirth, I guess. My dad hasn't been around for a while, but my mom and I are still close. I left for college and that was that."

"So, what happened with your dad?" he probes.

"I don't know for sure. He and Mom got into an argument one night and she kicked him out. He took his bags and went packing. I found out the next morning. She never told me what they fought about. He's probably in California somewhere living it up with his secret family we didn't know about," I lie. I don't know why, but I don't feel like telling him the story behind the man who's responsible for half my DNA. That's a piece of me I'm not willing to share yet, and he hasn't indulged much about his family either so I don't feel bad about it.

"What's your mom's name?" he asks.

"Um, Jaquelyn. Why? You want her social security number too?"

He pauses for a second too long, and I almost worry he's about to say yes.

"When's your birthday?" he probes.

"Are you worried I'm underage or lying about my identity, or something? I wouldn't stoop that low, but here, if it makes you feel better." I fish my ID out of my wallet and hand it to him, watching as he inspects it as if he's the bouncer at a bar.

"Piper Stevens," he mumbles to himself as he looks from the ID to me.

"I feel like I'm being grilled for something. What brought on the third degree?" I ask, growing uncomfortable with his questioning.

He hands me back my ID before running his palms over his face and sighing.

"I'm sorry. I just saw this story about a guy getting in trouble for messing around with an underage girl and it got in my head. Like I said, I haven't been with a woman in so long and this all just feels like new territory to me. I've just been in my head lately. I want to know everything I can about you. Not in a creepy way. God, I sound like such a perv. It's not like that. I just really like you and I want this to work." He sighs as he throws himself back into his chair defeated.

"Well, I haven't dated in a long time either, so this is different for me too. I think we're both trying our best to figure it all out."

He almost seems relieved at my answer as he nods. It's not like I should be surprised he's asking questions. That's what you do when you date someone. Speaking of dating.

"So, when's our next date?" I ask. Maybe I was overthinking his text message, and he wasn't running away from me.

"Who said there was going to be another one?"

Or not. My face falls and disappointment eats at my gut until he chuckles, indicating he was messing with me. Asshole.

"We both know you'd die of regret if you didn't take me out again," I reply.

"You're just full of yourself, aren't you?" he smirks, ridding me of any residual anger I was feeling

"I'd rather be full of you. Again."

He chokes on a sip of his coffee, and I look up to see his eyes wide, his knuckles white as he squeezes his thigh. Shit. Did I just say that out loud?

"Tread carefully, baby, or you'll be bent over this table," he says, answering my question. I'm ashamed to admit the idea is much more of a turn on than it should be, the result evident between my thighs as I cross one leg over the other.

"I'm free tonight, if you can manage to fit me in," he winks, smiling at his innuendo.

"I can manage just fine," I say. "Wouldn't be the first time." I wink back at him.

"But I don't want to go to dinner," I add.

"Okay. What would you like to do?" he asks, raising his eyebrows, gesturing for me to indulge him.

"I'm not giving you any parameters. I want to see what you can come up with. Something tells me you like a challenge." I smirk, having a feeling that creativity is not his strong suit.

"Hmm," he hums, eyeing me hungrily.

"I have to go," I say, tossing my bag over my shoulder and standing to leave.

He grips my arm as I try to pass him, his touch sending electricity through my body. He stands, bending so he's next to my ear as he whispers, "Baby, I can smell you from here."

"I—"

He cuts me off before I can try to defend myself. "Don't even try to deny it. You're dripping wet for me, and it's taking everything in me not to bury myself in that soaking pussy, baby."

I whimper but scurry out the door as soon as he lets go. As needy as I am for him to be inside of me again, a public sex fest is not on my agenda for today.

I make it to my car and send him a text: *Keep that thought for tonight ;)*

I smirk before looking up to see him stalking towards my car. I peel out of the parking lot before he has a chance to fuck me in the back seat in front of the security cameras.

Chapter 15

Lawrence

———————— ⋆ ★ ⋆ ————————

I watch her peel out of the parking lot, knowing she's laughing because she was all too close to getting what she secretly wanted. She pretends she's shy, but I have a feeling she's more like the women in her books than she wants to admit.

My mind reels with ideas for a date with her, but I also can't stop thinking about her name. My gut just tells me something is off. While her story tells me she can't be Starlette, I need to know for sure. So, I climb in my truck and head for the house I haven't seen in years.

For all I know, Isabelle doesn't even still live there. I haven't spoken to her since she returned my last check and told me to back out of their life. I have respected that until now.

The entire drive I ponder things I can do to impress Star/Piper, whichever one she is. I'm not a creative guy. I don't do extravagant dates. Hell, I don't date at all. This is the first time I've even given a damn about making a woman happy past a quick orgasm. But this is so much more than that. I want to be the reason that she's happy. I want her to think about what I did for her months down the road and smile. But screw my genetics for not giving me a creative bone in my entire body. Romance has never been my thing.

Going to the movies is a total cliché. I could take her shopping, but that makes me feel parental. Like, "Hey babe, I know everyone is gonna think I'm your dad but why don't you pick out something nice at Victoria Secret?"

I could cook for her, but that seems obvious. I would rather shoot myself in the dick than go bowling or roller blading. I'd probably fall and break my back anyway. What the hell do women want these days?

I wipe my hand down my face as I pull into the familiar driveway. A feeling of dread pools in my gut at the reminder of what happened here. Frankly, I have no idea why Isabelle didn't take Starlette and move miles away as soon as it went public. His abuse of Starlette remained a secret as I had hoped for, but his involvement with the drug trade didn't. He was a missing person that nobody cared to find. Likely a drug deal gone wrong, or he was hiding somewhere as far as anyone knew. I couldn't continue to live in a house that my spouse had abused my kid in, but that's just me. I got out of my house of horrors the instant I had the chance. I guess not everyone is like that.

I ring the doorbell, shoving my hands in my pockets as I hear the horrific chime on the other side of the door. I'm second guessing myself as I hear "Coming!" on the other side, wondering why I thought this was a good idea. She has no idea what I look like; our communication was always through texts on my burner phones, or letters I'd drop in her mailbox with the money I gave her. And if it isn't her, then I have to make up some lame excuse as to why I'm on their doorstep.

"Can I help you?" the familiar face asks when the door opens. She looks the same that she did all those years ago. A few more wrinkles on her face and her black hair has been overtaken with grays, but it's still her.

It takes me a second to formulate a response because I frankly don't believe I expected her to be here. I'm operating on a whim at this moment, not knowing any of my responses until they spill out of my mouth.

"Um, does Starlette still live here?"

Her skin pales, and an expression of recognition passes her face. "You're him, aren't you?"

I simply nod because I have no words for her. I don't want her getting sentimental on me. Surprisingly, she does the complete opposite.

"No, she doesn't live here. She's far far away from here and thriving. Leave her alone. She doesn't need anything from you," she insists, slowly closing the door so she stands in the small crack she's left open.

"So, you still talk to her," I ask. She hesitates before answering.

"We haven't spoken in a long time. After she left college, we became estranged. I don't agree with her career choices, but I know she's doing just fine where she is, and she's happy. You asked me once to keep a secret from her, and now I'm asking you. I don't want her to know who you are, what you did, or what *he* did."

Little does she know, that was never my intention. In fact, I came because I wanted to make sure I wasn't getting involved with her daughter. Knowing Starlette Reed is far from here, doesn't talk to her mom, and has a dead father gives me what I need to know that Star is not the same girl.

There are too many differences, the main one being their ages, and the name is just a big coincidence. But I didn't want to get myself in trouble digging where I didn't belong, so confronting her mother on her doorstep was the best option to figure out what I needed to know.

"I won't involve myself with her. I just wanted to know if she was okay and didn't know where she was." It's not a complete lie. I don't know where she is, and I would like to know that she's okay, but that wasn't the entire motive of my visit.

"I'm not telling you where she is. All you need to know is she's far from here, away from the hell this town was. Though from what I've gathered about you, it wouldn't be hard to find her. As her mother, I'm asking you not to go find her. She's healed and moved on."

She looks me up and down like she's judging me, but the look in her eyes is almost pleading.

"I won't go looking for her. I give you my word."

She gives me a slight nod before whispering a quick "Thank you." and shutting the door.

As I climb into my truck, I realize that over the years I probably should've been more concerned about Isabelle reporting me to the police, but I never worried about it. She had no idea who I was, and she never seemed to have any intentions outside of keeping her daughter safe and provided for which is what I helped with. I think she actually felt relief that her husband was dead rather than hiding away somewhere.

Relief floods through me as I make all the comparisons of Star, or Piper, I guess, and Starlette. It's gonna take me a minute to get used to using Star's name. Starlette is somewhere apparently far away from this shit town, doesn't talk to her mother, has a deceased father that I killed myself, and is a few years older. Star is in this town, is close to her mother, has a father who's presumably still alive, and she's younger. Knowing that I hadn't in fact started to fall in the love with the girl that I saved so many years ago made me feel a lot better and a lot less guilty. I should still feel guilty about falling in love with a 23-year-old girl, but I don't.

Throwing the truck in drive, I pull out of the neighborhood, cursing when I note the time on the dash. I'll be picking up Star in a couple of hours and have yet to come up with any ideas satisfactory enough for a surprise date. It shouldn't be this difficult when I know she's not high maintenance.

In fact, I'm pretty confident I could give the girl a dollar box of chocolates and tell her she's pretty and she'd be fawning over the gesture, which tells me she hasn't been spoiled enough in her life, and I plan to change that. So really, the standards I'm not living up to aren't hers, they're mine.

An idea sparks to mind, and I make my way to the local supermarket in pursuit of fulfilling my plan. I don't know when I became a romantic guy, but this woman's got me going crazy.

Chapter 16

Star

I'm shuffling around in the bathroom trying to get myself together, frantically working to calm my nerves as if I'm going on my first date as a 16-year-old. I've never been this jittery about going out with a guy, but Lawrence is different.

I have no idea what he's going to have planned for tonight. I don't even know why I put the pressure on him; I guess I just wanted to see how creative he could or wanted to be. I don't want to be with someone who has no idea how to be spontaneous or who only wants to do the basics. I don't want to come off as high maintenance because I'm not. But I also want to know how easy it is for him to crack. Judging by our entire interaction up to this point I'd say the man is nearly impossible to crack. But that doesn't always mean anything. A guy can jump through hoops like a trained rat to get you to sleep with him and then ditch the second you ask them for a glass of water while they're in the kitchen.

Don't get me wrong, I am all for a cuddle session on the couch or a simple coffee date, but I also don't think it's wrong to hope for a guy that is willing to do more than that. I fluff the hair sticking out of my messy bun and assess myself in the mirror. I look as flustered as I feel, but that's going to have to suffice because there's a knock on the door that has my heart thudding out of my chest.

Checking the clock, I chuckle to myself when I notice that it's ten minutes later than I told him to pick me up.

"Someone's learning." I smirk as I take in his delicious form standing against the door frame. He's in a black button down, the top two buttons undone showing off just enough of his chest, freshly shaven, his hair slightly tousled, and dark blue jeans that I'm almost certain look spectacular from behind.

"Gotta learn quickly with you. You seem to enjoy keeping me on my toes."

He smiles and I relax instantly. Something about his presence just makes me feel content. With him, it doesn't feel forced or awkward. It feels natural. It feels right. Maybe it shouldn't considering our age difference, and I'm sure my mom would have a heart attack if she knew I was dating someone closer to her age than mine, but I frankly couldn't care less.

"You ready, or was ten minutes not a long enough window?"

I roll my eyes as I snatch my keys from the counter and lock the door behind me. "Would you be impatient if I wasn't ready?" I ask as we make our way out of the complex and to his truck.

"I will always be impatient with you simply because I seem to lose all self-control with you. But I also know you're more than worth the wait, and I'll gladly rot on the couch waiting for you to get ready."

"You could try, but you'd probably get bored pretty quick. I don't have any streaming services, and the TV channels are pretty spotty, so the only thing that ever comes in is college basketball games."

His face turns up in a grimace as we make our way to the parking lot.

"What, you don't like basketball?"

"Not even a little bit. I actually hate it. Never found it the slightest bit interesting listening to the obnoxious squeak of their shoes on the floor. I'll survive on all the smut books you have instead."

He winks at me, and I feel my cheeks heat.

He flashes me his smile as he opens the passenger door for me, and I pretend that the simple gesture doesn't have me melting into a puddle. How pathetic is it that the standards have dropped so low that opening a door for a woman sends her into a horny tailspin?

I bite my lip concealing my grin as I climb in the truck. I notice he keeps it impeccably clean. I don't even see a single crumb on the floor. He gets in the driver's seat and starts the ignition, taking off out of the lot. Ten minutes pass of me jamming out to the radio before he turns it down and asks, "No questions about what I pulled out of my ass for this date?"

"Nope. I trust you. But I'm also looking forward to giving you shit about it if it's something lame. But I will have you know, if you're taking me somewhere to kill me, I will haunt you from the grave and make you hate yourself."

"Already do, sweetheart."

It's barely a mumble, but I still hear it. I try to ignore it and push it to the back of my mind. Not my business right now.

Another thirty minutes pass with light banter and singing (he sucks just as much as I do, for the record), before I'm turning to him and asking, "Okay, seriously, we've been driving forever and we're in the boonies. Are you actually planning on killing me? Because I would've at least liked to die in a sexier outfit than this," I say gesturing to my gray t-shirt, jacket, and skinny jeans.

Instead of a response all I get is a chuckle, and while I know that should send alarm bells flying in my head, it doesn't. I probably really do need therapy. At this point it's almost sunset and we're driving up some random hill with a winding road in the middle of nowhere, clear out of town. I haven't the slightest clue what he has up his sleeve.

Once we get to the top, there's a small parking lot that's little more than a patch of dirt and some tiny, abandoned brick building. There are no markings on it, and the sign that used to be on the door has weathered to nearly nothing. He parks the truck and hops out making sure to get to my door before I have the chance to open it myself. I jump out and take in the surroundings. For being absolutely nothing, it's beautiful up here.

Lawrence grabs a few large blankets from the back of the truck and a big reusable grocery bag. He cares about the environment. Cute. I try to grab the blankets from him to help, but he just smirks and pulls away from me. He leads me to a patch of grass about fifty yards from the building and starts fanning out the blankets, patting for me to sit down before pulling out a large assortment of snacks. I was right, by the way; his jeans do look phenomenal from behind. He got a little bit of everything: chips, salsa, a million types of candy, what looks like a chocolate fudge cake, strawberries, bottled water, wine, and I swear I snort when he pulls out a pack of Capri Suns.

"They're my favorite," he shrugs as he pulls one out and stabs it with the little plastic straw. It should not be this attractive seeing a man in his thirties with a juice box in his hand, but it's actually pretty sexy.

He leans back on his forearms, popping a strawberry in his mouth as I gape at him. This man planned a picnic. A fucking picnic on a secluded hill in the middle of nowhere.

"You planned a picnic?" I ask, the words getting caught in my throat. Not once has a guy done anything remotely this thoughtful for me.

"Shh," he says as he gestures out in front of him. "Watch."

I reluctantly turn my gaze and once again I am nothing more than a puddle on this blanket. Emotionally and literally. I'm scared to get off this blanket because I'm pretty confident that evidence would be left behind just how turned on I am by this man.

The sun is just starting to set behind the horizon illuminating the sky in moody hues of purple, yellow, and orange. A memory floods my mind that I didn't even know I had of a summer vacation with Mom on the beach in California watching the sunset on the sand. I don't know how I forgot about it. It was one of my favorite memories with her growing up.

I bask in the memory and the awe of it all until the sun sets completely and the only light illuminating the space is the full moon and a lantern that Lawrence must have pulled out when I wasn't paying attention.

When I look over, Lawrence is downing another juice box and snacking on a box of candy just smirking at me.

"Where did you go?" he asks. I want to hate that he can read me so well, but truthfully, I don't.

"To a memory with my mom as a kid. We were on the beach watching the sunset. It was right after Dad disappeared and the only vacation we ever took. Did you ever take vacations as a kid?" I ask as I drizzle some sour candy gel on a strawberry and pop it in my mouth. Lawrence raises an eyebrow at my snack choice but doesn't say anything.

"No, that wasn't something I had as a kid. I've never been on a vacation if I'm being honest."

"Not even like to the lake or something? An amusement park? You had to have done something."

"Nope. I didn't have an exciting childhood, and that's carried into adulthood. I mean I can remember doing small mundane things as a family like getting ice cream or going to the movies when I was younger. But that all went away when my mom took off and then my dad was just... Dad."

I gape at him because the thought of someone not getting to experience the joy of childhood is heartbreaking. I didn't get a lot, but my mom gave me the best she could. It's also the most he's given me about his childhood, and I'm thankful he's giving me more of himself.

"So, if you could vacation anywhere, where would it be?" I ask as I grab the extra blanket and curl it around me. It's barely spring so the air is still chilly.

"I have no idea. I've never really thought about it. I've been here the entirety of my life, and my focus hasn't really been on much outside of that. I guess if I had to pick something, maybe a waterpark. I remember seeing a commercial once about this place with a toilet bowl water slide and something about swimming in a toilet bowl piqued my interest."

I chuckle as I realize he's being serious. I truly think he thought the water slide was a giant toilet bowl. This poor, beautiful man.

"Thank you for this," I say as I pop another candy covered strawberry in my mouth. This time he doesn't keep his mouth shut.

"What's with that?" he asks, his eyebrows furrowed, sincerely bothered by my action.

"What? I like weird combinations," I shrug as I unashamedly grab the last strawberry, opting not to coat it in candy.

"No, not that. *That*!" he says as I chew up the juicy red fruit. "Who the hell eats a strawberry with the stem?"

I bust out in laughter, throwing myself back to the plush blanket beneath me and staring up at the sky.

"Is that a dealbreaker?" I ask, turning my head towards him. It's so dark now that I can just barely make out his face as he lies down next to me and cradles my face with his palm, running his thumb across my cheek.

"Unfortunately for you, sweetheart, I think our deal is sealed whether you like it or not," I close my eyes and relish the feeling of his rough skin against mine. "Even if you are a psycho strawberry stem eater."

He leans in, pressing his lips to mine, and I moan against him. He tastes sweet. His hand snakes to the back of my neck, his fingers gripping my hair as he leans closer, deepening the kiss. His tongue tangles with mine, moans escaping both of us as I push him to his back and straddle him. I can feel his hard length beneath me, and I grind my core against it, loving the friction as I kiss him, his scruff scratching at my skin. He nips at my bottom lip, and I groan as he cups my ass through my jeans.

I break away long enough to tear off my jacket and t-shirt, the cold air biting my skin before reaching between us and unbuttoning his jeans.

"You're going to freeze," he says. "You've got goosebumps."

I smile against his lips because no man I've known would be more concerned about a girl being cold than the fact that she's half naked on top of him.

"Those aren't from the cold, Lawrence," I whisper.

A feral growl leaves his lips as he flips us over so he's now on top. He rips my jeans down my thighs, along with my underwear so rough that I'm sure I'll have marks, and I can't wait to see them.

He frees himself from his pants before thrusting inside me in one go. I throw my head back as the pain mixes with pleasure as he starts to move.

"You don't know what you do to me, baby. I have no control with you," he moans, his forehead against mine, his thrusts picking up speed.

"Touch yourself. I don't come till you do," he orders as he grips my wrist and moves it to my center. The demand alone, along with his want for me to finish is nearly enough to make me orgasm on its own. I rub at my clit between our bodies, my toes curling as he pumps harder and sucks on my neck.

I let out a scream as I come, feeling him spill his release soon after. He stays inside of me, laying his body gently on mine before rolling us to our sides and wrapping us in the blanket.

"How did I ever survive before you?" he asks, though it seems more like a rhetorical question, so I don't answer as he caresses my face.

We bask in our private moment until the breeze picks up and I start to shiver. Lawrence cleans up the mess of food that got ruined during our sex session while I get dressed and fold up the soiled blankets.

He takes my hand in his as he leads us back to his truck, the lantern glowing just enough to keep me from tripping. As we drive back home, I think about the fact that I am so royally screwed with this man. He said our deal was sealed whether I like it or not, and I'm pretty certain at this point that I want it sealed with unbreakable chains.

"Was it sufficient?" he asks over the radio, turning to me. I can tell by the look in his eyes that he's worried I'm going to say no.

"The picnic or your dicknic?" I ask, laughing as I say the words unable to stay serious.

He snorts. "We both know my dick is more than sufficient, so yes, the picnic."

"Are you kidding?" I ask, gripping his hand on the console and squeezing. "A sunset picnic and sex is just about as romantic as it gets. It was more than enough, Lawrence. I loved it."

That seems to squash his concern as his face lightens and he moves his hand to my thigh, gripping it possessively.

He drops me off at my door, kissing me passionately against the metal before retreating out of the building.

"He's good for you," Gladys says as she smirks at me, peeking out of her door.

"I think so, too." I smile as I shut the door behind me.

Yup, I am royally screwed. Even Gladys knows it.

Chapter 17
Lawrence

— ★ —

It's been three weeks since our sunset date and I've been reeling ever since. Any time that I'm not working, or she's not in class, we're together. Being away from her feels like I'm suffocating, and I need her to breathe.

It's been stressful trying to balance my jobs with the time I want with her. Biggy has been handing me more work the past month than I feel like he ever did before. With my focus being on her, my jobs have become much quicker, the enjoyment in the torture dissipating as my enjoyment seems to only come from her.

I smile as my phone buzzes with a message from her: *Bitter cappuccino or would you like to try something new? ;)*

Smartass.

Surprise me.

I've been going to the café almost every day and sitting with her while she studies. I enjoy being in her presence because some days, being with her while she studies is all I get, and I will take any second with her I can get. I grab my latest book from the kitchen counter before snatching my keys and heading out the door.

I hate to admit that I've really started to enjoy these smut books of hers. She's loaned me two in the past three days, and I plan on finishing this one today. Though from what I've read, she may be holding expectations for me that I'm not sure I can live up to. While I do enjoy inflicting some pain and marks on her creamy pale skin, I think for me knife play is reserved for my torture sessions only.

I won't lie though that I have gotten some new ideas from the pages in her books, and I fully intend on playing out as many as I can with her. Due to conflicting schedules lately, our sex has consisted mainly of quickies when I drop her off at her apartment, or a quick riding session in my truck. That will be remedied soon. Not that there's anything wrong with a good quickie, but I need more of her.

I whip into The Creamy Pie parking lot, smiling at the sight of her at her usual table, a coffee in her hand and something that resembles a 4-year-old's milkshake in the other. It's bright pink with whipped cream and red drizzle on the top.

"I'm gonna guess this is my surprise," I say as I grimace, and she nudges the drink closer to me with a big smirk on her face.

"Sure is. Take a sip."

Reluctantly, I bring the straw to my lips, letting the cold sweet liquid coat my tongue. Her eyes light up, excitement plastered on her face. I love how easy it is to please her, and I will never stop doing everything in my power to keep her happy.

"You like it," she beams, and I hate to admit that she's right. I can feel my teeth actually rotting from the sweetness, but it is actually really good.

She leans back in her chair, taking a swig from her coffee, just staring at me.

"Do you want to grab lunch after this and maybe see a movie or something after? My class was cancelled, and I feel like we haven't had an actual date since the picnic."

I fully intend to say yes and spend the rest of my day with her, and in her, until my phone dings. Pulling it from my pocket I grumble under my breath. *Unexpected job. 987 W. Elm St. 3PM. Get it done.*

I don't even bother replying because I know it's pointless, and if I argue, it'll only put Biggy on my trail. So far, I've managed to keep him from looking into what I've been doing in my free time. I glance at the time and realize it's already pushing 1:00 and I still have to get back to the house to grab my things.

"You have no idea how much I want to, baby. But I can't. My boss on this job just called me into work." My heart clenches as I watch the excitement drain from her face, replaced with disappointment. This has been happening a lot lately, cancelling plans or leaving unexpectedly because Biggy can't seem to do anything himself. I knew this would happen which is exactly why I wanted her to know what she was getting into.

She shows that she's upset every time, but she never fights me on it anymore, and I haven't decided if that's a good or bad thing. We always keep my conversations about work brief, focusing instead on her classes or simple things like what she's craving for dinner. She hasn't pressed me on what it is exactly that I do, but I think she's realized she may not want to know.

I am the worst boyfriend ever. I haven't even asked her to be my girlfriend. I just decided she is whether she wants to be or not. I just haven't called her that to see her reaction yet. It all seems rather juvenile, the concept of labels, and I don't think she really cares about them, but I enjoy claiming her with one anyway.

"That's okay. I get it." Her gaze drops to the coffee in her hand as she scratches at the sticker on the side.

"You're a busy man. Independent contractor and all."

She emphasizes the word "independent". She's mad and I can't blame her. There's something else to her tone that I can't quite decipher. I don't know how much longer I will get away with not telling her the truth.

I stand from the table, taking my sugar shake with me and tilt her head up to look at me when she doesn't do it on her own.

"I will make it up to you, sweetheart. I promise."

I lean down, taking her lips in mine, and just get an "Uh huh" as a response. If I could, I'd be killing Biggy for being the reason my girl is hurting right now. I'd watch the life drain from his eyes as I strangled him. He may have given me a life, but he's taking the life I want away from me by keeping me from my girl.

At least with how things are now I can see my girl and hold her. Can't really do that behind prison bars, or buried in the dirt. She pops open her laptop and starts taking notes without acknowledging me. I take that as my cue and reluctantly storm out to my truck, cursing Biggy under my breath.

———————

Four hours later I'm back at the familiar dump, dropping off another body to be crushed to mush and left to decompose in a heap of metal. I didn't even bother to ask Biggy why I was after this guy. I've stopped caring. After the situation with Dante, I've become completely numb. That kid had so much potential, and now he's dead. I could've been in his position instead of the executioner. I used to think this was all for the greater good, weeding the garden. But I don't know anymore. Who decides weed from flower? We're all just stuck in the dirt.

I didn't even bother making a mess with this one. Simply put a bullet between his eyes and left it at that. The dude didn't even suspect anyone was after him. A quick glance around his place–which was in the middle of nowhere thankfully–told me he was a loner druggie with no wife or kids to worry about.

Granted, I knew that anyway from what Frederick had told me. It makes me thankful that I don't get put on the stakeouts much anymore. I don't think I'd survive watching these people for days or weeks on end to learn their schedule. After a while, I convinced Biggy to make his other minions do the prep work while I came in and finished with the dirty work. He gets more done that way and gets to utilize my capabilities more often. Of course it helped that nobody is as good at cleaning up the messes as me, so after a couple screw ups by some worker bees that resulted in people asking questions Biggy didn't like, he leaves most of the cleanup for me now.

I almost felt bad for killing this guy. Almost. But knowing I'm on my way to see my girl has me struggling to care. I know she's pissed at me, but I'm hoping she's not mad enough to keep me out.

As soon as I step onto her floor, I feel a sense of relief knowing that I'm close to her again. Even if she is pissed. I go to knock on her door and pause when I hear her voice on the other side.

"I'm fine, Mom. I've told you a million times that I know what I'm doing," she sighs, and I wish I could hear the other side of the conversation. "I am being safe. I wouldn't leave you. I just need you to trust me... I love you, too. I'll talk to you later."

Hmm, I wonder if that had anything to do with me. Is it cocky to think she was talking to her mom about me? Oh well.

I raise my hand to the door and knock, Star's dark eyes meeting mine moments later.

"What are you doing here?" she asks. I bring my other hand out from behind my back and present her with my creation. It's a bouquet of strawberries, sour candy, and tiny bags of spicy jerky. All of her favorites. I made it my goal to know her favorite everything.

"I come bearing gifts and an apology."

She snorts as she takes the bouquet and eyes everything in it.

"You don't like flowers, so this seemed like a better option. I contemplated a bouquet of diamonds too, but you don't seem very materialistic."

"It should piss me off that you know me so well." She steps aside giving me room to enter the apartment as she plucks a strawberry off a skewer and eats it. I cringe as she eats it stem and all. The look on her face tells me she did it on purpose just to irk me. I deserve that.

"I thought you had to work," she says, sliding the bouquet on the kitchen table.

"I did. It didn't take as long as I anticipated," I reply. She opens her mouth to say something, likely a question about my job but I speak before she can ask or say whatever she's planning to.

She's staring at the floor and I follow her gaze to my shoes. My shoes with blood splattered on the toe. How the hell did I forget to change my shoes? Her eyes find mine, questions filling her mind.

"I had a bloody nose earlier. It was a bad one," I explain, knowing it sounds like bullshit because it is.

"A bloody nose from what?" she questions.

"I've always had nose bleeds since I was a kid. Usually when the seasons are changing," I shrug hoping she doesn't keep pushing. She opens her mouth to say something else, but I don't let her.

"I owe you a date."

"Umm, I am nowhere near ready for a date." She gestures to herself, and I chuckle because she looks phenomenal even when she thinks she looks a mess. Her hair is piled in a messy bun on top of her head, her face fresh from any makeup, which she doesn't need anyway. She's got on a dark blue cropped tank and gray baggy sweatpants. They say gray sweatpants are a turn on for women when men wear them, but I have to say she looks sexy as hell in them, so I guess it goes both ways.

"That's okay. I brought the date to you. Well, it's in my truck."

"Why is it in your truck?"

I repress a sigh of relief that the crisis of the blood on my shoe has been forgotten. At least she's letting it go. For now.

"Well, I wasn't sure if you'd let me in or not, so I didn't want to be even more embarrassed if you slammed the door in my face."

She chuckles as if she's picturing slamming the door in my face, so I go out to the hallway and gesture at the door propped open.

"I'll go get it. Be my guest. I can see you drooling in your mind over the idea."

She giggles as she shuffles over to the door, gripping it so tightly her knuckles go white. "Fine! Go get it!" she yells before slamming the door so hard I feel the floor shake beneath my feet right before I hear her bust out laughing on the other side of the door. She props the door open just as the neighbor shoves her head out of her doorway.

"It's okay, Gladys," she says. "Thank you. I've always wanted to do that to someone." She smiles at me brightly before closing the door, gently this time.

I turn to go to my truck, ignoring the old woman's eyes burning into my back.

A few minutes later I return to her apartment, bag of ingredients to make eggplant parmesan and roasted potatoes in tow.

"You brought groceries?" she asks, peering in the bags that I set on the counter.

I snort. "I brought dinner. I wasn't sure what you'd have," I say as I take a few ingredients out and place them in the very empty fridge.

"But by the looks of your fridge I guess I should have brought you groceries. How have you not starved?"

Instead of replying she simply waltzes over to a cabinet and opens it to reveal a stash of chicken ramen and Pop Tarts. She grabs a foil packet from one of the boxes and takes a bite of the Pop Tart, hopping up on the counter and dangling her legs as I glare at her.

"Appetizer," she says as she shrugs.

"You're gonna kill me, woman."

She just chuckles as she takes another bite.

"That was phenomenal, Lawrence. Is there anything you can't do? I didn't peg you for a cook," she says as she props her legs up on the coffee table. I reach over and grab her legs, putting them in my lap instead, rubbing her calves.

"Ugh. If you're hoping to get in my pants doing that, you're gonna have to wait because I am stuffed," she huffs, putting her hand over her stomach.

I chuckle. It's then that I notice a stack of moving boxes in the corner of the room, photo albums and books piled on the floor in front of them.

"What's going on over there?" I ask, nodding my head at the boxes.

"Oh. My lease on this apartment ends at the end of next month so I've been slowly going through stuff packing. I can think of very few things worse than packing, so I'm taking my time."

"You're moving?" I blurt, louder than I intended. She grips my thigh and squeezes as she smiles at me.

"What? You worried I'm gonna leave you?" she chuckles but she doesn't realize how much that aspect terrifies me. "Just across town. I found a cheaper apartment for rent. It's a bit smaller, but I don't need much space anyway." She leans over and kisses my cheek before hopping up and heading for her room.

"I feel gross and need a shower. I won't be long. You can watch TV or whatever. I'm sure the game is on if you wanna watch," she chuckles as I glare at her. "If you wanna pick a new book, the second shelf from the top over there has all my steamy books." She smirks before disappearing down the hall. I hear the shower turn on a few minutes later and I fight the urge to join her, but I decide to give her space. I'll see her naked soon enough.

I make my way over to the bookshelf and skim through a handful, reading the synopsis and flipping through the pages before I settle on one that says it's a "reverse harem" about a group of mafia men who fall in love with the girl they kidnap. Kind of ironic given my job, but I'd chop another guy's dick off before he ever got the chance to touch Star, let alone share her.

I grab the book, and curiosity peaks as I bend down and see a photo album with *Star's pictures* scrawled in childlike handwriting across the top. I hear the shower turn off as I retreat to the couch, book and album in hand. I plop down on the cushion and start flipping through the photos. It's obvious a kid took most of these with some sort of disposable camera.

There are several blurry images of a dog in a kiddy pool, a few of a swing set at a park, and one of a dandelion sprouting out of the dirt.

Star comes walking down the hall, a towel in hand drying her hair, another towel wrapped around her body.

"Oh no. Please tell me you haven't gotten very far. There are some horrendous baby Star pictures in there that I'd really rather my boyfriend not see," she gasps, throwing her hand over her mouth as she realizes what she said.

"I mean not that you're my boyfriend. I mean we never really talked about it. I'm not really into labels, but I mean I guess you should actually ask me to be your girlfriend before I call you my boyfriend. I'm rambling. Sorry. I'll shut up. I just mean that if you don't want to be my boyfriend it's okay. Friends with benefits? Though I haven't even talked to another guy since I started seeing you, unless you count one of my professors or the students I teach, but that's kind of inevitable."

She's staring anywhere but at me, fidgeting with her towel as she shifts back and forth. I get up, tossing the photo album on the floor and storm across the room pushing her against the wall. She smells like her body wash, lilac, and honey. I snake my hand around her neck, gripping her wet hair in my fingers and yanking her head back to look at me though she keeps her eyes trained behind me.

"Look at me, Star."

When she doesn't, I grip harder. Not enough to really hurt her, but enough to make her wince as she looks at me.

"I will spend every day until I die proving that you're mine."

Her eyes soften and mischief fills her gaze. "Careful there. You're gonna make it sound like I'm your wife if you keep talking like that."

"Careful, or you will be."

She gasps at my confession like she doesn't think I'm serious, but I'd put a ring on her finger right now if I thought she wouldn't freak out. The time will come, though.

My knee slides between her legs, making the towel slip off her body and fall to the floor. I groan as I take in her damp skin. A stray drop of water is trailing down between her breasts which only draws my attention to her peaked nipples from the cool air of her apartment.

I lean down and use my tongue to lick the droplet of water from the valley between her breasts. The action makes her moan, her eyes falling closed as she throws her head back against the wall. When I retreat, she huffs, making me chuckle.

"What's the matter, sweetheart?"

She's looking at me like I'm an idiot as if to say, *You know what.*

"Were you hoping for a little more than that?" I ask as I lean down again to take one of her nipples into my mouth, licking over the tight bud before nipping at it gently with my teeth. She jumps at the sensation, and I switch to the other side.

"What about more than that?" I ask again as I slide down to my knees trailing soft kisses down her stomach to her pubic bone. Her fingers tangle in my hair and she tries to push my head where she wants me, but I resist her which only earns me another grumble of frustration.

"Stop doing that," she whines as I laugh, fanning my breath across her clit.

"I'm not doing anything," I say.

"Exactly! It's what you're not doing that's driving me crazy."

"And what is it I should be doing, baby?" I ask right before licking at her clit once with my tongue. She bucks against me, pulling my head as close to her as possible.

"That! That's what you should be doing. More of that," she moans.

"If you wanted me to taste you baby, all you had to do was ask." I don't give her a chance to respond before I'm burying my face in her core, licking and lapping at her clit as she writhes against my face. I grip one of her thighs and throw it over my shoulder so she's balancing on the toes of her other foot.

She's soaked, and I know it's not from her shower.

"You taste amazing, Star," I groan, resisting the urge to palm my erection through my pants.

"You feel amazing," she says. I use my tongue to lick up her slit before sliding my tongue inside of her. She lets out a small gasp, using both of her hands now to hold me in place. I can tell she's close, but I'm selfish and want to drag this out a little longer despite the fact that my dick is screaming at me.

I pull away from her and stand up, placing a rough kiss to her lips and loving when I pull back to see evidence of her arousal on her own lips which she eagerly licks off with a grin.

"Why did you stop?" she asks as she slaps my chest and throws her head back in frustration. I grip her arm and spin her around so she's facing the wall before smacking her ass hard. She yelps, but when I spin her to face me, she's got a smile on her face.

"You like when I mark you, baby?"

She bites her lower lip and nods while clenching her thighs.

"Needy little thing you are," I say before gripping her underneath both thighs and lifting her up against the wall, holding her in place with my arms so she's level with my face.

"What are you–"

"Oh! Oh!" she pants as I suck her clit into my mouth. She's leaned over gripping onto my shoulders, and our height difference is enough that I know she won't fall even though I have her pinned to where she can't.

I lick up and down her slit, sliding my tongue in and out of her before going back to circle my tongue around her sensitive clit. It only takes a few moments before her body is clenching and I know she's close. Her nails dig into my shoulder so roughly I'm almost confident she's drawing blood, but that only encourages me on more.

"Yes! Lawrence, don't stop. I'm gonna come!" she says right before her head slams back against the wall and she's riding her high out as she grinds against my tongue. I keep going until she's slapping at my shoulders.

"Stop, stop. It's too much." I lick at her one more time, feeling her buck against me before I lower her down, her legs wrapping around my waist as I carry her to her room and lay her on the bed.

"That was… " She throws her hands over her face, her chest rising and falling with her heavy breaths.

I climb over her, pulling her hands away from her face, loving the blush that's covering her cheeks.

"If I tasted nothing but you on my tongue forever, I'd die a very happy man." She grins up at me before pushing me off of her so she's straddling me, her thighs on either side of my hips as she pulls off my shirt.

"It's not fair you're the only one who got dessert," she says mischievously as she wiggles herself down to unbutton my jeans and pull my boxers down with them, relieving my hard dick from the confined space.

"These jeans are criminal, just so you know," she says as she tosses them to the floor and grips me in her hand, stroking firm, but gently from the base to the top.

"I'll be sure to stop wearing them," I say in a mumbled breath.

"Don't you dare." She glares at me just before she dips down and swirls her tongue around the tip of my cock. She moans when she licks a drop of pre-cum off of me and stares right at me as she flattens her tongue against the base and licks me all the way up before taking me down her throat.

It's unexpected so I unintentionally buck up, shoving myself further into her mouth causing her to gag. She comes up for air and I wait for her to stop, but instead she looks at me with hungry eyes and takes me into her mouth again, this time gripping my hips in her hands as she takes me to the back of her throat.

I can feel her tense up as I hit her throat, but she holds back a gag as I feel her throat relax and she sinks down further.

"Shit, baby, you gotta stop."

But she doesn't relent. She holds me in place down her throat for a few seconds before bobbing up and down my dick, gripping the base tightly in her fist. She swirls her tongue around the tip again and I know I won't make it much longer. I was already fighting the urge to come in my jeans while I was going down on her, but now she feels too damn good to hold back.

I sit up and grip her underneath her arms, pulling her off of me. I can see a pout start to form on her face, but I don't give her time to argue before I'm setting her on the ground and spinning her to face the mirror on the closet door at the end of the hall.

"I want you to watch how much I love being inside of you, what you do to me. You make me crazy, Star. I have no self-control with you."

A subtle blush covers her skin, and she tries to look over her shoulder back at me, but I force her face to the mirror and wrap my hand around her neck, squeezing enough to deprive her of some air as I bend down enough so I can sink inside of her.

"This is the only necklace I want to see around your neck," I growl into her ear as I pound into her, her breasts bouncing with the movement. She's on her toes trying to keep herself up, and the sight of her alone in the mirror is enough to send me over the edge.

"You have no idea how beautiful you are," I say as I thrust inside of her a few times before spilling my release. I watch her in the reflection as she pants heavy breaths. I pull out of her, stepping back to enjoy the view of our arousal dripping down her thighs.

She spins to face me. Realizing what I'm looking at, she cocks her head to the side and smirks before taking her finger and trailing it through the mess on her thighs. She stares at me with her soul stealing eyes before opening her mouth and licking her finger clean, making sure to swirl her tongue around her finger before closing her lips around it and pulling her finger free with a pop.

"Now, that is what I call dessert," she says as she turns and walks out of the room to turn on the shower again. My dick grows hard again at the sight of my welted handprint on the back of her ass cheek.

Ripping of my shirt, I follow her into the bathroom where she's already rinsing off in the steaming water. Grabbing the washcloth off the railing on the wall, I wet it and spin her so her back is pressed against my chest as I gently wipe her sensitive flesh clean.

She grabs ahold of one of my arms and gently kisses one of the scars she'd noticed before. That one in particular was surprisingly not from my father, but an altercation with Biggy many years ago when I was stupid enough to think I could get away from him.

"What's this from?" she asks quietly, her eyes trailing over the rest of my ink and noting how many scars there really are.

"A long time ago, baby." One day I'll tell her about every one of my scars, but we're not ready for that. More so, she's not ready. I worry she'll give me pushback, but she doesn't. She just stands under the water letting the water rush down her skin.

She lets herself lean against me as she hums with pleasure as I keep washing her. I finish cleaning her up before pushing her forward enough so I can grab the shampoo and massage some into her scalp. I'm pretty sure she washed her hair already, but I want to take care of her, so I wash it again. She moans as I massage it into her scalp.

"That feels nice," she says, swaying slightly until I pull her head back to rinse out the shampoo under the water.

"You have no idea what I feel for you, sweetheart." I realize after I say it that it was said out loud though I meant for it to be an internal thought. Not that I care if she heard it. She turns to face me and pulls me forward so I'm standing in the stream of the water as she grabs some body wash and starts washing me. I'm going to smell like a woman, but I couldn't care less because the smell will remind me of her, and her fingers on me feel too good.

"Tell me," she says, her eyes focusing on the task as she washes my torso.

"I don't want to scare you," I say honestly.

"Do it anyway," she says as she stops what she's doing to stare up at me, the universe in her eyes.

"Please," she pleads.

I don't respond as I wash off the soap and turn off the shower. Grabbing towels from the shelf on the wall, I dry us both off before wrapping her in a towel and usher her to the bedroom. I throw on my boxers and shove my shirt over her head before pulling back the covers and ushering her into the bed. I can sense the disappointment on her face though she's trying to mask it.

I climb in behind her, pulling her body to mine and press a kiss to her shoulder, using a finger to brush her wet hair behind her ear. I know it wouldn't keep her from hearing me, but I want her to hear every word with clarity.

"I can't remember the last time I cared about living another day in this world before I met you. I woke up every day not because I wanted to, but because something was telling me to keep going. Now I know it was the universe pushing me until I found you,"

I pause to see if she's going to say something or try to stop me, but she doesn't so I keep going.

"You are the reason I have a will to get up and keep living every day. I knew from the second you came up to me in that café that even if I tried to fight off the attraction I had for you, you were going to be a part of my life because in that moment I knew I was never going to be able to let you go. There are people in this world who never find happiness or love, and I was convinced I was destined to be one of those people. Someone never worthy of finding their person, of never knowing what it feels like to love someone so fiercely that you would go to the ends of the earth to make them happy. Being away from you feels like I'm drowning, like the breath can't find its way into my lungs. I didn't have much to live for before you, and now you're all I want to live for. You are my life now, Star. You are mine, and I am undeniably in love with you."

I continue to stroke her hair and worry that I've sent her into a tailspin thinking I'm some psycho for confessing my love for her after such a short time. I don't want to push her to talk to me if she isn't ready, so I just wait until she rolls over to face me. When she does, my heart sinks as I take in her splotchy face, silent tears streaming down her cheeks.

"Shit, baby, I–"

"No," she says, shaking her head to stop me.

This is why I didn't want to tell her. I mean I did, but I didn't want to send her running away from me.

"You're right. You do scare me. You scare me because I shouldn't feel as strongly about you as I do this quickly. In the grand scheme of things people would argue I don't know you at all. I don't know your favorite color, your birthday, what your first car was, or when you lost your virginity. But I also know that a lot of those little things are trivial and can come over time.

A lot of people don't get the luxury of finding love at all in their lifetime. I'm young, but I know something of value when I find it, and I know not to let it go. I don't want to let you go. I want to hold onto you with everything I have, even if that means being scared of the fact that I'm undeniably in love with you, too." She smiles as she sniffles, and I wipe away the tears on her face before leaning in and kissing her deeply.

I make love to her again before she's cuddled up against me trying not to fall asleep as her eyelids flutter.

"My favorite color is burnt orange. My birthday is September 19th, my first car was a blue Grand Prix, and I lost my virginity when I was seventeen, to a girl who I didn't even like." Her eyes flutter closed, a content smile gracing her face as she settles into sleep.

———

I wake up to light glaring in through the blinds. Star has since rolled away from me and is snoring, her body curled up in a ball facing the wall. I never intend to let her live it down that she snores. I gently climb out of bed to go pee, closing her door behind me before grabbing my jeans from the hallway floor. Nights like last night make me thankful she doesn't have a roommate, though I'd be lying if I said I'd have done anything different even if she did. I'm sure Gladys enjoys the entertainment through the wall.

It hits me then too that I slept better than I have in years. Not a single nightmare. No waking up covered in sweat, thrashing at the memories of my father. I'm grateful not only because I actually feel rested, but because I wouldn't know how to explain it to her if she witnessed it. I have no doubt that she's the reason I slept so well. She brings me peace and comfort.

I know she doesn't have much in the way of food, but there are leftover eggs that I brought for dinner last night, so I decide to make her a cheese omelet for breakfast. As I pad over to the kitchen, I notice the photo album that I dropped last night on the floor. I bend down to pick it up, the picture catching my attention as I bring it closer to my face.

I rub my eyes to clear them, sleep still fogging my vision. When the picture comes into focus, I nearly vomit. Staring at me through the picture is the little girl I saved all those years ago, her brown eyes burning through me as she smiles next to the woman I saw only a few days ago, Starlette's mother.

The woman I swore to protect and stay away from. The girl whose father I murdered and sent barreling into hell where he is rotting. The woman whose mother I swore I wasn't pursuing. I knew in my gut it was all so coincidental. But it doesn't add up. The ages, the relationship with her mom, her dad. My mind is reeling with the lies.

I am in love with Starlette Reed.

Chapter 18

Star

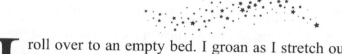

I roll over to an empty bed. I groan as I stretch out my body, soreness screaming at me, but as my memory from last night starts to come back to me, I smile. I'm sore for good reason. I stretch my arms above my head and rub my eyes as I remember everything Lawrence said to me and what I said to him.

He loves me. And I told him I love him, too. Which I do, but I'd be a liar if I said I planned on admitting that to him any time soon. I know I shouldn't feel so strongly for him when it's been such a short amount of time, but isn't the saying, "When you know, you know"? Well, I know in my heart that Lawrence has ruined me for any other man.

I sigh as I climb out of bed, my muscles protesting the sudden movement. I hold Lawrence's shirt between my fingers and bring it up to my nose, loving his scent. I throw on a pair of underwear underneath the shirt. I assume Lawrence is out in the kitchen cooking because the smell of food is wafting into my room.

across the hall to the bathroom, my bladder about to explode and relieve myself as I yell out from the toilet, "I hope it's something with cheese. I'm starving!"

I wash my hands and scurry out to the kitchen only to find it empty. His jacket is gone from the back of the chair, the dishes from dinner cleaned and put away. The only sign of him even being here is an omelet on a plate sitting on the kitchen counter. There's no note either, though I even check under the plate hoping I missed one. I check my phone to see if I missed a text, but there's nothing.

I peek out into the hallway to make sure he didn't get roped into conversation with Gladys since it wouldn't be the first time. When I come up empty, I check out the living room window just to confirm what I already know. His truck is gone. He left, and something tells me he's not coming back.

Chapter 19
Lawrence

———————— * ★ * ————————

Bile fills my throat as I pace around my room, fisting my hair and resisting the urge to punch the wall. How did I let this happen? I of all people know what to look for, how to cover my tracks, how to find information. My gut told me they were the same person, but after talking to Isabelle, I let myself be confident in believing it was all a coincidence, that I hadn't gotten myself buried–literally and figuratively– into the only woman I can't have.

I know it's only because I knew I wouldn't be able to let Star go, and I didn't want to, so I made up my own truth. But now the questions are reeling through my brain so rapidly that I can't even think straight. If "Piper" is really Starlette, then she's been lying about her age, among several other things. She's likely not actually going to school for what she says, and I want to know why. What is she hiding? Her mom says she doesn't, but does Star know who I really am?

There's no way she knows I killed her father. Not with the way she's been around me. But then again, I let all of this slip through the cracks. Could it all have been fake? No. I refuse to believe that. Something else is going on. Maybe it has to do with her dad. Maybe she changed her identity because she didn't want to be tied to him?

A pounding on my door shakes me out of my thoughts. I swear if Biggy sent one of his minions over here to get me to do a job instead of just texting me, I may actually rip their head off. I storm to the front door and rip it open, ready to tear into whoever it is until Star shoves her way past me into the house, her arms thrown across her heaving chest.

"Who do you think you are?" she asks, her voice full of venom and hurt. She doesn't give me a chance to answer.

"You think you can confess all of that crap to me last night, let me spew my heart to you, and then run away in the morning like a coward? Oh, but not before cooking me a freaking omelet. You don't care if I'm heartbroken so long as my stomach is full? Who does that? If you had a job, you could have woken me up to let me know. Though by your appearance and the fact that you're here tells me you didn't have a job."

She's pacing back and forth in my living room, her body shaking with anger, which tells me she really is hurt that I left. That only makes me think she has no idea who I actually am, but that doesn't answer the rest of it.

"If you slept on what you said and realized you actually didn't mean any of it, then at least have the decency to own up to it. What is it? Because of our age difference? I already told you I don't give a rat's ass about it. I don't care what your reasoning is for bailing, but I do care that you aren't at least man enough to say it to my face!"

She's seething as she stares at me, daggers firing at me from her chocolate eyes. She's stomping her foot awaiting an answer, but I'm too taken aback to even know what to say.

"How did you know where I lived?" I ask, suddenly remembering that she's never been here.

"Oh so you're the only one who gets to be a stalker? I never gave you my address but yet you found me. Uno reverse. Now answer me."

Fair play. My feisty little firecracker.

I go to step towards her, my heart aching over the hurt etched on her face. I don't know how I let this all get so screwed up. She steps back as I step forward, wanting space between us.

"I don't know how to explain it to you," I answer honestly. She's clearly hiding secrets, but so am I. It makes me a hypocrite to demand answers from her when I'm keeping some pretty massive ones from her. She doesn't speak or move, just stands there staring at me with her arms crossed over her chest awaiting more of an answer.

"There's a lot that you don't know about me, Star," I admit.

"Yeah, no shit. So, start explaining. Was this all just some screwed up mind game for you? Getting the young girl to naively fall for you, get in her pants and then leave?"

Her accusation stings more than it should.

"What? No, nothing I have said to you or done with you has been a game. I have meant all of it, including what I said last night." I run my hands through my hair and grumble at the fact that this is about to turn into the exact kind of disaster I wanted to avoid. This is exactly why I told myself not to pursue her in the beginning.

"Then why did you take off? What deep dark secrets are you keeping from me?" she asks, pain evident in her eyes. I hate that I'm hurting her.

"There's so much to explain, and for you to understand, I have to tell you what I do for work." I gesture at the couch for her to sit down, but she stands firm, her eyes not leaving mine.

"I haven't missed the fact that you've been cagey about what you do from the start, but I thought you were just a private person. I was trying to give you the benefit of the doubt but I've noticed the bruises on you. I've seen the blood and rips on your clothes. What, do you run a trafficking ring or something?" Her hand goes to her mouth like she's trying not to throw up at the thought.

"Fuck no, and I promise I will explain everything to you, but you have to promise you won't leave until I tell you all of it."

She creases her eyebrows as she looks me up and down like she's contemplating my request. "Why, if I try to leave, are you gonna kill me? I may not look like it, but I earned a black belt in karate as a kid, and I know how to fight. You'd still probably win, but I'll make sure you can't leave this house for days without people seeing the marks all over your face."

She says it with a slight smirk like her statement made her feel victorious. I don't doubt that she could put up a good fight, but she won't need to with me. I'd willingly let her draw blood if it meant getting to keep her, but my gut is telling me I'm in a battle I can't win, and she's already slipping out of my grasp. We both have questions that need answered.

"I'm not going to hurt you, baby. I just need you to trust me and let me explain everything first."

She huffs but relents and plops down on the couch, scooting as far away as possible when I sit down next to her. I can't say I blame her, but my body aches to feel hers close to mine.

I turn to face her, and she throws her hand out to me as if to say, "Well, go ahead." I take a deep breath, knowing that this may be the end of knowing the woman I love. That she may very well run out my front door before I've finished and report me to the police. I already know I won't stop her if she tries. There wasn't a lot keeping me motivated to start with until she came along, but living without her is a life I don't want. Not now that my heart only beats in time with hers.

I start from the beginning, explaining what happened with my mother and to my brother. She listens eagerly, absorbing every drop as I tell her about my dad and how I killed him. She doesn't interrupt once as I explain how I got wrapped into the shitshow with Biggy and how I've been trapped ever since.

I elect not to tell her about the truth behind her father's death because not only did I promise her mother I wouldn't burden Star with that pain, I also know it would only do more harm than good and what I'm doing now is enough.

When I've finished talking, I half expect her to get up and walk out the door ready to put me behind bars. Instead, she takes a deep breath as if she's been afraid to breathe this entire time and she pulls her legs up so she can clutch her knees.

"So, every time you've told me you had a job to do, you were going to kill someone?"

I shake my head. "Not always. They haven't always done something worthy of death. Sometimes they just need to be used as a warning to others, but I still hurt them, yes."

She nods slightly before asking her next question.

"Were any of them innocent people?"

"It depends on what you classify as innocent. They were all druggies, rapists, or murderers. Some of them were only guilty of petty drug infractions or theft, but none of them were innocent bystanders off the street if that's what you're asking."

She hums in response. "So why not just let Biggy turn you in to the crooked cops on his payroll? For one, you don't know that he'd actually do it, and two, there's plenty of clean cops out there who could help you.

Even back then, you could've testified about what your father did and claimed self-defense."

"Sweetheart, Biggy always keeps to his threats. He wouldn't be where he is today if he didn't. This town is far more corrupt than you'd like to believe, but money lines their very deep pockets. Besides, there would be no getting free from Biggy. Even if I served my time, he'd just put a target on my back to protect himself. I'm his most valued worker, but I also know the most. Knowledge is a death sentence in this trade, baby."

She's staring at the rug, picking at her nails silently like she's trying to think through it all. I don't want to push her further away, so I tell her the truth.

"I won't stop you from going to the police if you want to. I'd understand your motive. I begged myself to stay away from you, and I know you thought I was fighting the age difference, but I just wanted to keep you out of my fucked up messy world. I tried to fight it, but it was like no matter how hard I tried, the–"

"The universe wouldn't let you," she finishes, her eyes slowly dragging back up to mine. I nod because that's exactly what I was going to say.

"I get it. Well, not the murdering part, but I get why you couldn't walk away because I couldn't either. It was like this psycho connection that kept pulling me to you even when I tried to convince myself you were bad for me. You weren't the only one who played a part in us being together, Lawrence."

She sighs and I figure she's about to cut things off.

"I'm not saying you shouldn't have tried harder to keep me away, because I don't love that I'm involved in this now. But I also know myself, and I know I wouldn't have quit trying to have it my way either. I wanted you, and I fell in love with you. I'm not going to turn you in. Like you said, this town is apparently full of corruption anyway so it's not like it would do any good, and I can tell you already kill yourself inside more than a jail cell ever would. I don't blame you for killing your dad. From what you said, he was an evil man who deserved to rot for what he did. I only wish your mother would've tried harder to protect you."

Silence lingers in the air for several minutes. This did not go at all the way I expected it to go. She's far more understanding than anyone should be given her situation, and she's right. I hate myself every day for what I've done in this life. That's a jail sentence of its own. Self-hatred cuts deeper than any knife ever could, except for one wielded by her.

"So, what are you saying exactly?" I ask, wanting to move closer to her, but resisting the urge.

"I'm saying I don't know where we go from here except forward. I don't agree with your lifestyle, but I know that I love you, and I don't think I'm capable of walking away. I don't want my life the way it was before–before you. I only want the after, where you're in it. I want to find you a way out of this. As much as you want to self-deprecate, you deserve to be free and have a happy life, Lawrence. I want to stay out of it as much as possible, but I want to help you. You can't owe that Biggy guy forever."

I stare at her in astonishment. There's a million and one reasons why I will never deserve this woman, but now that I have her, I can't lose her. I still have a million questions, but after spilling my entire life story to her, I think it can wait a few hours.

"I'm gonna marry you," I say. Those words are enough to close the space between us as she lunges across the couch, putting herself in my lap and kissing me, her hands on both sides of my face. I kiss her back deeply, relishing in the feel of her against me. She pulls back and smiles, her eyes glittering with unshed tears that she refuses to let fall.

"I'm hungry. Are you gonna feed me or what?"

I throw my head back in laughter, her stomach grumbling in protest to her hunger as I move her to the cushion next to me. As much as I want to throw her over my shoulder and keep her in bed the rest of the day, she needs to eat first.

"And no perverted jokes about feeding me your dick!" she yells at me as I make my way to the kitchen. I can hear her cackling, and it makes my heart swell. I don't know how someone like me managed to get so lucky with her, but she's my four-leaf clover and I'm keeping her forever.

I'm scrambling some eggs while I wait for the pan to heat on the stove when I hear her padding into the kitchen behind me. She wraps her arms around my waist before leaning up and placing a kiss on my cheek. I swear it's like I didn't just spill the fact that I'm involved in a drug cartel and a murderer less than an hour ago.

"You're prickly," she chuckles as she runs her finger over my stubble. I usually don't like to have more than a shadow, but I've been a little careless with it lately.

"I didn't shave this morning."

"Hmm, yeah you were too busy hiding from me," she jokes as she steals some chocolate chips from a bowl on the counter.

"Those are for the pancakes," I scold her, swatting her on the ass when she turns away. She yelps but laughs before grabbing a bottled water from the fridge and sitting at the island behind me.

"I could get used to this," she says. I glance over my shoulder at her before pouring the eggs in the pan and watching them sizzle.

"What? Living with me? That can be arranged." I smirk.

"I actually meant staring at your ass while you cook for me, but yeah, that too."

I give my ass a little extra wiggle which earns me a chuckle.

"I have to pee. Where's the bathroom?"

"There's one right next to the living room, or you can use the one in the master. It's nicer. It's down the hall, second door on the left."

Fifteen minutes later, a plate of scrambled eggs and pancakes in hand— yes, I made breakfast for lunch, sue me–I walk out to the living room to feed my girl, but the room is empty. I set the plate down on the coffee table and check the bathroom closest to me, but the door is open.

I head down to my bedroom figuring she's taken to snooping. Not that I have anything to hide. She'll be disappointed that she couldn't find any childhood photos to mock me with. Turning into my bedroom, I see her standing in front of my dresser across the room. Her back is to me, but she must not sense me at first because she doesn't move.

"Hey–" I say, but she whips around, her hair fluttering around her head from the force. Tears are streaming down her face, cheeks red from crying.

"Baby, why are you crying?" I go to cross the room to her, but she holds up her hand, the object in it screaming at me from her palm. I didn't even realize she was holding it, and I guess I did have something to hide.

"How do you have this?" she asks, her breaths uneven as the tears continue to fall. She holds up the pocket watch I had taken from her dad so many years ago. I forgot I even had it, and I'm not sure why I kept it, but it doesn't matter now because she found it, and the engraving on the inside makes it clear that it was his.

215

"It's not what you think."

"Don't lie to me! I gave this to my dad when I was seven," she yells. Her eyes flicker across my face, and my heart sinks as I watch the very moment realization dawns on her.

"Did you kill him?" she asks, a sob racking her body.

I try to get closer to her, only wanting to hold her but she shakes her head.

"Don't come near me. Did you kill him?" she asks again.

My head drops as I simply nod because no words are going to be enough for her.

"You piece of shit!" she screams. She throws the watch at me, narrowly missing my face, and I have a feeling the tears clouding her vision are the only thing I have to thank for that. She storms past me, and I hear the front door slam shut seconds later. As much as I want to chase after her, I know it's no use. She needs some space, and not giving it to her will only make it worse. I know I should be angry that she's mad at me without offering any explanation as to why she's lied about who she is, but I'm not. I'm mad at myself for letting this turn into the mess that it did.

In this moment, I know I just signed my death sentence. Star is mine no more, and that is a pain worse than death.

Chapter 20

Lawrence

———————— * ★ * ————————

S everal hours have passed since Star left, and I've fought it long enough. I need to find her. Whether she listens to what I have to say is up in the air, but I at least need to know she's safe. Yet again, I ask myself how I let things get so screwed up. Not only did I drag her into the hell that is my life, but I broke the one promise I made to her mom.

There's no way of explaining to her why I had her father's watch without explaining why I killed him. I don't want to tarnish any memory she has of him with the truth, but she deserves to know all of it.

I drive by her apartment, expecting that to be too easy, which proves to be true when her car isn't in the lot and she doesn't answer the door. As I turn to leave, her neighbor pops her head out, her eyes glaring me down from behind her bifocals.

"You were supposed to be good to her. I don't know what you did, but she's out for revenge."

She's slamming the door in my face before I even have the chance to ask her what the hell that means. Is she at the local police station, turning me in, eagerly waiting to see me in cuffs? A drive by there tells me that's not the case either.

I'm cursing myself for not bugging her phone at this moment. I had planned on it, just so I could always know where she was, but I hadn't done it yet. I hit my hand on the steering wheel as I try to think about where she could be.

I try the café with no luck, and even check every parking lot and garage on the college campus. I head back home, making my way inside in the hopes that she's waiting for me when my phone rings. I'm not smart enough to look at who it is before I answer.

"Star, baby please–"

"She can't hear you, Lawrence." Biggy's voice sends chills down my spine like ice.

"What are you talking about?"

"Did you really think I wouldn't check up on you? Especially with how lazy you've been on the job lately? How long did you think you could keep your little toy a secret before I found out?"

"It's none of your business what I do in my personal time," I spit.

"Everything is my business, Lawrence. I own you. I let you play your little game with her in peace until you started getting sloppy. I knew she had to go, but lucky for me she made it easy and came to me herself. Shame I didn't get to chase the little mouse though."

"Don't you dare put a finger on her or I swear–"

"You swear what? You have been under my thumb for a very long time, and you still are. She's better off this way. She's at the warehouse if you're stupid enough to try me." He chuckles before hanging up the phone, and I scream as I throw my phone at the wall, watching it shatter to pieces. Why would she have gone to Biggy? How would she have even known how to find him? And how could I have been so stupid to not check the cameras? That place is rigged with them.

I grab my bags from the hallway closet and throw them in the back of the truck before peeling out of the driveway. I swallow bile in my throat as I make the drive to the warehouse. It should be crossing my brain that this could be an entire setup and he doesn't even have her, but the gnawing feeling in my gut tells me he does. I could check the cameras but I'm sure Biggy has shut them off by now, and I shattered my phone anyway.

Red blurs my vision as I speed down the roads trying to get to her. I don't trust Biggy with a fiber of my being not to hurt her, and I already know I'm going to kill him. His body will be six feet deep before the night is over.

I slam the truck into park as I pull into the warehouse lot and shove a pistol in my back pocket, one in my waistband, and my pocketknife in the front of my jeans. As much as I'd like to bust down the door, guns blazing, I have to be smart. Though the thought of Star being in there is making it hard to focus.

The door creaks open, dim lights flooding the space as I enter. I strain to listen for any indication of screams or voices but I hear nothing. As I make my way to the basement, I wait for one of Biggy's goons to attack me from behind a corner, but it never comes. It's not until I get to the door that leads to the basement that I see someone. Several of his men are posted in front of the door, arms crossed and bullet proof vests on their bulky forms. I don't recognize any of them, but I also do most of my jobs alone, so it doesn't surprise me that he's hired on new lackeys.

I don't even bother pulling a gun on them. I'm extremely outnumbered, and I already know if Biggy had ordered it, I would've been dead before my feet hit the gravel in the parking lot. I may be his go to killer, but I'm not stupid enough to think I could take on all six of these men and win without Star being hurt in the process if she's behind that door.

"Toss your guns. You won't be needing them," one of the men says, nodding his head down towards his feet, a sickening grin on his face. Reluctantly, I pull the gun from my back pocket and toss it at his feet.

"Both of them."

I grumble as I pull the other out of my waistband and drop it to the floor.

"Knife too," another says pointing at my pocket. I've killed several before without needing a weapon, but that doesn't mean I like the idea of going in here empty handed. I throw the knife down in front of them before the one on the end lunges forward and pats me down feeling for anything else I may be carrying.

"She's a pretty thing, but is she worth dying for?" one of them asks.

My heart doesn't beat for anything other than her so if she's hurt or dead, then I'm already dead with her.

The door is shoved open, and I'm shoved into the basement, the bright lights causing my eyes to struggle momentarily. Two more men stand on either side of me inside the basement door. Biggy is pacing in the middle of the room, but my eyes fly behind him where Star is tied to a chair, her head hanging forward, her hair covering my view of her face. Her arms are bound behind her, rope around her middle, and ties around both ankles. I can't see any visible wounds, but that doesn't mean anything.

"Star!" I yell.

Her head tilts up, her eyes meeting mine. I growl and step forward when I see her face. Her lip is busted, her nose is swollen, likely broken, and there's blood trickling down the side of her face from a cut by her eyebrow. She stares at me with tears in her eyes and I nearly shatter.

"You sorry son of a bitch," I say, directing my gaze to Biggy. I haven't seen him in years. Most of our communication is done over the phone or through one of his worker bees. He doesn't like to get his hands dirty, so he sends a messenger.

His age is showing, wrinkles marring his skin, gray overtaking his hair. His short stout form stands as he looks at me, and I can't help but wonder how I let this shriveled piece of man control me for so long.

"Now, now. No need for that," he says, still pacing back and forth.

"She has nothing to do with any of this," I say between clenched teeth, trying to reel in my temper at the sight of my girl hurt by their hands.

"You know, it's funny you say that. I was actually willing to let you have your fun with her. You've been a loyal worker to me for a long time and I figured so long as you kept up with your work, there was no shame in you having a little ass on the side."

He looks over at her, licking his lips, and I nearly snap, but her eyes plead with me to stay calm.

"But you know if there's one thing I really hate, Lawrence, it's a liar."

"What are you talking about?" I hardly speak to Biggy. It's mainly one-sided communication so my ability to lie to him is small.

"I would've killed you a long time ago if I'd known back then, but you're sneaky I'll give you that."

"What the hell are you talking about?" I ask, growing frustrated with his roundabout talking.

"You remember Terry don't you, Lawrence? Kind of a twit that one was, but my brother nonetheless."

My stomach churns in knots at the mention of his name. It's been so long since I killed Terry, there's no way he figured it out now.

"Yes." I say. "I remember him."

Biggy hums, putting his hands behind his back, taking a few steps closer to Star as he continues to pace.

"Yes, and do you also remember how he died? According to you that is."

221

I stay silent because it seems like the best choice at the moment. Biggy takes my silence unkindly and puts himself right behind Star, pulling a gun from his pants and putting the barrel flush to her temple.

I clench my fists, her eyes not leaving mine as a tear falls down her cheek. If he kills her, there will be nothing left of him when I'm done.

"Remind me how he died, Lawrence."

I growl under my breath but answer him. "We didn't know Reed had a gun in the car when we took him. Terry got hit."

"Hmm. What did I just say about lying? Tell me the truth! Or this pretty little head is going to be blown to pieces," he threatens, pushing the barrel harder into Starlette's temple. She flinches, but I can tell she's more pissed off than she is scared.

I can't fathom how he knows anything more than what I told him about Terry's death years ago, but somehow, he does so there's no point in denying it.

"I killed him," I admit.

"Right, you did. Now why did you kill him? He'd done nothing to you other than what, be a pest? He was my brother!"

"He was a pedophile!" I yell. Star's eyes widen as she looks at me. I don't think Biggy knows her connection to that night, that it's the same girl, but I don't know that for sure. "The guy you sent me to take care of that night had his daughter in the car. He'd snuck her in without our knowledge and when I was taking care of Reed, I caught Terry trying to fucking touch her."

I glance down at my feet before looking back at Star, and I don't know how I know but the tears streaming down her face tells me she knows the truth. Sometime between her finding the watch and now, she figured out the truth.

"So, you killed him? Over a girl? A kid you didn't even know?"

"He was a disgusting, vile human being! She was a child!"

"You kill and dispose of people, Lawrence, and you didn't think to just let him have his fun and get rid of the girl? There's an awful lot you didn't disclose."

"We didn't involve the wives or kids. That was the rule."

"No, it was your rule!" Biggy replies as he lifts the gun pointing it to me.

"I didn't care so long as you got shit done because you were valuable, but I think that value has since expired. And to think, you're throwing your whole life away for a cop," he scoffs.

"What?" I ask, my eyes darting from Star to Biggy.

"Oh, don't tell me you didn't know, Lawrence. She that good in the sack you didn't figure it out? Cause she sure as shit knows who you are. She may be a pretty piece of ass boy, but she's been stringing you along like a damn puppy on a leash. She doesn't love you. She's been using you. You were nothing more than a pawn to her to get to the king." He laughs, and I look to Star expecting to see her spewing her denial, but she isn't.

Tears stream down her face as she shakes her head.

"Tell me he's lying!" I scream.

She flinches and finally forces her eyes to meet mine. I feel sick to my stomach as I stare at her, waiting for her to say it's all a lie. I knew she was hiding something, but I wasn't expecting it to be *that*.

"It's not like that, Lawrence, I swear," she hiccups between her sobs, but that answers my question. She's a cop. Starlette Reed is a cop, and I've been playing into her game this whole time.

"Maybe I should just let you kill her, Lawrence. After all, you are so good at cleaning up messes and seeing as *you* made this one, it only seems fair."

My brain feels like it's short circuiting and I can't catch my breath as I balance on weak knees. Everything is a blur, but I do know I can't kill her because looking at the girl in that chair, I still know that my heart loves her. I catch myself shaking my head.

"What do you mean, no? You owe me, boy! I've raised you. Put clothes on your body, food in your stomach, money in your pockets. I created you. Without me, you'd have nothing, and you think you can tell me no? She played you!" he growls, his face laced with fury, his gun going back and forth between pointing at me and pointing at Star.

The sad thing is he's right. Without him I'd likely have nothing. But now that I've experienced loving her, take that away and I am nothing.

I keep my eyes trained on Star's. I wait to hear the sound of a gunshot, but it doesn't come.

"What a waste," Star scoffs.

"What was that, sweetheart?" Biggy asks, leaning down closer to her.

"You are a sick twisted waste of space," she spits.

Biggy busts out into a full belly laugh. "Enlighten me. Why is that?"

"You ruin people's lives and thrive on it. You're too cowardly to do any of the dirty work yourself so you drag other people into your endless pit of misery. Except no matter how much money you make, no matter how much blood is on your hands, you will never be able to outrun the hatred for yourself or be able to crawl out of the pit of hell where you'll rot when your useless body finally breathes its last breath."

"I see why you liked this one. She is a firecracker," Biggy says, circling around her as he taps the gun on his thigh.

"Just kill me and get this over with," I say.

"You'd rather die than kill her? After everything, you're throwing it all away for a piece of ass that doesn't even want you?"

Maybe he's right. Maybe she doesn't want me. But I want her. I can't bring myself to look at her, though I can hear her sniffling as she says "I'm so sorry" over and over.

"I'd rather die than listen to more of your bullshit. You think she used me? What the hell have you done for more than a decade? We both know I am nothing to you. I've been a convenience, someone you kept around to make your life easier. But don't act like you've ever cared about me. If I wasn't so good at getting rid of your messes, I'd have been dead a long time ago. Maybe it was all a lie, but she gave me more in this life than you ever did. So yes, just get this shit over with."

"Yeah, I could. But you'd get off too easily with that. I want to watch you suffer when you have to watch her die in front of you."

"No!" I scream as I lunge for Biggy.

I hear yelling and commotion on the other side of the door just as Biggy turns the gun on me.

"DEA!" is all I hear before a burning sensation grows across my chest and I'm falling to the floor.

"No! Lawrence!" I register Star's voice, but I can't think past the pain radiating through my body. My vision is spotty, and it's hard to breathe. I try to make myself move, but I can't. The lights on the ceiling burn my eyes, and my chest heaves as I cough, the taste of copper flooding my senses.

I'm not a doctor, but I'm pretty sure that's not a good sign. I feel clammy and disoriented like everything is jumbled. I can hear the commotion around me. Stomping feet on the concrete floor, voices yelling, gunshots in the distance, but none of it is registering.

I let my eyes drift closed. Someone grabbing my face stirs me, their fingers smacking at my cheeks.

"Lawrence, please. Look at me, baby. You're gonna be okay. I need you to fight for me baby."

My eyes open slightly, and I see her staring at me, blood and tears covering her face.

"I gotta keep pressure on it, but you're gonna be okay. You have to be okay. It's not what you think. I promise it's not. It was real." Her blood-covered hands go to my chest, presumably where I was shot, but I can feel myself drifting away. I can't fight it. I know I'm dying but it's strange.

I always thought when I died that it would just be pain and then nothing. It's peaceful. The pain is gone, and I think I can feel my heart slowing. I feel content.

I struggle to speak through the blood and lack of air, but I need her to know.

"I love you," I cough.

"No! No! Don't do this, Lawrence. Fight damn it!" she says, pushing harder on my chest, her tears a constant stream down her face.

I smile, or at least I think I smile at her. Even in her current state she's the most beautiful thing I've seen and though I don't want to leave her, I know she'll be okay.

"Tell me, please," I muster slowly between breaths.

"No. I won't because I'll tell you after. You can survive this."

I know she means she'll tell me when I wake up from this nightmare, but I learned a long time ago you're never promised your next breath.

"Please," I croak.

Her hands leave my chest and go to both sides of my face.

"I love you, too," she whimpers as she places a kiss on my lips.

I soak in as much of her as I can. Her scent, her skin on mine, her face. I absorb as much as I can to take with me wherever I'm going. Her head falls to my chest, her body shaking with sobs and as I draw in my last breath. Everything goes dark as I hear her last words: "I forgive you. Please forgive me."

Chapter 21

Star

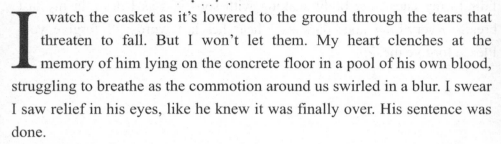

I watch the casket as it's lowered to the ground through the tears that threaten to fall. But I won't let them. My heart clenches at the memory of him lying on the concrete floor in a pool of his own blood, struggling to breathe as the commotion around us swirled in a blur. I swear I saw relief in his eyes, like he knew it was finally over. His sentence was done.

He had a lot more life to live, and he could do so without worry of Biggy or the threat of prison. The thought of the lifetime I could have had with him almost makes the tears fall, but I hold them back.

He wouldn't want me to cry.

I'm the only one here. Not that it's a surprise. Lawrence didn't have anyone else. I tried to track down his mother but wasn't successful.

I can't help but smirk as the sun pokes out from behind a cloud and illuminates the sky. When you think of funerals, you think of gray skies, dark clouds, and maybe even rain. You think of gloom and doom. Death. But today is anything except gloomy.

The sky is blue, clouds white as cotton. The flowers of early summer are in full bloom, accentuating the cemetery as the birds chirp in the trees.

If you'd asked Lawrence, he'd say he wasn't worthy of this. A funeral. Especially not one in the bright sun and beauty of the world. He'd say he deserved the doom and gloom rainy burial.

But I'd say he deserved all of this. While he hated himself for many reasons, and thought he was unworthy of everything good, he was worthy of it all. He loved me deeply and fiercely. He showed me what it meant to give your entire heart to someone, even if it's in pieces. I don't know what my life would've been like without him. Stuck in the before. All I know is what it's like after him.

I never expected to fall for him. I never expected to picture my future, and only see him in it. I never expected to be seen and wanted in the way he did. But in the end, I learned it was all inevitable. Our souls were bound long before either of us knew, and my choice to love him was only strengthened when I learned the harsh truth.

Lawrence was one of the unlucky souls who was dealt a crappy hand with seemingly no way out. Until me.

Chapter 22
Lawrence

———— • ★ • ————

They say death is peaceful. That, or it's just nothing. An abyss that you float off into, your mind and being just cease to exist.

I knew I wasn't going to get the bright lights and angels. If anything, I expected fire and brimstone. I'd done nothing to earn my place up top, so I figured down below it was. I didn't expect peace.

But I definitely didn't expect this either. And I have to say, it's pretty damn frustrating.

Time doesn't exist here. I have no sense of anything actually. A day is a year. A year is a day? Damn if I know. All I know is that I am constantly tormented with her voice. It's mixed with a handful of others, but I only focus on hers.

It's just darkness. A dark empty void. And her voice. I guess whoever's in charge down here has a cruel sense of humor because I'd much rather burn than suffer the fate of hearing her, but not being able to see or touch her.

Her words have become a tangled mess over time. It feels like months have passed, just listening to her talk to me as if she were right next to me. There's bouts of her speaking, spread out by long stretches of silence.

Silence has the ability to drive you mad. Especially when you're staring into a darkness that never ends, with nothing but the silence. But hearing her is worse. Hearing the woman I left behind is a cruelty like no other.

Once I swore it was like I could feel her holding my hand. But as quickly as it came, it was a phantom.

I know I deserve this screwed up twist of fate. With the way I lived my life, I knew I'd earned an afterlife of misery, but this is a torture worse than I imagined.

She's talking now. At least my mind is making it up that she's talking to me. I've come to the conclusion that it's what this all is. Just my mind playing screwed up tricks on me in the afterlife.

I cling to her words, not really absorbing what she says, but just basking in the sound of her. For the second time I swear I feel the faintest touch of her. I grasp onto it, praying that it doesn't go away.

"Come back to me," she says.

You have no idea how much I want to, baby.

I try to hold her back, to squeeze her hand in mine. I focus on the feeling, her fingers in mine and the feeling gets stronger.

I think she gasps and speaks again, but I can only focus on the feeling of her hand in mine. The harder I focus, the more real it feels. If only I could make myself see her, too.

"Lawrence. Open your eyes."

No. Shut up. Leave me alone. I'm spending time with my girl. The closest I've felt to her in an eternity.

"Lawrence, baby. Look at me."

Her voice echoes through my mind. I hold onto the feeling of her and focus on seeing her. Even a dream of her is better than nothing.

Suddenly everything is bright. Blindingly bright. The contrast from the constant darkness I've been living in is painful to my eyes. I close my eyes and try to open them again slowly.

I swear I can see her this time, but it's still too bright and blurry to make out anything.

"Turn down the lights," I hear next to me as I squeeze my eyes closed again.

Slowly I start to recognize more sounds. The movement of feet on the ground, an obnoxious beeping from beside me. The sniffles of a woman crying and hushed whispers.

I open my eyes again, slowly, and am pleased when my eyes aren't assaulted with blinding lights. It's duller now, though my vision is still blurry. I blink rapidly to focus my eyes and I see her.

Her face is right in front of mine. My Star. Her face is streaked with tears, and she smiles at me. She squeezes my hand in hers, and I swear if I'm yanked back into the darkness, this is a cruel cruel dream that I'll hold onto forever.

"Hi baby," she says through her cries. I try to speak but nothing comes out.

"Oh. Here." Someone passes me a plastic cup and holds the straw to my lips. I take it eagerly and groan when the cold liquid coats and soothes my sore throat.

This isn't real.

"It's real, Lawrence. You're here. You're alive." I guess I said that out loud though I didn't mean to.

"You're going to feel groggy and disoriented for a while, but it'll go away. I need to take your vitals and do some tests and then I'll let you rest and we can talk later. I'm sure you have a lot of questions," an older woman in a long white coat says as she approaches me.

Star never leaves my side as the doctor does her tests and explains what happened.

232

"You should have died. You are a very lucky man. Count your lucky stars, sir."

I chuckle at her comment as I look directly at my lucky star and squeeze her hand in mine. Turns out I did die. I was shot in the chest twice and lost large amounts of blood. My heart stopped, but they managed to bring me back. Well sort of. I've been in a coma for several months. I guess they had me on life support for a while and didn't think I would wake up, but Star was persistent that miracles happen every day. They took me off the ventilator and I managed to keep breathing on my own.

The doctor leaves the room, reminding me she will be back later to discuss plans going forward and tells me to rest. I've been resting for months. I'm not falling back to sleep. Not when I have my girl right next to me.

I place her face in my palm, and she leans into it.

"I was so scared I'd lost you," she says.

I wipe the tears from her face and smile at her. "Over my dead body," I chuckle.

She slaps my arm. "Not funny!" she says, though she's smiling too. It's kind of funny.

"I've missed you."

"I've been right here. I couldn't leave you," she says. It's then that I register the fact that I was hearing her talk to me all those months I'd been unconscious.

"I heard you."

She looks at me questioningly.

"In my head. I could hear you talking to me. I thought I was being tortured. Getting to hear you but not see you."

She takes a moment before she responds. "What all did you hear? Do you remember anything before you got shot? In the warehouse?" she asks.

"I don't know. I mean there was a lot, and I couldn't make sense of a lot, so I just clung to the sound of your voice. Some of it seemed crazy, like I was just making it all up. It's all fuzzy, and I can't tell what was real and what was a dream."

"Like what?" she asks, concern marring her face.

"Umm let's see," I sigh as I lean back in the bed and stare at the ceiling.

"Like that you're a cop, you faked my death, and my mom is dead." I can't help but laugh at the things my mind concocted while I was in a coma. I'm only met with silence, so I look at her, but she's staring at me like she's scared.

"Why are you looking at me like that?" I ask. Now I'm the concerned one.

"You didn't imagine it."

I bolt upright, the motion making me nauseous, and my hand finds my head as pain shoots through it. She pushes me back and hands me the cup of water which I take and gulp down, closing my eyes to push down the nausea.

She sighs but scoots closer to the bed.

"I don't know how much you remember, so I'll just tell you everything and you can ask whatever questions after okay? If you want me to leave once I tell you everything, I will."

I just stare at her because I'm not sure what to say.

"I didn't know who you were when we met in the café. I mean, I knew who you were, and the role you played in Shotty's drug ring. But I didn't know who you were to me, what had happened between you and my dad that night."

I don't say anything because I'm beyond confused about where she's going with this.

"We'd been trying to take down Shotty for a while, but he was hard to catch. Every time we tried to infiltrate, we failed. We even almost lost an agent trying to smuggle him in to get information. When they found out about you, that's when the whole undercover thing came into play. I get in cozy with you, and we bust the ring that way."

Suddenly it all starts flooding my mind. I remember Biggy blowing her cover in the warehouse. I remember her sobbing as she said she was sorry.

"So, it wasn't real. You're not 23, and you're not a student," I say scrubbing my hand down my face, my heart sinking. No, this can't be right. She shakes her head, defeat lacing her features.

"I'm 27, and no. I mean at the very beginning it wasn't. Real, I mean. But I figured out pretty quickly it was going to be real, that I was being pulled to you like a magnet. I knew I was falling for you, and I was at war with myself for falling for someone who..."

She trails off like she's afraid to finish her sentence, so I finish it for her.

"Who's a murderer."

"Yeah," she sighs.

"But I knew in my gut that wasn't you. It wasn't who you wanted to be. And I knew I was falling in love with you even if I didn't want to. Even if it was wrong. I was trying to figure out how to keep you from getting caught up in everything when we took Shotty down.

"And then you told me your story. You filled in the blanks, and I knew I had been right, that that's not who you wanted to be, but you were stuck. But when I saw the pocket watch in your room, I freaked out."

I try to lean forward. "Star, I'm sorry."

She puts her hand up to stop me and shakes her head.

"You couldn't have talked sense into me in that moment. I thought everything from you had been a lie. And yes, I know that makes me hypocritical given everything, but I went to see my mom after I left your house. She broke down and told me everything, all of what my dad did, and how she made you promise not to tell me. She told me about you helping us over the years, and you showing up at the house after we'd met. She knew I was undercover, but she didn't know I was involved with you."

She's crying now and I just want to hold her, but I know she needs to get this out. It's all starting to add up now. Why she lied to me, why her mother lied.

"I get why you both kept it a secret. It's not like I thought my dad was a great guy. I knew he'd been into drugs, and despite how hard my mom tried to keep it from me, I knew he was hurting her, too. I had a vendetta against Shotty; well, all of you really because the drug trade is what got my dad into the hole he couldn't climb out of."

There's a knock on the door and a nurse pops her head in.

"I just need to get some blood for a couple more tests," she says.

Star clears her throat and we both sit in silence as the nurse stabs me with the needle and gets the vials she needs. She looks back and forth between Star and me like she can sense there's something going on, but she takes the vials and leaves without a word.

"After my mom told me everything, I understood why you killed him. He deserved it, and I'm glad he's gone if I'm being honest. I want to thank you for killing Terry, too. I mean it's not like I'm a fan of killing people for sport, but I'm glad you were protecting me."

"I've always protected you. I always will," I say. Though knowing now that she's a cop I don't think she's ever needed my protection.

"When you died on that floor, a part of me died, too. It felt like a piece of me had broken off. It had all gone wrong. I was so angry after I found out about my dad that I diverged from the plan, and I went after Biggy myself. I told my team where he'd be, but I went alone, and I wasn't thinking clearly."

"You could've gotten yourself killed," I say, my voice clogging in my throat at the thought.

"But instead, I got you killed," she says through a sob.

It takes her a couple minutes, but she gets her composure back, wiping the tears from her face. "Your heart stopped, Lawrence. You were gone. But I begged and pleaded that you not be taken from me. We finally had a chance."

She looks at me with those chocolate brown eyes and I can't help but wonder.

"What happened with Biggy?"

She blows out a breath, throwing herself back in her chair.

"He's dead. He wouldn't lower the gun when the rest of my team converged on the scene. He was stupid enough to try and turn the gun on me, but they got him first."

The thought of him trying to kill her makes me seethe with rage. She must notice because she reaches out and grabs my hand giving it a light squeeze.

"I'm okay," she says, a slight smile on her face. "When the paramedics somehow got your pulse back, I knew you'd be okay. I didn't know if you'd want anything to do with me once you found out the truth, but I still wanted you to be free. I had connections. A little bribing with an old friend down in the morgue, and as far as records show, you no longer exist. You bled out. Your body is in a casket over at Park Memorial."

"There's no way they'd let you get away with that. Did you quit?" I ask.

She nods and hands me my chart hanging on the foot of the bed.

I flip it open and look at my file.

"Michael Jordan? Seriously?"

She snorts and smiles as she shrugs. She knows how much I hate basketball so that's a cruel joke.

"I thought it was fitting. It was also the name of some poor guy who tried to kiss the grill of a bus while it was moving. He gets to live on through you. It's just a precaution, but I gotta admit I like the idea of you having to ward off 'Like the basketball player?' comments every time you show someone your ID."

"Well, that's why I didn't die from the gunshots, because you're gonna be the death of me," I smile and she smiles back. I wouldn't have it any other way though. "What about my mom?"

"I tried to track her down for your funeral. I knew it was too risky to tell her the truth, but I thought she might at least deserve some closure. But when I looked into it, I found out she passed from cancer three years ago."

She looks at me sympathetically as if she expects the news to break me. I don't blame my mom for leaving. I hate that she left us behind, but I

238

know why she ran. It's just unfortunate she ran from one unfortunate fate just to be taken by another.

"I know this is a lot to take in. Especially given everything." She motions to my hospital room. "And if you want nothing to do with me now, I completely understand." She looks at the floor and tries to hide her sniffle, but I catch it anyway. I grab her arm and pull her onto the bed next to me, holding her close and relishing in her scent.

"I knew you were hiding something when I found the photo album the night before you came to my house. That's why I'd left. I figured out who you were and didn't know why you were lying. But I also knew I had to tread carefully since I was also hiding some big secrets.

"I think we were both dealt a pretty crappy hand in life, but I think we were two unfortunate souls bound to share this life together."

She glances up at me, her eyes twinkling, and my heart feels full. She looks back down, staring at our hands entertained together.

"Marry me."

"What?" she asks, her head snapping back up so forcefully I'm afraid she might break her neck.

"I've been given a chance at freedom that I never thought I'd get. I'm not screwing it up. Marry me?"

Her eyes fill with tears, and she nods, grabbing my face in her hands.

"Yes," she says, and I take her mouth with mine, devouring her with a kiss that I never want to end.

"I love you. You'll always be a part of my universe. My lucky star."

"I love you too, Michael Jordan."

The room fills with her mischievous laughter and for the first time in a very long time I feel complete.

Epilogue
One year later
Lawrence

I 'm too old for this. I'm gonna break my back or something."

Star rolls her eyes at me, pushing me towards the line.

"You act like you're ancient. And stop pretending like you aren't dying inside to try it."

I can't help but grin because she's right. "I am ancient."

"Don't remind me. I'm married to a decrepit old man. Now go," she laughs as I turn and head for the end of the line.

A boy probably about 6 stands in front of me and turns when I get behind him.

"What's your name?"

"Michael."

"Michael what?"

"Jordan," I answer without thinking because what 6-year-old asks for last names?.

"Like the basketball player?"

I hear Starlette chuckle from where she's standing, and I shoot her a glare over my shoulder.

Luckily, it's only a short fifteen-minute wait, and I giggle like a little boy when I make it to the top. I stare into the green and orange striped bowl and sit down with my arms crossed like the lifeguard instructs, a smile plastered on my face. It looks nothing like a toilet, but I can't wait to try it anyway.

"What, have you never been on a water slide before?" a smart mouth teenager behind me says, apparently noting my excitement.

"Nope!" I say right before the lifeguard pushes me into the ice-cold water with his foot.

I should've known after I told Star that I'd never gotten to go down a water slide that she'd remember that tiny tidbit of information and fulfill my childhood dream.

Shivering from both excitement and the chill of the air against my wet skin, I pad my wet feet across the hot concrete to a smiling Star, a knowing grin on her face. I grab her cheeks between my wet hands and kiss her.

"Thank you," I say.

"You're welcome baby. You gonna go again?"

I can't help but smile and she grins back, waving me towards the line again.

"Have fun, baby," she says, swatting my ass before I take off eager to go down the slide again.

"This is awesome!" a young child yells as they run to the line in front of me. Yes, it is, bud. Yes, it is.

Dedication

To my husband, thank you for giving me the push I needed to find my passion. Without your encouragement, I would've never put these words to paper. Without you and our boys, I am nothing.

To my mom, there's no words good enough for you. I love you. Thank you for being my biggest cheerleader always.

About the Author

Emma Humfleet is a self-published author who discovered her unknown love for reading and writing romance after despising anything book related for most of her life.

When she's not reading the latest romance book release, or daydreaming about being a future New York Times bestselling author, she's taking care of her (soon-to-be) two boys in her Indiana home that she shares with her husband.

Made in the USA
Monee, IL
24 May 2025

17764254R00152